An Excerpt from *Wanderlust*

Date: *September 19*
From: *KateBogart*
To: *VioletMorgan*
Subject: *Balls in the Air*

Oh Vi! Got back to NY yesterday and so much to talk about, but have no idea where you are. Anyway, at Mom's advice decided it is better to have two of a kind than a bum hand and have decided to keep things open with both Jack and Maxwell.

That's right. I'm playing the field, with my ex-husband and my editor's drinking buddy. Haven't figured out exactly how this is going to work yet, or really how to juggle them, but not at all willing to throw either one away. There were e-mails waiting from both of them when I got home, and I have to admit, it feels kind of great, though also scary, as both are a bit intense.

. . . Does any of this sound crazy to you?

Wish You Were Here,
Kate

A first-time novelist and proud member of several frequent-flyer programs, **Chris Dyer** lives in New York City, in a location convenient to all its airports.

Harper

wander *lust*

CHRIS DYER

A PLUME BOOK

PLUME
Published by the Penguin Group
Penguin Putnam Inc., 375 Hudson Street, New York, New York 10014, U.S.A.
Penguin Books Ltd, 80 Strand, London WC2R 0RL, England
Penguin Books Australia Ltd, 250 Camberwell Road,
Camberwell, Victoria 3124, Australia
Penguin Books Canada Ltd, 10 Alcorn Avenue, Toronto, Ontario, Canada M4V 3B2
Penguin Books (N.Z.) Ltd, 182–190 Wairau Road, Auckland 10, New Zealand

Penguin Books Ltd, Registered Offices: Harmondsworth, Middlesex, England

First published by Plume, a member of Penguin Putnam Inc.

First Printing, February 2003
10 9 8 7 6 5 4 3 2 1

℗ REGISTERED TRADEMARK—MARCA REGISTRADA

LIBRARY OF CONGRESS CATALOGING-IN-PUBLICATION DATA

Dyer, Chris.
   Wanderlust / Chris Dyer.
      p. cm.
   ISBN 0-452-28379-5
      1. Women travelers—Fiction. 2. Travel writing—Fiction. 3. Travel—Fiction. I. Title.
PS3604.Y46 W36 2003
813'.6—dc21   2002074948

Printed in the United States of America
Set in Times New Roman

PUBLISHER'S NOTE
This is a work of fiction. Names, characters, places, and incidents are either the products
of the author's imagination or are used fictitiously, and any resemblance to actual persons,
living or dead, business establishments, events, or locales is entirely coincidental.

BOOKS ARE AVAILABLE AT QUANTITY DISCOUNTS WHEN USED TO PROMOTE PRODUCTS OR SER-
VICES. FOR INFORMATION PLEASE WRITE TO PREMIUM MARKETING DIVISION, PENGUIN PUTNAM
INC., 375 HUDSON STREET, NEW YORK, NEW YORK 10014.

For Celia

CONTENTS

ACKNOWLEDGMENTS

Endless thanks to my editor, Kelly Notaras, and to my agent, Craig Kayser, for all their insight, patience, and support. I am also blessed with friends devoted enough and crazy enough to have followed the first draft of this story as it developed day by day, and page by page. No writer could ask for a more encouraging—or better looking—row of cheerleaders than Suzanne Collins, Alexa Junge, David Rakoff, Laura Walsh, Jim Chamberlain, Joanne Dolan, Joanna Kulesa, Laura Howell, Paula Curtz, and David Zaza. My sincerest thanks also to David Evans, Wendy Silbert, Dan DeLuca, and Jaime Wolf for all the help they provided. Thanks to my family and the Flahertys for their constant support, and to Robert Francoeur for years of friendship and life-sustaining long-distance phone calls. Finally, miles and miles and miles of gratitude to the delightful Deborah Davis, for her bright ideas, for her boundless generosity, and for having the confidence in me to write this story in the first place.

wander *lust*

CHAPTER 1

✈

In Lisbon

Date:	July 11
From:	KateBogart
To:	VioletMorgan
Subject:	A Fine Mess

Dear Vi: Pardon my typos. Trying to do this as quietly and quickl as possible. It is 5 AM in Lisbon. Am in very posh Hotel da Lapa, a restored 19th-century palace. Lisbon's finest. Bathroom bigger than NY apt. and towels for giants. Glorious views to the Tagus, lush gardens, palm-shaded pool, marble tiles, antques, frescoes, but also, stuffy diplomats and trophy wives everywhere.

Paolo stil asleep. Paolo being Portugese bullfighter who dedicated his match to me. (Did you know that Portuguese bullfighters are called "Cavaleiros"? They perform on horseback too.) The room is his treat, as it is way beyond my budget. Having a great time, but Paolo cannot seem to grasp that travel writing is job not hobby, and it is high time for me to hit road. Last night was our 3rd "last night together" in a row.

Fear I have fallen behind in itinerary so have quietly packed and am leaving him a goodbyeitwasgreatfunbutitismuchbetterthiswayforbothofus farewell note. I figure by the time he gets it translated, I'll be on train for Bilbao. I know this seems weasely, but I just dont think I could bear any more tears, kisses, desperate clinches, etc. Still, thought

I'd take advantage of the computer hook-up. Who knows when I'll be in such accomodating digs again?

To tell the truth, I do regret leaving Paolo. It's been a heady week. But how can I stay with a man who still lives with his parents *and* grandparents, taunts and skewers befuddled bulls for a living, and looks better in second-skin crimson tights than I do? Never mind the language barrier. And yet, looking at his smooth brown skin all tangled up in 300-ct damask sheets . . .

If only you could see him, Vi. He's curled up all fetal and lovingly clutching a sumptuous down pillow. Every now and then he makes this soft little cooing noise low in his throat, the sound of utter human contentment. He's got those I-can't-believe-it's-not-mascara kind of eyelashes and thick black silky hair. Even at rest his muscles seem flexed, and as the room is starting to brighten a shade, there are two droplets of dawn's blueish light caught in those adorable dimples at the base of his spine. I know it sounds crazy, Vi, but it's the perfect moment for leafing. I want to remumber him just the way he is right now.

As always thanks so much for taking care of apt, cat, plants, mail, bills, banking, landlord, and all else, and for keeping up regular e-mail correspondence. It helps me so much to maintain rooted feeling whil on the road. You are even better than a best fiend. I do hope Truman has been well behaved; he can be a persnickety little kitty, but I'm sure that he appreciates your effffffff uh oh oh no. the cavaleiro awakens. oh. he just beamed at me. oh darn. he's stretching. oh god he's loovely. oh crap. he's coming over here. wearing nothing. but that smile. great. he's reading over my shoulder. luckly can't grasp word of English beyond basic make-out vocab. oh drat. kissing my neck. ooo . . . again? hard to concentrate Vi. jeez I wish he wouldn't do that! so well. oh damn! he's got such great hands oh VI. damn him! no use oh well back to dddrawing board I geuss yikes!.////////..///,,,.//sorrydon't forget to fertilllize plntas!,,,,,feed cat! soooooooooooooooo sorrrry Laterrrrrrrrrrrrrrrrrrrrrhhhhjjjjjjjjjjjjjjjjkkkkkkkkkkkkkkkkkkkk kkkkkkkkkkkkkate

Date: July 11
From: VioletMorgan
To: KateBogart
Subject: RE: A Fine Mess

Hey, Bogie. How awful for you and your delectable Portuguese bull-fighter, but rest assured, your life could be less enviable. Just think, you could be waging a losing battle against your own good sense by continuing to work as the assistant to a crazed and belligerent pro-ducer of unwatchable movies. You could also be married to a 30+ struggling rock 'n' roller—and his four noisy, untidy, and stubbornly single bandmates by default. Or, you could be sitting in your best friend's NY studio apartment staring down one overfed misanthropic housecat by the name of Truman Capote, who always seems to regard you as if you were a delicious little sparrow.

So you see, there are worse things in this life than contemplating the subtle gradations of a European sunrise in your Portuguese lover's ass. Nevertheless I admit some genuine concern, and truly hope that macho bullfighter has not taken you as his permanent sex slave, so do e-mail as soon as possible. Otherwise, I am contacting the authorities, and none of us want to suffer any further embarrassment. Do we?

Toro!
Your Violet

PS: Knowing you as well as I do, you might want to save that Dear John letter as a template.

Date: July 11
From: VioletMorgan
To: KateBogart
Subject: RE: A Fine Mess

Kate? Have you thrown your Portuguese bullfighter yet? Or are you still "in the ring," so to speak? If so, please come up for air to let me know where and how you are.

    Vi

Date: July 12
From: VioletMorgan
To: KateBogart
Subject: RE: A Fine Mess

Yoohoo! Time's up! It has now been one whole day since your last message. You have had an obscene amount of time to finish your business. You leave me no choice but to forward your e-mail to the US embassy, as I am seriously concerned for your safety.

    Vi

Date: July 12
From: VioletMorgan
To: KateBogart
Subject: RE: A Fine Mess

Okay, US embassy guy thinks I'm insane and I am now on official crackpot list. So, on to next tactic: Forthwith I am putting Truman Capote on a starvation diet until you e-mail to assure me that you are free and safe. (I'd endure the starvation myself, of course, but I think I might be borderline hypoglycemic.)

    Nervously yours,
    Vi

Date: July 12
From: KateBogart
To: VioletMorgan
Subject: RE: RE: A Fine Mess

Violet Morgan, you feed my cat immediately, or *I* will report *you* to the authorities!

Thanks for your concern, by the way, but I'm perfectly fine. In fact, I feel quite rich. Paolo and I had another farewell romp, and then another, and another, and, well, you get my drift. He finally agreed to see me to the train station, but as departing time grew nearer, two perfectly formed teardrops, the kind that look as if they might have been drawn by Disney animators, positioned themselves on the precipitous curve of those eyelashes. In a flash, I imagined myself living in a restored vineyard villa in the Portuguese countryside, where all my sun-dappled days are split between working on my great expatriate American novel and reading Iberian folk tales to my three olive-skinned children, all blessed with their father's athleticism and romantic looks, their mother's inquisitive mind, and, most attractively, dual citizenship in the US and the EU.

Then I caught a double reflection of myself in those glistening twin tears and I remembered something: I am *Katherine Alison Bogart! Travel reporter, cultural adventurer, citizen of the world, and the freest woman alive!* I will be tied down by no man, confined by no geographical borders, limited by no conventional nine-to-five desk job! Never! The world is my all-you-can-eat buffet, and I'm on a shameless, unrestricted diet!

But how can I be the freest woman alive if I have to look after a sprawling vineyard, a small army of farmhands, a bullfighting husband, the horse he rode in on, his disapproving family, and his three Portuguese brats? You know me, Violet; I have a very low threshold for domestic drudgery.

While I was tearing my hair out trying to explain this to the weeping, clinging Paolo, the train whistle sounded. Let me remind you, Violet, that actual rip-snorting bulls tend to lose their disputes with this man. I thought for sure I'd never be able to get away from him, when fate intervened in the form of some noisy fans who recognized their hero from the bullring. They'd set upon him for the usual hand-shakes, ass-pats, autographs, etc., when suddenly, a gaggle of Swedish PETA protesters who have been tailing Paolo for weeks took the plat-form by storm. A melee erupted between Paolo's fans and his detrac-tors, with poor dazed Paolo being yanked between them in a heated tug-of-war.

I seized the opportunity to hop aboard the train and claimed my seat just in the nick of time. As the train was leaving the station, I caught sight of poor Paolo running alongside it, his shirt torn, one shoe missing, and his tears flowing like the Tagus in rainy season. He made a foolhardy leap for the train, but one of the PETA protesters, an absolute Valkyrie of a woman, caught him in a tackle that would do any Green Bay Packer proud. I do believe the brave cavaleiro fi-nally met his match. As the train gathered speed, Paolo and the Valkyrie were still rolling and wrestling about in their own angry lit-tle cloud of dust. And that was the last I saw of my dreamy Portuguese bullfighter. . . .

Really feel as if I dodged a bullet, Vi. After all, I'm still getting used to the idea of myself as a "divorcee." I rushed headlong into that situation and look what it got me—a date with a smirking judge who looked like he'd much rather be golfing than presiding over another disaster everyone should have seen coming in the first place. It's a life lesson that's not wasted on me.

So, now I am safe at the Oporto station. Lunch here, a good night's sleep on the train, and Bilbao by morning. Sorry for the wear and tear on your nerves. You're an absolute doll. I'll try to stay out of trouble. Promise. Love to Truman.

Wish You Were Here,
Kate

CHAPTER 2

✈

In Bilbao

Date: July 13
From: TedConcannon
To: KateBogart
Subject: Deadline

Kate: As the reluctant travel editor of this glorified tabloid, it is my unfortunate duty to remind you of your deadline. Please send me something to run on Sunday, a bus schedule, a couple of parking tickets, anything. Just save me from my ulcers and the dirty looks I keep getting from the 12-year-old managing editor. Excuse me, 12-*and-a-half.*

Dyspeptically Yours,
Ted

Date: July 13
From: KateBogart
To: TedConcannon
Subject: RE: Deadline

Dear Ted: Still working on Lisbon pages. Portugal was a lot more fun than I could handle. Now I'm in Bilbao trying to whittle it all

down to a manageable article. The rest of the piece will be in your
e-mail box when you roll into work an hour late and cranky tomorrow. I swear.

Wish You Were Here,
Kate

Date: July 13
From: KateBogart
To: VioletMorgan
Subject: A Fine Mess, Pt. II

Dear Vi: Hellish ride on the train from Oporto last night. Booked an
overnight sleeper, but one of my couchette mates was afflicted with a
whistling sinus, making a high-pitched noise that fell somewhere
between a tea kettle and a hair-trigger car alarm. Miraculously managed
to doze off a bit, when my blanket slipped from my bunk down to hers.
First I tried to do without, but my goosebumps would not be denied.

So, tired and shivering, tried to retrieve my fallen blanket as gin-
gerly as possible without disrupting her big solo. This, however, caught
the attention of her husband, who accused me of trying to rob her, in
very excitable Portuguese. Things got even messier from there, with
conductors, interpreters, gawkers, etc. Even those perpetual widows
who board at each local stop to hawk fresh bread and chocolate bars
somehow got caught in the fray.

And what noble and majestic peacemaker should suddenly stride
into this scene to settle the conflict deus ex machina–like? You guessed
it: undefeated cavaleiro supremo and Portuguese national treasure,
Paolo Caetano. I could have smothered that woman with her pillow,
hacked her to bits, then tossed her piece by piece from the moving
train, and still my infractions would have been overlooked, because I
was *with* "The Great Caetano." Such is the importance of the bullfight in Iberian culture. Whistler's sister and her crazed husband even
gave me a generous length of home-cured linguiça and some very
tasty wine as a peace offering.

It seems that the PETA Valkyrie did some real damage before she could be subdued by Paolo's fans and the Lisbon police. With his arm now in a sling, it's not safe for Paolo to get on his horse and venture into the ring. Taking full advantage of this unscheduled recovery time, Paolo thought he would seize the day and track me down. With all the hyperactive sign language and crude picture-drawing going on, I'm not exactly certain how he caught up with the train, but it looks like a hang-glider. Maybe a whirligig.

Paolo is very, very, very happy to accompany me on my travels, and we have checked into the hotel together for the next two nights. Oh, Vi, what am I going to do? He's just a boy who can't hear no, and I'm in an awful fix.

Wish You Were Here,
Kate

Date: July 13
From: VioletMorgan
To: KateBogart
Subject: RE: A Fine Mess, Pt. II

Dear Bogie: Didn't you learn your lesson last year with that flamenco dancer in Seville? There's no resisting Iberian passion; it's an ineluctable force. My advice: savor it while you can, sister. After all, Paolo sounds like a positively yummy antidote to the solitude of life on the road. Meanwhile, I will look into Bilbao chapter of PETA. Maybe they can scare him off. Glad to hear you're safe, even though I was so looking forward to starving your cat.

Hasta luego.
Vi

Date: July 13
From: TedConcannon
To: KateBogart
Subject: Deadline Looming

Kate! Time marches on! Now where is the stuff on Lisbon? We're trying to run this toot sweet, as the French say. You haven't run off and
married some Portuguese bullfighter, have you?

　　Ted

Date: July 13
From: KateBogart
To: TedConcannon
Subject: RE: Deadline Looming

A Portuguese bullfighter! *Hah!* If your ulcer is as overactive as your
imagination, Ted Concannon, you're in serious medical trouble. Sit
tight. Article on its way.

　　Kate

Date: July 13
From: GamblinRose
To: KateBogart
Subject: FREE PRIZE!

Congratulations, Kate Bogart! You've just won a free guilt trip! As
you have not written or called your loving mother since Madeira! Or
was it Lisbon? It's so hard to keep track of you sometimes and it's not
like you to go so many days without an e-mail.

　　My life of late hasn't been nearly as interesting as yours, I'm sure.
You'll be pleased to know that the "Sisters of Perpetual Bingo"—if I
may borrow your phrase—have been grounded while Althea's van is
in the shop. We haven't been on any gambling adventures beyond the

usual Thursday night bingo at His Holy Blood High. And our regular Tuesday night poker game, of course. What good company the Sisters are. We're really lucky to have each other as friends all these years, though Ina has had some varicose veins removed from her left leg and she's had to miss the last few functions.

You'll also be pleased to know that I took your advice, and I've been volunteering at the halfway house literacy program. You were right, Kate. It's very rewarding, and it's touching to see people who've had such hard lives work so diligently to improve themselves. When we get tired of Dr. Seuss, *Goodnight Moon,* and whatnot, I like to treat my students to a little game of whist, or some five card stud. Not for money, mind you; just to keep a hand in. I can hear you tsk-tsking all the way across the Atlantic, Kate, but everyone needs a little diversion. I don't think I have to tell you that play is good for the mind and the spirit.

I'm dying to hear your impressions of Portugal and Madeira, and since I am your mother, I don't feel as if I should have to go hunting for them in a newspaper or magazine. You don't know how proud I am to have raised such an adventurous daughter. I brag to the Sisters of Perpetual Bingo all the time—and they even seem to like it!

By the way, Moira asked that you bring her back an autograph of the Pope from Rome. I told her it's not like he's James Brolin or Barry Manilow. You can't just walk up and ask him to sign a glossy. Can you? Anyway, I promised her that I'd ask. What a nut!

Love,
Mom

Date: July 13
From: KateBogart
To: GamblinRose
Subject: RE: FREE PRIZE!

Dear Mom: Thanks for the guilt trip. Maybe I can write a travel article about it. Hmmm . . . Let me see . . . A Guilt Trip Around the World? Guilt Trips the Whole Family Will Enjoy? Guilt Trips by Rickshaw?

I am sincerely sorry about my shabby correspondence, but my days and nights have been crazy beyond my expectations. I'm in Spain now, writing up the Portugal stuff. I know you worry about me, but rest assured I'm very safe, and not at all lonely.

I am also a bit concerned about you, and really wonder if you should be tutoring your students on when to hold 'em, when to fold 'em, and that sort of thing. Maybe with this particular group you should place more of an emphasis on phonics? Just a suggestion. But you are the teacher, and the best mother in the world, so I defer to your expertise.

I'll do what I can re: the Pope, but it seems a real long shot. I'll try to be a better correspondent/daughter. As always . . .

Wish You Were Here,
Kate

Date: July 14
From: VioletMorgan
To: KateBogart
Subject: PETA, PETA, PETA

Bogie, have been on-line as much as time and nosey, suspicious boss will allow, but can't seem to find anything on Bilbao PETA. However, I have struck up an e-mail correspondence with one Joseba Ixtarry, a proud member of ETA, the Basque Nationalist revolutionary movement. I bet he'd know how to get rid of an unwanted bullfighter. Shall I tell him that Paolo is only pretending to be a Portuguese bullfighter and that he's actually a spy in the service of Juan Carlos and he's using an innocent redheaded American turista as his beard? Just let me know and I'll fire off a message to Ixtarry now. This is fun!

Violet

Date: July 14
From: KateBogart
To: VioletMorgan
Subject: RE: PETA, PETA, PETA

Violet, you've *got* to get another job. Thanks for the offer, really, but I've had enough of activist/terrorists for one week. Besides, it's been great fun discovering Bilbao on Paolo's broken arm, and he's been such help, believe it or not.

While I worked on the Lisbon piece, Paolo scoped out Bilbao for me. Just as I was finishing up a day of hard work, he returned from the marketplace with a bundle of fresh fruit, flowers for the room, and reservations at Goizeko Kabi, a very fine restaurant. But before dinner, he drew a bath, which he thoughtfully freshened with verbena leaves, also from the marketplace. After a warm, lemony soak, we strolled through the Casco Viejo, the city's lively old quarter, then went on to dinner: leg of lamb for him, langostinos for me, a nice rioja, and a perfect nutty/ sweet oloroso with a flan so good, calling it "flan" is an insult.

Today was museum hopping, which I thought might bore Paolo, but he enjoyed the Guggenheim at least as much as I did. It turns out that Paolo has collected some contemporary art himself, so he knows his Schnabel from his Kiefer.

Ever since I got to Bilbao, Vi, I've been sleeping that deeply satisfying sleep you get after a day of productive work and warm companionship. It's funny, but life on the road is so hectic, so distracting, so wondrous really, that I rarely think about how solitary it is until I find myself in such outstanding company. Last night, Paolo even took me for an impromptu evening of dancing—on Santiago Calatrava's glass footbridge of all places. It was like dancing on the surface of the river while Paolo hummed some pretty fado tune in my ear.

Maybe it's the sherry, but that damn Portuguese vineyard is starting to look better to me with every passing minute . . .

WYWH,
Kate

Date: July 14
From: VioletMorgan
To: KateBogart
Subject: Basqueing in It

Okay, Barbara Cartland, I get the gauzy, soft-focus picture. Do you want to know how I spent the last couple of days?

Yesterday: Went to dry cleaner to drop off my favorite jacket, which your cat puked on. Then, went to work, where insane boss asked me to drop off his dry cleaning. At night, went home, where husband and bandmates were ecstatic about upcoming out-of-town gig and wheedled me into taking all their bizarre fetishy tights and pleather camisole thingys where else? To dry cleaner.

Today: Went to dry cleaner to pick up above items.

I love my dry cleaner. He's such an adventurous, kind, thoughtful, impulsive and well-rounded man. An artist, really. Why, his dry cleaning solution smells sweeter and sweeter to me with every transaction. I'm just dancing on fumes . . .

Anyway, I'll call off PETA, ETA, IRA, PLO, etc. Killjoy!

V.

Date: July 15
From: Manowar
To: KateBogart
Subject: Portugal

Dear Ms. Bogart:

I hope that this e-mail doesn't come as a brazen intrusion, but I wanted to take the opportunity to introduce myself. My name is Miles Maxwell and after reading of your Portugal travels in yesterday's *Standard*, I realize we have several things in common: 1) a career in Journalism 2) a love of things Portuguese 3) a mutual friend in irascible old Ted Concannon, who suggested I send my admiration on to you directly. Perhaps I am being presumptuous, but do I also detect 4) a restless spirit? I think so.

Madeira is also one of my favorite places in the world. Been visiting regularly since boyhood. Isn't Reid's a remarkable resort? Truly civilized. I'm glad you had a chance to include it, though I'm a bit surprised you didn't mention the restaurant, Les Faunes. Top rate! Must admit, however, that I'm afraid my childhood paradise will be overrun with Yankee tourists now that it has been so highly praised in a major American daily.

You are absolutely conscientious to have warned your readers that Madeira isn't a beach lover's island. You might have advised them, however, that nearby Porto Santo has some truly enviable beaches, and it is quite easily reached by ferry or boat-for-hire from several spots on Madeira. Perhaps we can meet there someday for a swim.

Well, thank you again for your most illuminating impressions and advice. As always, I look forward to following you in your travels.

Sincerely,
Miles Maxwell
London, England

Date: July 15
From: KateBogart
To: TedConcannon
Subject: The Inquisition

Dear Editor: Forgive my Spanish "*pasion*," but today I received a most annoying e-mail from some Englishman who calls himself "Manowar" and mentioned you as his old friend. Is this legit, and if so, why on earth would you give my personal e-mail address to him? I am trying to enjoy my Spanish idyll, Teddy. But my otherwise perfect days have now been adulterated by this snooty fellow and his condescending message.

Kate

Date: July 15
From: TedConcannon
To: KateBogart
Subject: RE: The Inquisition

Kate: Miles Maxwell is an old friend of mine, back from the days when newsmen were newsmen. A real gentleman and a hotshot to boot. Think Afghanistan, Baghdad, Sarajevo, Chechnya, Somalia, and Rwanda. He was kidnapped once in Beirut and once in Colombia and decided he didn't want to die in a ditch. Now he's writing freelance travel pieces. Howzat for a career arc? Thought you'd like to meet him.

Maxwell is a great guy! Think of me, only 15 years younger, a little taller, quite a bit trimmer, with a full head of hair, crisp British diction, suave manners, and a single, well-defined chin. Okay, don't think of me at all, but would it hurt you to be a little cordial to him?

    Ted

Date: July 15
From: KateBogart
To: TedConcannon
Subject: RE: RE: The Inquisition

G-R-R-R-R-R-R-R-R-R-R-R!

Date: July 15
From: KateBogart
To: Manowar
Subject: RE: Portugal

Dear Mr. Maxwell:

Thanks so much for your flattering e-mail. If you do indeed follow "Wish You Were Here" regularly, you know that the column is aimed at travelers of mostly ordinary means. While we always try to mention some high-end splurges, putting too much emphasis on a place like Reid's might push the column into the realm of elitist "fantasy" travel. No?

I am also well aware of the beaches at Porto Santo, but as the article was already a sidebar to a feature piece on Lisbon, it was narrowly focused by necessity. Your points are appreciated nevertheless.

While your invitation for a swim at Porto Santo is most gracious, I'm a sensible woman who would never venture into the water with the deadly "man o' war." Nor would I ever want to tread on your quasi-colonial childhood paradise with my crude Yankee feet.

Best,
Kate Bogart

Date: July 16
From: Manowar
To: KateBogart
Subject: RE: RE: Portugal

Ms. Bogart: So sorry if my last e-mail was rude or untoward in any way. I confess to being a bit of a naif in this field, and I am merely trying to establish some professional contacts.

As to the "Manowar" matter, it's a vestige of my erstwhile profession as a war reporter. Every configuration of my birth name was spoken for, you see, and "Manowar" seemed to be the easiest for my e-mail correspondents to remember. (I tried "hotspots" for a time, but it proved far too suggestive in the long term. Very problematic, that.)

I apologize if my e-mail seemed inhospitable to you or your compatriots. I am in fact sincerely fond of you crude-footed Yanks. Rest assured that I am duly embarrassed by my faux pas and I am now going off to give myself a sound flogging, as that is the way of my elitist, "quasi-colonial" tribe. Or perhaps I shall have my manservant see to that unpleasant task.

Yours in Contrition,
Miles Maxwell

Date: July 16
From: KateBogart
To: Manowar
Subject: RE: RE: RE: Portugal

Maxwell: Tell that manservant to give you one for me!

    Best,
    Kate Bogart

Date: July 17
From: KateBogart
To: GamblinRose
Subject: A Long Story Short

Dear Mom: Had a wonderful time in Bilbao. Also made a new friend in the person of an injured Portuguese bullfighter named Paolo (he's the long story) who has been escorting me through the Basque country.

    Yesterday we rented a car and drove out to explore some of the outlying countryside and fishing villages. Very pretty, lovely food and scenery. Not much doin' of course, but it's just a matter of time before these humble little villages are discovered by the overflow of Guggenheim pilgrims.

    Am beginning to think I was crazy for agreeing to Rome assignment in summer, with its baking heat and hordes of tourists. Frankly, having a hard time tearing myself away from the ease and charm of the Basque country, and the sweet and verrrry attentive Paolo not making it any easier. Oh well, he's planning to join me in Positano after Rome, so I have that to look forward to.

    Wish You Were Here,
    Kate

Date: July 17
From: JackMacTavish
To: KateBogart
Subject: Happy Anniversary

Katie! Just down from Pichu Pichu, and still high from the experience. Of course we never found any "lost Incan gold" (selling point
of trip). I don't even believe in it, but it's one way to separate crazy
city dwellers from their money.

We almost lost a Wall St. trader along the way. He had some kind
of wacky vision up there and became convinced that it was his spiri-
tual home. I don't know if it was the physical exhaustion, or the
thin air, or the ayahuasca (sp?). Told him not to touch the stuff!
Heckofa time getting him off the damn mountain fighting wind and
sharp, stinging granizo the whole way. Actually had to strap him to a
stretcher to get him back to the city. Now his wife is here in Lima
with an American deprogrammer who looks like Johnny Cash. It just
goes to show that the only thing more fragile than our ecosystem is
the human mind.

Except for that casualty the expedition was amazing, Katie, and
I'm already itching for another adventure. Thinking about skiing the
backcountry of the Rockies and trying to round up more rich crazy
people to back it. Though feeling sort of mercenary as it is still pretty
much virgin territory. Maybe should try to stick to eco-adventures from
now on.

By the way, do you realize that today is the second anniversary of
our divorce? Wow, right? I think we did the right thing, Katie, but I
gotta admit, there are still times when I miss you like a spleen or
something. I still feel deeply connected, y'know? In a really soulful
way. Anyway, I'm getting all sappy and ungrammatical, and I know
you don't have patience for that.

So! I'm ripe for a shower and going in search of some modern plumbing. Talk about an adventure! Hope you're well! Happy
Anniversary!

Love always,
Yr old buddy, Jack

CHAPTER 3

✈

In Rome

Date: July 18
From: KateBogart
To: JackMacTavish
Subject: RE: Happy Anniversary

Oh, Jack, there's not a mercenary hair on your manly head, and your idealism is one of the many reasons I married you in the first place. As to your backcountry skiing expedition, I am much more concerned about you smashing all those big rugged bones to bits without any proper medical professionals to put you back together again. Can't you just go to Aspen where there are modern niceties like hospitals and telephones?

As for me, just finished up Iberian travels escorted by a popular Portuguese bullfighter. (Not kidding.) Am now in beautiful, chaotic, crowded, steamy, delirious Rome, so you are not the only one devoted to insane and risky travel. Paolo had to take care of some legal business in Lisbon (PETA run-ins an occupational hazard) and he is to join me later in the week for a trip to Positano.

I think you would like Paolo almost as much as I do, though you would no doubt have a problem with his day job. At least the bull becomes dinner eventually, so its slaughter is not totally gratuitous. Oh my God, that kind of cheap rationalizing is the first sign that things are getting serious, isn't it? Yikes.

While I also miss you terribly, Jack, I do think we made a mistake. And we fixed it. Let's face it, our differences are as striking as our similarities. We share the same instincts, but play them out with very different agendas, and we need to find partners who fit into the scheme of our crazy lives more naturally.

I see you with one of those incurably athletic, apple-cheeked women, probably blonde, probably German, probably a Gretchen, or maybe a Petra. The kind of woman who practically lives on trail mix, has no problem wearing Patagonia purple fleece 365 days a year, and who knows a thing or two about yurt-building. I just don't fit the pro-file. I'm more likely to spend my life living on continental breakfasts, room service, and frequent flyer upgrades.

That's not to say I don't get wistful too, Jack. Do I ever! I figure I always will have to fight off some amount of wistfulness for you, but it's a condition that's decidedly on the sweet side of bittersweet for me. I don't regret our time together at all and I treasure our friendship more than ever. I truly think the best is yet to come for both of us, and I look forward to many many years of celebrating our matrimonial liberation day. (So much better than "divorce," don't you think?)

In the meantime, ford ev'ry stream, baby.

Wish You Were Here,
Kate

Date:	July 18
From:	JackMacTavish
To:	KateBogart
Subject:	RE: RE: Happy Anniversary

Wow, Katie. That made me cry like a baby, but it felt great too, y'know? You're so wise and so right. We're just both too independent and too much in love with our own restless souls. We sure did make each other crazy when we were married, didn't we? I was always trying to drag you to the Himalayas and you were always trying to drag me to some spa resort, or civilize me with your opera and museums.

It sounds like you might've already found someone to help you get over our thing, and I wish you all the best with bullfighting dude. Think I know what I have to do now. I've gotta stop feeling sorry for myself. Gotta stop comparing every woman I meet to you and just move on. When I get back home to SF, might go to a sweat lodge up in Marin to expel you once and for all. Then we can enjoy a pure, easy, unpolluted kind of friendship, just like we agreed to do, and I can get on with my life.

Meanwhile, if you meet any Gretchens or Petras while in Europe, tell 'em to drop me a line.

Love,
Jack

Date:	July 18
From:	Manowar
To:	KateBogart
Subject:	Roman Holiday

Dear Ms. Bogart: My friend and yours, Ted Concannon, tells me that you are in Rome this week, as am I. Isn't it fortuitous? I fear we got off on a bad foot and I would appreciate the opportunity to make it up to you with dinner. Perhaps on the roof of the Hotel Eden? I find it quite comfortable there. As you know, I'm just a fledgling travel writer, and so far, I'm not having an easy go of it. I would be most grateful for any guidance or advice you might impart.

Eagerly,
Miles Maxwell

Date: July 19
From: KateBogart
To: Manowar
Subject: RE: Roman Holiday

Dear Mr. Maxwell: Who wouldn't be "comfortable" at the Hotel
Eden? While I do have a very hectic schedule in Rome, I would be
happy to meet you there, as long as you're picking up the bill, that is.
The truth is "my friend and yours" doesn't pay me enough to afford
such a splurge.

  Don't know how much I can help professionally, but I'm looking
forward to trading war stories. Call me at the Hotel Navona.

  Sincerely,
  Kate Bogart

Date: July 19
From: KateBogart
To: TedConcannon
Subject: For the Record

Ted: This is just to let you know that the only reason I'm agreeing to
squeeze Miles Maxwell into my crazy Roman schedule is that he is
picking up the tab for a meal at a swell establishment. I could never
afford a place like the Hotel Eden on my budget, yet I will be able to
include the invaluable travel information in the article. Do you see
how dedicated I am? How I suffer for my work?

  While I'm semi-grateful for this opportunity, please don't make a
habit of siccing your crazy cronies on me—unless of course they can
come through with dinner reservations along these lines. I just hope
the company doesn't negate the pleasures of the meal.

  Ciao,
  Kate

Date: July 19
From: • KateBogart
To: VioletMorgan
Subject: *La Dolce Vita*

Dear Vi: Much too hot in Rome and hard to leave air conditioned comfort of my room, but a travel writer's gotta do what a travel writer's
gotta do. This morning, went to see Bernini's sculpture of St. Teresa in
Ecstasy at a wonderful little church where a kindly old monk sells
mystical oils and waters in a room behind the altar. From the look on
St. Teresa's face, I had to wonder if she too ever had a romance with
a bullfighter. After all, she was Spanish. Later, visited the beauti-
fully restored Galleria Borghese. An incredible collection, but its un-
cannily good trompe l'oeil ceiling creatures will probably keep me up
all night.

Oh well, can't get used to a bed without Paolo in it anyway, and
can't wait till he joins me at the end of the week. Right now, he is in
Lisbon testifying in the arraignment against PETA Valkyrie and following up with his doctor. Had a tearful, messy good-bye with him in
Madrid. He is due here at the end of the week for more seaside frolicking and some further negotiations re: "us." Paolo is dead set on
joining me in my travels. Don't know where this is going, but I'm all
wrapped up in it just the same. Sigh.

Received a sentimental greeting from Jack just down from a Peruvian mountain trip and planning his next adventure before he has
even gotten home. Sound like someone else you know? That man is
one sweet hunk of homemade pie, Violet, but one of us has to be sensible, so I took the lead. Reviewed the usual drill about how we're too
much alike and how we have to move on blahblahblahblah. At the risk
of being callous, even mentioned Paolo to him, just to show that *I'm*
getting on with *my* life. I think it might have worked, but I'm not entirely convinced.

At Ted's introduction, made a dinner date with Miles Maxwell,
that unlucky British correspondent who was kidnapped by terrorists
a couple of times. Remember that? He should be interesting, and
he's taking me to a very posh restaurant on the roof of the Hotel

Eden. So why am dreading it? Love to Truman, and to you too, of course.

Wish You Were Here,
Bogie

Date: July 20
From: VioletMorgan
To: KateBogart
Subject: RE: *La Dolce Vita*

Rooftop Roman dinners with a dashing war correspondent, a heartsick Adonis aching for you thousands of miles away, and a seaside tryst with a sinewy, sensuous Latin lover willing to give up the bullfight for a life spent wandering the globe with you. La Dolce Vita indeed!

Q: Is there a statue in all of Rome as beautiful as your ex-husband?

A: No.

As you know, I have always been very fond of your ex, and while I love my own sweet and constant mate, I'd poison his Oatios tomorrow for just one kiss from that gorgeous slab of male pulchritude named Jack MacTavish.

So, I think you're crazy for divorcing him in the first place. Nevertheless, I understand your reasons, as you are both already married to impossible lifestyles. What I don't get is your rationale for hanging on to this cruel and unusual housecat. But that is apparently my cross to bear.

Wish You Were Here Too,
St. Violet in Misery

Date: July 20
From: KateBogart
To: TedConcannon
Subject: Last Night

Dear Teddy: Dined with Miles Maxwell last night atop the Hotel Eden. Glorious views at sunset as the city lights emerged through a soft pink haze. Maxwell's not at all dull or hard to look at. A bit supercilious, but I guess that's part of his charm. Still, he doesn't seem to have adjusted to life away from the war zone. Seems to think everyone he meets is a terrorist, a tool, or a tyrant. Can't grasp that sometimes a waiter is just a waiter and really just wants to take your order. He bristled at the suggestion that this attitude might not be a boon to a career in travel writing, but he bristled graciously just the same.

After dinner, we went to hear some lovely music in the Borghese Gardens. Since it was such a warm night, I wanted to walk home, and Maxwell, gentleman (or cad) that he is, insisted on seeing me to my hotel. Maybe it's my imagination, but I do believe I detected a moment of hesitation, the kind in which the walker expects the walkee to invite him up to her room. Of course no such invite was ever extended, and Maxwell had to settle for a cordial handshake. I know you're busy, Ted, but this is where it gets good . . .

I hit the bed right away but as I was dozing off to a well-earned sleep, I heard my name being called from the street. At first I thought I was dreaming, but this was really happening. I opened my shutters Juliet-like, and sure enough, there in the glare of the streetlight stood Miles Maxwell, wearing nothing but his underpants and a desperate expression. "So, the gentleman *is* a cad!" methought, and a pathetic one to boot.

But Maxwell wasn't trying to get into my pajamas at all. It turns out that just a few blocks away from here, in one of those charming little alleyways in the Centro Storico, poor Maxwell was approached by a gang of robbers who took everything from him, including his Rolex, his best Harvey Nichols shoes, and his very sharp Ermenegildo Zegna summer suit. Ah, Rome! Even the street criminals have good taste!

Maxwell tried to get a taxi, and he apparently appealed to quite a few passers-by, but would you help a raving Englishman roaming the streets in his underpants in the middle of the night?

Once he explained the situation, I had to let him up to my room. He spent the night sleeping on the cold tile floor, or trying to, anyway. Every time I thought of him standing out there depantsed and sputtering with rage, while tourists made indiscreet detours around him, I got a fit of teenaged giggles. I think there were even a few guffaws. Okay, there were quite a few guffaws. In fact, I'm guffawing right now. Maxwell, however, was not amused.

This morning, I tried to make up for any further damage I did to his precious male pride. Went out and bought him some clothes, then took him to the police station to file his complaint. When we left the station, you could hear the *carabinieri* laughing for blocks. Remarkably, except for a few snide anti-Italian remarks that involuntarily escaped from the corner of his mouth, Maxwell was a good sport when all was said and done. I do feel sorry for him, naturally, but there aren't too many tears in my espresso. After all, if you can afford a Rolex and Ermenegildo Zegna in the first place, you can afford to lose them, too.

Thanks for the introduction, Teddy! I had great fun. It may be the highlight of my trip!

Wish You Were Here to Share It,
Kate

PS: He wears garters! (Guffaw!)

Date:	July 20
From:	KateBogart
To:	Manowar
Subject:	How's Your Portuguese?

Dear Maxwell: Thanks again for a lovely dinner, and for the er . . . entertainment afterward. I hope that you have recovered from the indignity of it all. You really are cute when you're humbled.

I'm wondering if you could do me a favor. I received the attached e-mail from my Portuguese bullfighter friend today, but I don't know the language at all. So I'm offering you the chance to see how much you retained from those childhood summers in Madeira. He's due here in a few days, so if you can't make sense of it soon, can you let me know? I'm quite anxious about this.

Kate

Date:	July 20
From:	Manowar
To:	KateBogart
Subject:	RE: How's Your Portuguese?

Dear Ms. Bogart: Thank you so much for helping me in my hour of need. Let me say that I particularly appreciate the canary yellow trousers you selected for me to wear to the police station. Very smart those, and a big hit with the *carabinieri*. I also take great satisfaction in having presented you with the opportunity to laugh yourself into a deep and otherworldly slumber. I now count you as a true friend and I am only happy to return your kind gestures. I will attack the enclosed missive with my feeble childhood Portuguese straightaway.

Gratefully,
Miles Maxwell

Date:	July 21
From:	Manowar
To:	KateBogart
Subject:	Sonnets from the Portuguese

Dear Ms. Bogart: I am so sorry to bring you this bit of unpleasant news, but it seems that "your little Portuguese" (if I may borrow from the Brownings) has done you wrong. Following is an approximation of his words:

My Kate: Please forgive me, but I cannot be with you in Rome. When I hear (sic) Inga's testimony in court, I realized that I have dedicated my life to cruelty, suffering, and injustice. I now see things clearly. I have excused the charges against Inga and I am going with her to Sweden so that we can be married as man and wife. Like you, she is a strong, noble, and beautiful woman, and we are very much in love. Together we will follow the way of St. Francis and dedicated (sic) our lives to protecting God's innocent creatures against needless torture and harm. I only hope he will accept my penance.

It is a difficult choice to make, but I am very happy for our time together, my Kate, and hope that you are too. I pray one day that you will also find what you are searching for. Until then, I beg for your forgiveness and understanding. I know that we will meet again, if only in our dreams.

Always,
Paolo

Date:	July 21
From:	KateBogart
To:	Manowar
Subject:	RE: Sonnets from the Portuguese

Ouch! Now who's been depantsed? Luckily for you, Maxwell, I don't believe in killing the messenger. Thanks just the same.

Kate

Date: July 22
From: Manowar
To: KateBogart
Subject: While Rome Burns

Dear Ms. Bogart: Since I have already unwittingly intruded on very private territory, I am going to risk further impropriety by being frank. As I see it, you're better off to have it over with this man sooner rather than later. If you'll pardon my saying it, he seems to me no more evolved than the bulls he puts down from week to week. Anyone who would turn his back on a woman as intelligent, as attractive, and as spirited as you are might even be criminally insane.

I have very recently separated from my lover of many years, a war photographer who decided that the world's danger zones were far more compelling subject matter than yours truly. I sympathize with the pain of your situation all too well, but I do hope you won't make it worse by sulking about Rome in despair.

Tonight, I intend to take in the sights of the Palatine and Colosseum lights and go in search of a good wine, live jazz, and wanton Roman nightlife. You are more than welcome to join me. You won't be able to reach me until then, so if you are feeling up to it, just meet me under the oculus at the Pantheon at 8:00. I'll be the bloke in the yellow trousers.

Sincerely,
Miles Maxwell

Date: July 23
From: KateBogart
To: VioletMorgan
Subject: That's Amore!

Well Vi, Paolo has indeed given up the bullfight, but not for me. It turns out that he was deeply affected by the Valkyrie's courtroom testimony. He is going to Sweden to dedicate himself to her and the animal rights cause. It would be so much sadder, if it weren't so laughably absurd. Feel like a fool, and don't know why I ever let my guard down.

At least Miles Maxwell has supplied some diversion. Last night, he thoughtfully surprised me with a rented Vespa. We cruised through the city in true Roman fashion to see the ancient sites with their nighttime glow on. We took in some jazz in a beautiful garden near the Colosseum, then we went nightclub-hopping in Testaccio, where Maxwell kept my mind off my broken heart by making an ass of himself on the dance floors of some very hip, very loud discos. He's really not a bad guy at all, once you get to know him, and even sort of sweet.

Paolo "prays" that someday I might "find what I am searching for." What I am searching for right now is a big damn gun so I can hunt him down and shoot him. But I have to admit that I am a bit lost, at least in the short term. I'm not so sure if I should go through with the seaside trip alone. It might just aggravate my heartsickness.

One thing's for certain: there'll be no more men in my life. They just make things messy. I'm taking a vow of celibacy, starting right now. If St. Teresa could do it, and still muster up all that ecstasy, so can I.

Oh, how I wish you were here!
Kate

Date: July 23
From: KateBogart
To: Manowar
Subject: *Arrivaderci Roma!*

Maxwell! Thanks so much for showing me Rome's nightlife. I'm still reeling from it. Or is that a hangover buzzing inside my head? Oh well, working right on through it. Thanks so much for your offer to join me down South. It would indeed help to defray the cost of that pricey resort, and I'm sure we could have a time of it, but I couldn't take advantage of your generosity or friendship any further. Nor do I think I could handle one more negroni headache.

Have to confess that when I first met you I thought you were one dry crumpet. Boy, you proved me wrong! What a pal you've been.

I'm sure our paths will cross again sometime. In London? In New York? Wherever it is, I hope it's soon. Until then, keep writing and keep traveling.

Your friend,
Kate

Date: July 23
From: Manowar
To: KateBogart
Subject: RE: *Arrivaderci Roma!*

I'm afraid the loss is all mine, Ms. Bogart. I do believe I enjoyed our days in Rome together even more than dodging sniper bullets in Beirut in my reckless youth. Much more, in point of fact, and I was so looking forward to spending some time with you by the sea. I do sympathize with your reasoning, however, even if it works counter to my selfish desires. I too hope our paths cross again, and I find it extremely gratifying to know that I am not a "dry crumpet."

Fondly,
Miles

Date: July 24
From: KateBogart
To: TedConcannon
Subject: Backing Out

Ciao, Ted! Said good-bye to Maxwell last night. You were absolutely right, by the way; he's a prince. After his run-in with those outlaws, he showed me Rome at night from the back of a perky Vespa and even did some translating for me. All right, it was a farewell letter from a

Portuguese bullfighter who was supposed to join me in Positano this week. So you were right on all counts. No gloating! But you'll be pleased to know I've taken a vow of celibacy. And this time, I mean it.

Ted, I want to skip Positano. It's so romantic and I'm afraid that I'll get all torchy and blue there. It's just not for me. Can't you find someone else to file a story next week so I can come home early and get drunk with my cat and plan my next escape? What about one of the sports writers? They're always on the road. Those guys can whip up stuff on places like Cincinnati and Tampa–St. Pete in their sleep. Or that scary old mummy in Lifestyles? Maybe she can do an update on the Hamptons, or Boca in the off-season or something. C'mon, Ted, have a heart. I'm homesick and lovesick and just plain sick of it all.

Signed,
Through with Men (Except for you, of course, and Jack, and Truman.)

Date: July 25
From: TedConcannon
To: KateBogart
Subject: RE: Backing Out

Dear TWM: Lucky for you I used to write advice to the lovelorn back when I was just a lollipop-wielding Fauntleroy in short pants. In your plea to skip Positano, do I detect at least a little bit of self-inflicted punishment? Maybe as payment for making a bad choice in a particular Portuguese bullfighter? Tsk-tsk-tsk. That's not my fiery and resilient little redhead.

Don't beat yourself up, kid. Take your tired, swollen feet and your battered heart to recover by the sea. You've earned it. Once you're face to face with that deep blue ocean I bet you'll forget all about the rat bastard. Plus, I won't have to find a pinch-hitter for you. Besides, that "scary old mummy in Lifestyles" was a featured item in the obits over a year ago. Where the heck have you been?

I know it's expensive in Positano, and I have a feeling Señor Bull-fighter was probably laying out the euros for this splurge. No? It raises the question as to where those guys carry all that money in those tight little pants. I'll see what I can do re: getting you a little more for your budget, but don't expect the moon, as my clout around here seems to depreciate by the minute.

Miss Lonelyhearts

PS: Take it from me, if you were serious about celibacy you would've just stayed married.

Date:	July 25
From:	KateBogart
To:	TedConcannon
Subject:	RE: RE: Backing Out

Dearest Ted: Nothing to revive a girl's broken spirit like a budget increase. I know just the place to spend it, too. I'm on the next train out. Sorry about the mummy.

Positano, here I come!

Kate

Date:	July 26
From:	GamblinRose
To:	KateBogart
Subject:	I Bet!

Dear Kate: I bumped into Violet last night at the grocery store loading up on cases of beer and giant bags of potato chips. I think that's all Shane and his band live on, so I'm going to send them over a nice lasagna. Violet is wearing her hair fuschia pink and spiky short this summer. I think she's trying to get fired from her job.

She told me that the Portuguese bullfighter stood you up in Rome.

Typical. Some men are just unreliable and I hope you're not taking it
too hard. I know how it feels, having put up with your saxophone-
blowing, artistic genius of a father before he went on that neverend-
ing "European tour" back in the 70s. After years of feeling abandoned,
neglected, and just plain duped, I eventually learned the value of this
piece of good old Brooklyn wisdom: *"Fuhgedaboudit!"*

Violet tells me that you have taken another vow of celibacy. I told
the Sisters of Perpetual Bingo all about it at our weekly poker game,
and we've all placed a wager on how long you can go. Violet's in on
the bet, too! She only gave you five days, though. I picked eight. Moira
went the highest at fifteen, but that's just because her granddaughter
was born on the 15th of June. Althea picked seven and Ina's got
eleven, I think. This is so exciting! Keep me posted, honey.

Love,
Mom

CHAPTER 4

✈

In Positano

Date: July 26
From: KateBogart
To: GamblinRose
Subject: RE: I Bet!

Thanks for that heartwarming support, Mother dear. It's always comforting to know that your mother regards your love life as just another horse race. I can tell you now that Moira, being the most confident of my supporters, is about to make you all a little poorer, and she could have chosen a much later date, too.

Anyway, after trains from Rome to Naples to Sorrento, hopped the bus for the twisting, death-defying, and insanely scenic ride along the Amalfi Coast. Quite a thrill, and well worth all the shuttling. Am now at a very sweet hotel called La Fenice, on the outskirts of Positano. There are amazing views of the Tyrrhenian from the grounds here and the room is even larger than I expected, as it is distinctly lacking the Portuguese bullfighter that was supposed to come with it. Another story from the heartbroken files of Kate Bogart, I'm afraid. But at least it's a short one.

There's nothing to cure a broken heart like solitude, scenery, and sea air. I'll be resting and recovering here for the rest of the week, then heading back home. Can't wait to see you!

Wish You Were Here,
Kate

Date: July 26
From: JackMacTavish
To: KateBogart
Subject: Culture Shock

Hey, Katie. Back in SF since last week. Having a hard time adjusting. Of course. Every time I come back from a trip, it takes me longer to acclimate (sp?) to all the Banana Republicans sucking on their cell phones and power-driving those gas-guzzling SUVs. (Someday someone's gonna have to sit me down and explain the appeal of those things.) What's worse, everyone's into road rage, even when they're not in their cars. This ain't the San Francisco of freelovin' yore. Janis and Jerry must be rolling in their early graves.

Maybe I'm just not cut out for the 21st century. Fighting the impulse not to run back to the jungle tomorrow.

Wonder how you're doing with that bullfighting dude. The more I think about it, the more the match just doesn't make sense. I know you dig the old world charms and all that, but that guy sounds a little too Eurocentric even for you.

Going up to Marin in a couple of days to that meditation retreat where I'm really going to try to figure myself out. In the meantime, you're all I think about. Where are you and what're you doing there?

Love,
Yr Jackson

Date: July 27
From: KateBogart
To: JackMacTavish
Subject: RE: Culture Shock

Dear Jack: I'm in Positano now. On the outskirts, actually. Much easier to take than Rome, thanks to merciful sea breezes. Sorry to hear that your old hometown feels so strange to you, but if it's any comfort you'll be pleased to know that Rome is the cell phone capital of the world and Positano is crawling with the conspicuously rich, tanned, and bethonged. (Someday somebody's gonna have to sit *me* down and explain the appeal of *those* things.)

To catch you up: The bullfighter was supposed to meet me in Rome and accompany me here, but instead, he left me for a Swedish animal rights activist. He threw me, along with the bull, so to speak, and he plans to join her in the fight to protect defenseless animals against senseless humans. Noble, right?

Feel a bit foolish, of course, but decided to come to Positano anyway, just to shake off the stress of the city. Have sworn off men for now, much to the amusement of Violet, my mother, and the Sisters of Perpetual Bingo, who all have a wager riding on how long I can go without breaking my vow. I'm sure you can get in on it if you're so inclined. Just give 'em a call.

Wish You Were Here (Even If You Are a Man),
Kate

Date: July 27
From: KateBogart
To: VioletMorgan
Subject: *La Dolce Far Niente*

Dear Violet: Thanks so much for filling Rose in on my vow of celibacy. Thanks also for giving me five days in the sick little wager you've all made. Too bad you're going to lose that bet.

You'll be displeased to know that day two has passed without the distractions of a man, unless you count the waiter who served the tender calamari and cool, citrusy wine I had at lunch, or the kindly bus driver who shuttled me up the vertiginous roads to the village of Montepertuso. There, I walked off my lunch with a late-afternoon hike to the precious cliff-clinging hamlet of Nocelle and drank in the wondrous views over Positano and the Amalfi Coast as the sun set gloriously over the water, with nary a man in sight.

Here in Positano, I've been enjoying what the Italians call *"la dolce far niente."* It means "the sweetness of doing nothing." And oh, how sweet it is! How're things at the office, by the way?

Don't You Wish You Were Here?
Kate

Date: July 27
From: Manowar
To: KateBogart
Subject: Personal and Confidential

Dear Ms. Bogart: When I got to Fiumicino Airport, my conscience would not let me board my plane. Perhaps our Roman holiday does not bear the same significance for you as it does for me. Be that as it may, since you left I have not been able to think of anything or anyone other than you. Most unusual.

I have not been in this situation for quite some time, frankly, and these feelings have taken me completely by surprise. I am not at all certain of any proper course of action, as things are especially complicated due to the recent unpleasantness with your bullfighter. While a wiser man might have just gone home to wait for a more opportune moment or for his childish infatuation to subside, I have never been a very practical sort. I booked a flight to Naples, and will be arriving in Positano tomorrow morning.

I am hoping that you will be so kind as to give me an afternoon of your time to help me sort out my condition. I am staying at the Palazzo

Murat, but it might be better if we meet in neutral territory. Let's say the pizzeria, Lo Guarracino, at 2:00 tomorrow. It is quite popular, so you can ask at your hotel for directions. If you don't come, I will simply take it as a gesture that I have seriously overstepped all proper bounds, and I will return to London as scheduled.

Anxiously,
Miles

Date: July 27
From: KateBogart
To: Manowar
Subject: RE: Personal and Confidential

Maxwell: Your e-mail sure has caught me by surprise. I'm flattered and touched and at a total loss. Since you've already been silly enough to follow me here, don't top yourself by running off to London without letting me explain my situation in person. Lo Guarracino it is.

Kate

Date: July 28
To: VioletMorgan
From: KateBogart
Subject: Day 3, and counting . . .

Well, Violet, my oldest and most devoted friend, day three has passed with my vow unbroken, despite some serious temptation thrown in my path. It turns out that Miles Maxwell developed a little schoolboy crush on me while we were running about Rome together. He actually followed me here to make his feelings known and to see if I returned his affections. Imagine that!

Honestly, I hadn't really looked at Maxwell that way, as I thought him initially to be an arrogant twit. Told him so, too. I also told him how pleased I was when he turned out to be such thoughtful and entertaining company once we'd actually spent some time together. Just as honestly, he told me that he had pegged me for an uptight, hard-hearted, castrating man-hater, and he was just as surprised to learn that I wasn't nearly as bad as all that. As you can imagine, all of this honesty seems to have cooled any of the heat that was building in the love-starved loins of Miles Maxwell.

We laughed over what an impossible match we'd make, and we agreed that we'd last much longer as friends. He admits to being a little out of sorts since giving up the career that defined his life for almost twenty years, along with his last lover, a war photographer named Odette. He thinks I might even be a substitute for Odette, who's actually more addicted to danger than he ever was. They'd been engaged for years, but when Maxwell finally called her bluff and quit his job, she got cold feet and refused to leave the battlefield. Even though I felt sorry for him as he was telling me this sob story, I have to admit, I sympathize more with her. Why give up a fascinating, extraordinary career for something as pedestrian and constricting as marriage? (No offense.)

Poor Maxwell. He attributes his infatuation and his impulsiveness to a Darwinian biological midlife impulse beyond his control, and I don't think that's a bad analysis of the situation. I acknowledged that I am in no position to get involved with anyone no matter how attractive he might be, as I am very deeply attached to my own itinerant career. Besides, I have made some serious errors in that direction in the past, the very recent past even, and we both wondered why we tend to fall for the most impossible people.

So, there we sat at the most romantic pizzeria in the world, a sort of twig and stone treehouse with the obligatory view of the sea, the sunlight beaming off the water, the fishing boats and pleasure crafts bobbing in the bay, and Maxwell staring into his salad plate all brave and abashed. For a brief moment I thought I must be out of my mind. After all, there was an accomplished, intelligent, well-to-do, well-dressed man with plush bangs, a winning smile, and a perfect arrangement of character lines. He went to a great deal of trouble to put his heart and pride on the line for little old me, and my first instinct was to talk him out of it! But then I remembered my vow, and St. Teresa, and I realized I was doing the right thing.

It would be unfair to lead Maxwell on. Just because he's a catch, doesn't mean he's my catch. Maxwell came around to see that following me here was just a lark, and probably just a way of putting off his new career and a desperate attempt to get over his last lover. We said a very civilized good-bye, promised to check in with each other from time to time, and to never talk about it again.

He is setting sail for Naples tomorrow. Honestly, I'll be surprised if I ever see him again, as I think his embarrassment over this incident will just increase with time and distance. There's something just a little sad in that, but also a little sweet. What's most important is that I remain fancy free, and true to my vow of celibacy. So there!

Wish You Were Here, My Faithless Friend,
Kate

Date: July 29
From: VioletMorgan
To: KateBogart
Subject: RE: Day 3, and counting . . .

Dear Bogie, nice to know that you're prejudiced against all marriages and not just mine. As always, I think you're looking at everything all wrong. Marriage isn't a trap, and I haven't bet against you; I've bet *on* you.

It must be hard for you being chased, I mean chaste, all the time, but you seem to have handled yourself with uncharacteristic control and maturity. Still, I can't believe that there's not one man in all of Positano able to make a dishonest woman of you. C'mon, Bogie, vows are for breaking! Gather ye rosebuds while ye may and all that. I could really use the extra cash!

V

Date: July 30
From: KateBogart
To: VioletMorgan
Subject: Oops!

Dear Violet: Maxwell hired a boat to take him back to Naples yesterday, but before he was even out of sight of Positano, he ordered the boatman to turn around and come to La Fenice. He wanted to see me one more time. Here we go again, I thought, but you and St. Teresa would have been very proud of me. That guy only thought he'd dealt with terrorists until he met me! I was stubborn and steadfast and battlefield fierce.

Then he trotted out a secret weapon. That's right, our Miles Maxwell, hardened survivor of public school spankings, various and sundry tribal skirmishes, several murderous jihads, and a couple of extremist kidnappings, actually started to well up a bit. You know I can't fight it when men cry, Violet.

The boatman was watching the Englishman come apart with devilish amusement, so in defense of his pride, I brought him back to my room. Maxwell finally seemed to get a grip and was about to march off to the beach, soundly defeated but having pitched a noble fight.

That's when I made the fatal mistake. I gave him an encouraging parting embrace, a strictly friendly gesture, mind you. But in an instant it melted into a bona fide clinch, which lead to a surprisingly passionate kiss. If there's anything I find harder to resist than a good-looking man in tears, it's a good, deep, heartfelt kiss. A few kisses later, I heard the boat's motor rev, grumble, then fade away into the distance, in a way that told me this is a common occurrence here in Positano. Just like the boatman, I think you can fill in the rest of the blanks.

Just as knowingly, the boatman returned today, still loaded up with Maxwell's luggage. This time, Maxwell, more embarrassed and apologetic than ever, agreed to give me some time to think and room to breathe. Of course, he also wants to see me again. Even invited me to stop in London on my way home.

Oh, Violet, what is my problem? All I wanted was to simplify my life, but despite my own good sense, here I am right smack dab in the middle of another quandary. Do I take Maxwell up on his offer and get deeper into another doomed affair, or do I call it one of those things, go back to New York, and start all over again?

One way or another, I guess you can collect your damn winnings. Congratulations, by the way, Miss Smugface. I don't know which I'm dreading more, the wrath of St. Teresa or the wrath of my mother when she finds out she lost a bet on my account.

Wish You Were Here,
Kate

Date: July 31
From: VioletMorgan
To: KateBogart
Subject: Jackpot!

Oh, Bogie, we both got lucky! The only surprise is that you broke your vow with Maxwell. That, I didn't see coming. I thought for sure it would be some sort of shiny, suntanned European import/export guy all got up in designer sunglasses and linen clothes that catch the breeze just enough to accentuate his languid manhood, or someone like that. Not at all my image of Maxwell, but now that I think of it, he does fit the basic profile: handsome, successful, interesting, difficult, and maybe a wee bit messy on the inside.

You don't know how happy you've made me. I just bought a pair of Miu Miu's I cannot afford at all, even on a summer sale with a lot of exclamation points after it. I really need that money. I'm calling your mother right away.

Who knows you even better than you know yourself? Me, that's who! Oh, and don't run off with Maxwell. I miss you, and I hate your cat.

Love,
Your Psychic Friend

Date: July 31
From: KateBogart
To: Manowar
Subject: Simplicity

Dear Maxwell: I'm guessing you're back in London by now. As you asked, I took some time to reflect and I really don't think I should join you there. It is such an exciting city and such a tempting offer. Still, things are much too complicated.

After all, you don't seem to have really recovered from your relationship with your war photographer, and I'm as unlikely to give up my rambling ways as she is. As for me, when it comes to matters of the heart, I'm my own worst enemy, and it's time to change. Be that as it may, I simply don't see myself running off to some drafty London estate to sip port with a blanket on my knees, while the dogs snore and fart by the fire. Cozy as it may be, it's not the life for me. Too English.

That doesn't mean that I regret our spontaneous little slip in Positano entirely. But really, we're not a couple of randy college kids on Spring Break, and in retrospect I wish that we had been able to control ourselves.

I will always think back fondly of the laughs we shared in Rome, before things were complicated by sex. I hope that we can return to that level of pure, platonic friendship in time. Toward that end, I feel that we should keep the Atlantic between us, and let time and distance work their healing magic. I hope you feel the same.

Wish You Were Here, But It's Probably Better You're Not,
Kate

Date: August 1
From: Manowar
To: KateBogart
Subject: RE: Simplicity

Dear Ms. Bogart: Just to clarify some points:

1)   Not all Englishmen live on estates. I actually inhabit a hastily furnished loft dwelling in a renovated factory on what once was the unpopular side of the Thames. Now that the Tate Modern and the new Globe have come along, however, I have quite a lot of company in the flocks of American tourists asking me where they might find a public bathroom. To which I always reply, "Tokyo, as the British prefer to bathe in private."

2)   I am allergic to dogs. Even if I were able to tolerate them physically, I am not especially fond of any creatures that stare at me enviously while I dine, or have at themselves while I entertain guests. It's most discomforting.

3)   When I asked you to come to London, I was not proposing marriage, or scheming to turn you into some dispirited prisoner-of-love-gone-stale out of some Brontë novel. I was merely suggesting that we take some time to figure out what might be occurring between us. Perhaps our little "slip" in Positano was not a mistake at all but, rather, something genuine and enduring. Perhaps we two peripatetic souls might some day find that we are indeed capable of experiencing the ease and comfort of friendship along with the joy of passion and tenderness, which as I see it, is why we were born. Is it not?

Nevertheless, no one understands better than I that restless spirits make for irregular bedfellows. I have already paid a dear price trying to deny the hard truth of this with my former fiancée. Turbulence comes with the territory of our chosen paths, I'm afraid, and I sympathize strongly with your desire to make your personal life less chaotic. Your prudence and foresight may prove wise in the long run.

Yours,
Miles

Date: August 1
From: GamblinRose
To: KateBogart
Subject: Win Some, Lose Some

Hello, Honey: Just off the phone with a gloating Violet. The Sisters of Perpetual Bingo and I have mixed feelings regarding her news. We are depressed to have lost our bet, but impressed by your way with men. Love 'em and leave 'em, baby, and don't ever take out any joint accounts. That's my advice. In the meantime, that wager's coming right out of your inheritance.

When will you make your mother happy and come home? *I* wish *you* were here.

Love,
Mom

Date: August 2
From: KateBogart
To: GamblinRose
Subject: Homeward Bound

Mom: Don't know how much bigmouth Violet may have told you, but you will be pleased to know that I am in Naples now waiting for a flight home. Can't wait to see you and tell you all about my travels. Also, must kill Violet.

Love,
Kate

Date: August 2
From: KateBogart
To: TedConcannon
Subject: The Truth About Positano

Ted: You might as well hear it from me. After a very long and deep exchange with Maxwell, sent him back to England to straighten himself out. A great guy really, but things got a little out of hand. Luckily, we are both mature, sophisticated adults who know a mistake when we make it, and we've both come to our senses.

Will be in New York soon. So find yourself a substitute for at least one week, preferably two. Maybe even three. I'd like to get reacquainted with my cat.

Kate

Date: August 2
From: TedConcannon
To: KateBogart
Subject: RE: The Truth About Positano

Gee, Kate, I hoped you guys would hit it off, but I'm sorry if it turned into such trouble for you. Miles is a great guy when you get to know him. He just got into the racket too young and spent too much time in the hot spots. He's never had a chance to work up the social know-how necessary to deal with women who aren't training a Glock on him. His last girlfriend was no help, a real tough cookie who was a little too proud of her battle scars. Odette got him into all kinds of dangerous scrapes, and I think he's better off without her.

I thought a worldly woman like you might be able to set him straight. But what do I know? My own wife is like some mysterious Sphinx to me. Where does she get all that energy to run her consulting firm, and sit on committees, and boss around her staff, and go to parties, and make to-do lists, and run the world the way she does? She's even been toying with the idea of political office. It's scary!

Oh well, my matchmaking days are over. From here on in, it's strictly don't ask/don't tell when it comes to the subject of you and Miles Maxwell.

Hope Positano was good for you otherwise, and don't worry, you can take as much time off as you want. Miles is going to pinch-hit for you. A lucky break for all of us. Can't wait to have you back in New York.

Ted

CHAPTER 5

✈

At Home

Date: August 3
From: KateBogart
To: TedConcannon
Subject: Say What?

Ted: Last night I arrived home exhausted and bleary-eyed to a month's worth of mail, a stack of unpaid bills, and a cat so happy to see me, or so pissed-off that I left him behind, that he shredded the toilet paper into a million fluffy bits. Then, this morning I checked my e-mail and learned that a certain newspaper editor has handed over the column that I usually write to a former war correspondent suffering from a premature midlife crisis in which I just played a cameo role. Why, Ted, why?

I know that I shouldn't mind so much. You need to fill a space, I need a break, and Maxwell needs a favor. Just for the record, however, it makes me uncomfortable.

Kate

Date: August 4
From: KateBogart
To: Manowar
Subject: Congratulations

Dear Maxwell: I heard the news that you are going to write "WYWH" while I lay low. At first, I wasn't sure how I felt about it. Frankly, I'm a bit territorial, as it is about the most reliable job someone with the travel bug and no career ambitions to speak of can find. Still, I wish you well, and if you need any advice, feel free to contact me. But tell me, are you really going to stay at budget lodgings and eat at cheap restaurants? Or do you plan to get around researching the "low end" somehow?

    Kate

Date: August 5
From: Manowar
To: KateBogart
Subject: RE: Congratulations

Dear Ms. Bogart: Might I remind you that I once spent three weeks blindfolded in what I surmise was a former meat locker in Beirut, and that I also once kept lodgings in a church belfry in Tegucigalpa, where the return of the resident bats at dawn served as my morning wake-up call. That was far preferable to The Kandahar Ritz, the small dirt cave I called my home in 1991, but I will spare you those details.

    As for alternative dining options, I once ate an ant sandwich to win over some very imposing tribal leaders on the warpath outside Mbuji-Mayi. After that, I think I can handle anything that even the lowest of the "low end" purveyors can toss my way.

    Must be off now. There are articles to be written! Hope you are well.

    Miles Maxwell

Date: August 6
From: VioletMorgan
To: KateBogart
Subject: *Wilkommen, Bienvenue,* etc.

Welcome Back, Bogie! I don't dare call, as the Evil Lord of Independent Cinema keeps one dark, distrustful eye trained on me at all
times ever since he caught me booking an out-of-town gig for the
band. E-mail is safer because he has no idea how to monitor it. He's
still learning how to use a push-button phone. At last count, he has
gone through 23 cell phones because he smashes them all in frustration. Now I just order them by the case.

Anyway, miss you like crazy. But you're probably still smarting
over that bet I won from your mother and her friends. Let me make it
up to you later with a bottle of champagne. Your roof or mine?

Vi

Date: August 6
From: VioletMorgan
To: KateBogart
Subject: Sweet Freedom!

Bogie: Wish you would pick up, but you'll be pleased to know I won't
be haranguing you with any more e-mails, because I just got fired.
That's right. The giant reptile I work for is indeed unable to monitor
the e-mails. I guess his webbed feet get in the way or something, so
he has been paying some junior high cybergenius fifty cents and a
footlong to go through them once a week. Turns out he doesn't much
like personal e-mails on the job and he wants to know who "this Kate
Bogart" is. Also doesn't much like being called "a giant movie-
producing reptile," "the Evil Lord of Independent Cinema," "His
Worthlessness," "Ol' Fat Bastard," or "a waste of precious plasma."
Has asked me to pack my things and go. It's the first time I've attacked any of his orders with gusto. Afraid, however, of having to live

in subway tunnels. It doesn't help that I also seem to have lost my best friend.

Violet

Date: August 6
From: KateBogart
To: VioletMorgan
Subject: RE: Sweet Freedom!

Oh, Violet, you weren't fired; you were liberated! That job was a waste of your potential anyway. This is the best thing that ever happened to you, after that time you won those Duran Duran tickets on the radio.

This calls for a celebration. Let's make it my roof. Bring Shane and the band. We can keep the neighbors up, then flirt with the cops when they report us. Oh, fun, fun, fun!

Your Best Friend Always,
Kate

PS: By the way, apology accepted.

Date: August 7
From: JackMacTavish
To: KateBogart
Subject: Spirit Rocks!

Katie: An amazing experience at Spirit Rock. Met a Buddhist nun who used to run a brothel up in Saskatune (sp?). Not kidding, either. Her name is Sharmi Shotu (sp?). Not her given name. That's Willow Peterka-Pyczstek (sp?). She really helped me see through my illusions more than any therapist, guru, bartender, or anyone I've ever talked to about you.

She got turned on to the Buddha in prison. Showed me some new meditation and breathing techniques and told me about concentrating on the "Holy I." She helped me realize that I don't need you to live my life, that I was just clinging to you to fill my inner emptiness and my fear of solitude. Sharmi says I need to open up to these things and cherish them, which is what she thinks all my wandering around jungles and mountains and deserts is all about, a yearning for this inner peace. I think she has a point.

Marriage, she claims, is an earthly delusion in which we believe that we have been miraculously united with some other person through some sort of ritual, when really we are always alone, and it is far more truthful to the laws of the universe to accept and embrace our solitude. Only then can we ever experience true love. Whew!

I know you think a lot of this is just a bunch of New Age claptrap or something, but this woman was the real thing, Katie. She was educated and worldly and wise, quoting Rilke and Jung and Plato and L'il Kim right along with Shantideva and Chandrakirti (sp? sp?). I left feeling stronger and more centered than ever.

Of course I love you. I will always love you, Katie. But I will always love my mother too, and my first grade teacher, and the guy who sold me my bus ticket, and that teenage Satan worshiper who blew away his shop instructor in Fresno today. Love, in its purest form, knows no bounds and no hierarchy, that's what Sharmi says; and it's possible for me to love you purely without feeling as if I need you to exist.

What a freakin' breakthrough! What a freakin' relief! Finally, after two years I feel like I might be able to get on with my life.

Purely Yrs,
Jackson

Date: August 7
From: KateBogart
To: JackMacTavish
Subject: RE: Spirit Rocks!

Jackson, What happy news! Your Sharmi sounds like a wise and extremely interesting person, the kind no writer could invent. Glad to
hear she got you feeling so clear headed and full of platonic apprecia-
tion for me.

By the way, in my perpetually foggy-headed way, I was thinking
of you today. It's been too long since I've been to SF, which is still my
favorite American city (after NY of course). It seems high time that
"WYWH" paid a visit. Would love to do the research before you go
running off on some nature trek or rafting adventure or something.

However, I only want to do this if you think you're really, really,
really ready for a reunion. I don't think either of us wants a repeat of
that scene in Buenos Aires last year. (That poor waiter. Oh well. I'd
feel even worse if I'd hit *you* with that chair.)

Anyway, I can do SF any old time. It's not like it's sitting on some
shaky fault line or something. I'm home catching up and plotting my
next move, so let me know if it's okay.

Yours in Purity,
Kate

Date: August 7
From: JackMacTavish
To: KateBogart
Subject: Ready, Set, Come!

Great idea! SF doesn't seem quite that horrible now that I had all that
bad energy weeded out. Can you think of any other major US city that
has a clothing optional beach within its city limits and accessible by
public transportation?

I am totally confident that things won't get sticky between us. I
swear. I even have a date with this woman I met at a Critical Mass

demonstration last week. You know, that's the bicycle activist organization that stages shutdowns and protests all over the city. Totally empowering. She's one of the organizers. And her name is Gretchen!

I am over you like the mumps, baby, and I can't wait to see you again.

XOXO,
Jackson

Date:	August 8
From:	KateBogart
To:	TedConcannon
Subject:	Can't Keep a Good Woman Down

Ted: It's not that I don't love my hometown. I do. Had every intention of staying put for a whole month, but then I got to thinking about San Francisco and how refreshingly cool it is in the summer fog. Then, my mind wandered over to that swoony fragrance of lemon pittosporum that catches you by surprise as you turn any corner.

Soon enough, I was overcome by a bona fide jones. I started calling the airlines and the consolidators and nosing around on the Internet, and wouldn't you know it, I found a cheap airfare! In peak season, mind you. Need to book it superfast. Give me the go ahead, I'll jump on the ticket, and do a piece on San Francisco.

I know I should probably stay put for a bit, but it's just for a week or so and you know I can't resist a great deal. Besides, I don't like the idea of you handing the column over to that upstart Maxwell.

Kate

Date: August 8
From: TedConcannon
To: KateBogart
Subject: RE: Can't Keep a Good Woman Down

San Francisco? Again? Aren't you and that ex-husband over each other yet? You know that tree-hugging, vine-swinging, Nature Boy just isn't good for you. Every time you go there, you seem to forget you've already been married and divorced, and everybody you have ever known gets sucked into the vortex of your love quandary. Then we go over the whole spiel about whether you're attracted to Tarzan because he's attractive, or because he's impossible. And if you're attracted to him because he's impossible, then what does that say about you? And will you ever be able to fall in love with any one man, or will you grow old all alone with your yellowing snapshots, your dusty souvenirs, and your beloved stuffed cat?

Go to San Francisco and make yourself crazy if you want, but I've made my case.

Concerned,
Ted

Date: August 8
From: KateBogart
To: TedConcannon
Subject: RE: RE: Can't Keep a Good Woman Down

Dear Editor: Let me start by saying "Hmpf!" For your information, Jack MacTavish and I get along very well on a platonic level and I think we've both grown up quite a bit in the past couple of years. While I appreciate your concern, I do not at all appreciate your insensitive, harsh, and patronizing tone. Although it's futile, I'll ask that in the future you refrain from using it in our business and personal interactions.

I will be leaving for San Francisco next week, like it or not. And thank you, by the way.

Kate

Date: August 9
From: GamblinRose
To: KateBogart
Subject: Pick Me a Winner

Kate: The Sisters of Perpetual Bingo and I have a new wager going. How long will Kate stay in New York? Don't you love it? I picked 11 days, Ina picked 25 days, Althea went with 17 (based on a 14-day advance purchase, plus three days of restlessness), and Moira took the longshot with 39. Gutsy.

> Love,
> Mom

Date: August 9
From: KateBogart
To: GamblinRose
Subject: RE: Pick Me a Winner

Mom: I hate to enable what I think could be a serious addiction, but even more, I hate having you place bets on the twists and turns of my personal life. You'll be pleased to know, however, that you won the bet, as I already booked a cheap flight to San Francisco for next week. Go collect your winnings.

> Predictably,
> Kate

Date: August 10
From: GamblinRose
To: KateBogart
Subject: RE: RE: Pick Me a Winner

Congratulations on snapping up that cheap airfare. Told the sisters that I won the bet, and Althea's accusing me of cheating. She thinks that you were giving me inside tips. She hasn't said it in so many words, but I know how to read her silences.

Be sure to give my former son-in-law a big kiss for me. But not too big a kiss. You know what that can lead to, and we don't want to go through that again. Do we?

Love,
Mom

Date: August 10
From: Kate Bogart
To: VioletMorgan
Subject: S.O.S.

Violet: Left three messages on your phone today. Where are you? Maybe you're out on a job interview. Already? You? Maybe you're shopping.

Anyway, just letting you know that I am going to SF next week. Jack is back home. Have not seen him since last winter, so I'm looking forward to it very much. Still, a little nervous. He claims to be over "us," but he has made that claim before.

He sounded composed when I called to tell him I was coming. Happy, but not *too* happy. Still, I'm a little leery. Do you think I should put it off? Hate to do it. Scored a rare bargain airfare, but having second, third, fourth thoughts, etc.

Wish You Would Help,
Bogie

Date: August 10
From: VioletMorgan
To: KateBogart
Subject: Go West, Young Woman!

Bogie: Not shopping. Couldn't hear phone ringing. Band is practicing. Very loud. Ear plugs useless. Send help!

Anyway, I thought you were taking a break, but of course you should
go to SF. As long as you are prepared to have Jack's gorgeous head
crying on your alabaster shoulder telling you how much he loves you
and wants to run away with you and live on tubers and berries in a
tree house he has built in the rain forest with his own rugged hands.
Besides, the sex is first-rate, isn't it?

Allowing for his chronic untidiness, husband has been nothing but
a giant lump of sugar during my first week of unemployment. Very
supportive and does not want me to jump back into another job that I
loathe. If things take off, he wants me to be The Killer Abs' manager.
I pointed out that I already *am* The Killer Abs' manager, but would
happily make the transition from de facto to in facto if compensated
for my troubles. What do you think of that as a career move?

Vi

Date: August 10
From: KateBogart
To: VioletMorgan
Subject: RE: Go West, Young Woman!

Vi: Thanks for those perceptive and worldly words of support.

As to your question: Of course I think you should manage The
Killers. As long as you are prepared to keep five messy, flatulent, arrested adolescents in junk food, fishnets, and depilatories for the rest
of your life; and you see to it that all of their groupies are of legal age;
and make sure to put them in taxis in the morning before the boys
wake up and have to commit to breakfast or something.

We obviously have things to discuss. I'll talk you into your bad idea if you talk me into mine. Wine on the roof at 8:00. Attendance mandatory!

K

Date: August 11
From: KateBogart
To: JackMacTavish
Subject: Truman Capote's Bladder

Jack: Don't think I'll be coming to SF after all. Truman has come down with an infection. Have to stay and administer unpleasant medication. Hate to think of how I'd feel if something happened to him while I was away. If I left him with Violet, she'd just let nature take its course. So sorry. Maybe in the autumn?

Wish I Were There,
Kate

Date: August 11
From: JackMacTavish
To: Kate
Subject: RE: Truman Capote's Bladder

Katie, I know how much that cat means to you, but I'm really disappointed. I'm so looking forward to seeing you.

Gretchen and I really hit it off the other night. Had a great meal at Delancey (sp?) St., a restaurant staffed by ex-cons, homeless people, recovering addicts, etc. Would love to take you there. Plus I want you to meet Gretchen. You know how I respect your skeptical, distrustful East Coast social instincts. Maybe I've been blinded by the physical attraction, y'know? (You should see this woman's calves. So hot!)

But you are responsible for Truman's life, and you need to take care of the big tiger. I just hope that you're not having second thoughts because you think I'm still hung up on you. That would be a silly mistake, Katie. Everything's okay. I swear. Please come as soon as Truman gets better. I'm going to do some healing chants for him right now.

Wish You Were Here Too,
Jack

Date: August 12
From: KateBogart
To: VioletMorgan
Subject: Pants on Fire

Vi: Followed your devious, wine-fueled advice and took the deceitful way out. Postponed SF trip due to Truman's "sick bladder." Feel very lousy and afraid of jinxing poor Truman. Don't know how I let you talk me into it.

Once again, Jack assured me that he's over me. He even went on about this woman he's been seeing recently and he sounds totally smitten. Don't feel right avoiding one of my favorite cities in the world because Jack is there and *might* make things messy. What is all this apprehension? All this bellyaching? Truman's feeling better already and I'm going to San Francisco, dammit! Must call hotels.

K

Date: August 13
From: KateBogart
To: JackMacTavish
Subject: California Here I Come!

Surprise! Those healing chants did the trick. Truman is showing signs of much improvement, and after some arm-twisting and some unreasonable payola, Nurse Violet has agreed to administer the rest of his medications. For some crazy reason, I actually trust her. Will be checking into the Milano the day after tomorrow. Call me there. Can't wait to meet Gretchen!

Kate

Date:	August 14
From:	Manowar
To:	KateBogart
Subject:	The Grate Dictater

Dear Ms. Bogsrt: Please forgive any eras in this message you see I am actually dictating it to Mynah my domestic sharge dafare (Good Day, Miss!) Im afraid shes an innocent in the ways of the computah. although she swears she spend some time in sercretarial school in the Outer Hebrides (True, mum) tis highly doubtfull sush institutoins even exist. Alimentry gramma and spelling also seem uterly beyond her ken, but she is quite indispensible otherwise yes your quite welcome Mynah.

Had a bit of misfrtune researching my first artickle for Ted. Peraps the idea of a bicycle tour of the dystilleries of Speyside was not entirely wise. Although I tasted some topnotch whiskeys (Too much is the truth of it, mum) I took a nasty tumble off my bike. Yes, thank you for that illiminating insite Mynah you are right I should have known better. Broke my left arm, 2 ribs, and some asordid fingers. I am now trussed, plasterd, and swaddled like a mummy with only limited use of my too hands. Thus Mynah.

The injuries have prooved an inconveenyance that cannot compare to the hard ship of my convalesence. (Nothing wrong with him the love of a good woman wouldn't help, as I see it.) I do not appresheate idleness yet have difficulty even turning the pages of thee newspaper. Ocashunaly Mynah will attempt to read to me, an arjewous sharade that only exaserbates the pain.

I have, whoever, been aforded more than enough time to reflect on our incounter in Ittaly. You'll be pleesed to know I have come round to see your version of things and i agree that we would make a most impossible match. (He fancies you, mum.) I do believe that I behaved impechewously and immeturely and I am quite embarassed by it. (Embarassing, all right. Been moping about like a bloodhound straight on two weeks. The likes of it!) I still have warm feelings for you sorry Mynah I am still acceptionally fond of you, but I do agree tis best we except ourselves, our diffrences, and the impossiblity of our sichewation. Twas in the end nothing more serious and nothing less preshus than our own brief incounter. (He'll love you forever is what he means.)

As soon as I find a more capible amanewensis never mind what it means Mynah and stop typong ever word I say and look athe blasted keybroad for bloody I intend to finish my work on Speyside. I do look forward to your comments. Until then, I remain your admirerer and friend, Mile s manxwell, Now let's runs a spellchekc Mynah up there Press that key No not that one stop are you daft Myn now press NO not the send key the other one no not that blasted key. The left the left thelfet no

Date:	August 14
From:	Manowar
To:	KateBogart
Subject:	strike that

ms bogart—pecking keys with pencil btw teeth slow and humbling but more efficient than mynah. please ignore her insane interjections. she drinks. so sorry.

miles

Date:	August 14
From:	KateBogart
To:	Manowar
Subject:	RE: strike that

Maxwell: Sorry to hear about your Highland fling. Though the idea of bicycling from distillery to distillery is indeed intriguing, I have to say I agree with Mynah. Not to pour whiskey in your wounds, but you do have to think of your readers' safety as well as your own. Imagine the lawsuits if legions of bicycling maltophiles were suddenly to wreak havoc on the roads of Speyside all because they were following your careless lead.

Glad to hear you are feeling better re: our "brief incounter." Have hardly had a chance to give it a moment's thought myself. Hope you recover from your other injuries before Mynah does even more damage.

Get Well Soon,
Kate

Date: August 15
From: Manowar
To: KateBogart
Subject: RE: RE: strike that

not even a moment's thought. that disappoints. cuts like knife actually. can not pretend otherwise. please take moment to give some thought and report back. jaw hurts. must close.

painfully, m

Date: August 15
From: KateBogart
To: Manowar
Subject: RE: RE: RE: strike that

Oh, Maxwell, of course I remember you fondly, but my head has been full of so many things. Bills and banking and laundry and such. I am also responsible for the welfare of one large elderly housecat, a mother with a troubling gambling addiction, and a best friend in serious need of career counseling. Also have been making arrangements to go to San Francisco. Leaving today, in fact. I just haven't had the time to dwell on the Positano incident. In retrospect, it was quite sweet. Badly timed, but sweet. I am, however, deeply intrigued by Mynah. Can't get her out of my mind. Do think I'm in love with her.

Kate

Date: August 15
From: Manowar
To: KateBogart
Subject: major mynah

then you are in love with a rump-fed, one-eyed, halitosic Gorgon who bludgeoned her parents to a bloody pulp over a forbidden bit of toffee when she was not yet ten. upon her release from the reformatory mynah became the pet project of my parents who, in a rare fit of human kindness, hired her to run their summer cottage in the hebrides. although i have been terrified of her since boyhood, i much preferred her to the joyless wax figures who claimed legal parentage over me. in those long dank childhood summers bereft of toys, playmates, parental affection, and central heat, mynah became my sole source of comfort, security, and amusement. as soon as i came into my own means, i easily outbid my penurious parents for her services. thereupon the mercenary mynah hefted her considerable girth, her favourite shiny hatchet, and the shoe boxes that hold her parents ashes and brought them to london. here she spends her days subsisting on crunchies and tepid mugs of whiskey-infused pg tips, chortling at things that aren't funny on the telly, and putting the fear of god into bothersome solicitors. her parents, may they rest in peace, named her mynah apparently for the alarming high-pitched squawk that makes a forced detour through the nether regions of her sinuses before escaping from her mouth in some crude version of english. that was before their massacre of course. i too love her and would be lost without her.

now you know of our grim early years. what of yours, my dear ms. b

Date: August 16
From: KateBogart
To: Manowar
Subject: Enough About Me

Maxwell: You're getting a bit too proficient with that pencil. It can't be good for your teeth. And I seem to recall hearing something of your childhood summers in Madeira, so I have to question your honesty, if not your sanity. But since you asked:

I was born and raised in Carroll Gardens, Brooklyn. My father was a jazz musician. I have vague recollections of his music, but none of him. I also recall his disruptive friends who would occasionally take over our long narrow apartment with their bleating instruments and their outlandish get-ups. He was famously unhappy with his rent-paying gigs in Broadway house orchestras and went on a tour of Europe with an avant garde combo in 1972. Letters came to my mother and me for a while, then they stopped.

My mother waited tables by day, finished college at night, then went to work as an English teacher in NYC public schools. When she's not teaching, she spends her afternoons volunteering in literacy programs and her evenings gambling with her best friends, all veteran workers of the NYC public school system. I call them the Sisters of Perpetual Bingo. They are, to the woman, a "hoot."

My summers were spent in the tiniest whitewashed cottage in the world, a one-room shack situated like a toll booth on the sandy strip between the two highways leading into Provincetown, at the tip of Cape Cod. It felt more like the desert than the seaside. My mother cleaned rental properties, and when I was a teenager, my best friend Violet and I joined her. I have been all around the world and still don't think I've ever been so happy as on those nights when we would make meals from the food the summer people left behind, dine under the stars, and wave to the cars zooming past us on their way to their suntan-and-saltwater-taffy vacations.

Mynah sounds like a peach and you are very lucky to have her.

Speedy Recovery,
Kate

Date: August 16
From: Manowar
To: KateBogart
Subject: RE: Enough About Me

touching account of your girlhood. i particularly relish the image of you in your nubile youth and abbreviated summer togs brandishing a salvaged ear of slick buttered corn at all those lucky motorists. far more effective than any painkillers the chemist could provide. you have a lovely bedside manner indeed.

gratefully,
miles

Date: August 16
From: KateBogart
To: Manowar
Subject: RE: RE: Enough About Me

Dear Mr. Humbert: I hate to spoil your lecherous daydream, but I have to tell you that as a kid, I was the anti-Lolita. So if you want to get the picture of me in my "abbreviated summer togs" right, you might also want to add spindly legs, bony knees, a rack of shiny braces, shinier skin, and all my daring, but self-defeating, early experiments with make-up and hair mousse. At that time in my life, if someone had told me that someday a handsome, well-known, and well-to-do British journalist would be weaving fantasies about me, I probably would have laughed milk through my nose. But today, I can't help but be flattered.

Wish You Were Well,
Kate

CHAPTER 6

✈

In San Francisco

Date: August 17
From: KateBogart
To: VioletMorgan
Subject: Jack in the City

Vi: Here I am in San Francisco. Foolishly agreed to go on a bike ride with Jack and Gretchen, his new love interest. What the heck was I thinking, riding a bike in San Francisco? It's like riding a bike straight up the flipping Matterhorn! Jack was patient, of course, but Gretchen was all forced sympathy masking competitive superiority. If she wasn't so much stronger than me I'd strangle her, but this woman is exceedingly fit. She's a cable technician for the phone company and she refuses to use a cherry picker. That's right, she scales those suckers the old-fashioned way, tool belt and all.

Of course, it makes me a little jealous. After all, he's my Jack and I'm not used to seeing him kiss another woman or absent-mindedly stroke her ropy forearms the way he did at least twice during our picnic. Still, it's such a huge relief to see him happy, and I may yet warm up to her. I'm trying.

Spent the rest of the day pampering my aching legs, writing, and corresponding with crazy Maxwell, who has had an even worse run-in with a bicycle on the other side of the world. An odd man, but he sure is amusing. Tomorrow: a rest and beauty day at the Kabuki Springs and Spa. I have earned it.

Wish You Were Here,
Bogie

Date: ·   August 17
From: VioletMorgan
To: KateBogart
Subject: Good News and Bad

Bogie: The good news is the Killer Abs are going on tour, opening for Potty Mouth. Great exposure and there's the promise of a record deal. The bad news is, I'm going with them and someone else is going to have to take care of you-know-who, or you're going to have to change your career, or donate him to science or something. Won't be going for another couple of weeks. No need to come rushing back or anything. Sorry.

V.

Date: August 17
From: KateBogart
To: VioletMorgan
Subject: RE: Good News and Bad

Oh, Vi, you just spilled a milky fog over my perfect sunny California day! How can you abandon Truman and me like that? We need you so much more than Shane and those needy, untidy androgynes. After all, they can conceivably work their own can-openers, if they'd just take the time to learn.

    Who will I get to care for Truman? I can't imagine my mother climbing the five flights to my apartment. Oh God, I'm going to have to get a regular job. I can't get a regular job. I'm a travel writer, forgodsake. I have no marketable skills!

Wish You Would Stay Put,
Kate

Date: August 17
From: VioletMorgan
To: KateBogart
Subject: RE: RE: Good News and Bad

Bogie: Hmm. Hadn't thought of that. Maybe it's time to practice saying, "Would you like to supersize that?" Just a thought. Sorry again.

Love ya,
Vi.

Date: August 18
From: JackMacTavish
To: KateBogart
Subject: Superfreak!

Katiekatiekatie! Where the heck are you, babe? Called The Milano. You checked out. What's up? Really need to talk. Turns out that Gretchen comes with a catch. I knew she was too good to be true. She's bisexual. Big deal, right? It's not the first bisexual woman I've been involved with. In fact, at this point I'd start to be suspicious if I met a college-educated woman who hasn't checked out the same-sex scene.

But this isn't something Gretchen is doing for extra credit for her Women's Studies elective. She has a lover. *Now.* A woman she actually lives with. She's named Plover or Piper or something like that. Can't remember. They have an open relationship and they are looking for a third wheel, preferably one with a penis. She thinks I'm the perfect candidate. Wants me to meet her and Plover or Piper for dinner tomorrow night.

You know I pride myself on keeping an open, questioning, and progressive outlook, but I've never been in a manage a twois (sp?). Is there something wrong with me? Am I secretly square? Have you ever tried it? I feel like this uptightness is something I should overcome, but I'm nervous as hell about it. Do you think anything lasting could ever come of such an arrangement anyway? Do you think I should go through with it?

Freaking,
Jack

Date:	August 18
From:	KateBogart
To:	JackMacTavish
Subject:	RE: Superfreak!

Jackson: Moved to The Phoenix to enjoy rare break in summer fog by swimming pool. A lot of rock 'n' rollers and other long-haired, tattooed types here. Must make a note of it for Violet, who is about to abandon poor Truman to hit the road with Shane and his band. Devastating news.

To answer your questions:

1) There is nothing wrong with you at all, although you are possibly the only heterosexual man in the world who would rack his conscience and search his soul before jumping into bed with an incredibly fit, good-looking blonde and her female lover. Your own superlative good looks notwithstanding, this quality is a huge part of your personal appeal and very likely the basis for this privileged invite.
2) You are in fact today's secret square.
3) Upon our divorce, I was freed from the obligation of divulging to you any information regarding my personal sexual habits and practices. *Hah!*

4) Things will last only on the chance that all three participants are equilaterally weird. But freak not, my fair dude, as the chances of this are always higher in the state of California. Otherwise, memories of the pure physical fun of it all are sure to linger long after the whole damn thing falls apart like a house of cards in an earthquake.

5) I can't say if you should or shouldn't go through with the offer, but meeting Piper, or Plover, for a harmless dinner will surely help you make a more educated decision.

Wishing You Luck,
Kate

Date:	August 19
From:	KateBogart
To:	GamblinRose
Subject:	San Francisco Treat

Dear Mom: Sorry I missed your call yesterday. Very busy exploring San Francisco's secret walkways. They can be very hard to find, even with a map, but Jack has been a very helpful navigator and host. He sends his love, by the way.

It's been so long since I've seen him, I had actually forgotten how good looking he is. But when he showed up at my hotel the other day and I saw that face and those eyes and that smile, my heart literally skipped a beat and I felt a mighty surge of adrenaline.

Can't tell if it's just a vestigial response because we were once in love, or if it's some deep-seated Darwinian physical impulse all women have to such primo mating material. Thankfully, it passed in an instant, and you will be pleased to know that we remain firmly divorced. Haven't actually seen too much of him since my arrival, as he has his hands full with a new love interest, or two. How long can a man like Jack stay single?

Lovely as it is here, thinking of skipping down to Big Sur for a couple of solitary days. I'll keep you posted.

Wish You Were Here,
Kate

Date: August 20
From: JackMacTavish
To: KateBogart
Subject: Double Trouble

Katie! First you weren't at the Milano, now you're not at the Phoenix! Where the heck are you? Can't you stay in one place for more than a couple of days? Really need to talk to you.

Had dinner with Gretchen and Piper, not Plover. I liked her a lot. She teaches sign language and she didn't seem crazy at all. Just sexy and smart, and really beautiful.

Anyway, I took your advice. Told them that I didn't want to put any pressure on the situation, but that I'd keep myself open to experimenting with them sometime. Said that I still needed to sort out my feelings for Gretchen and then figure out this whole situation. They thought that was cool, and a lovely dinner was had by all.

So, on my way out the door I kissed Gretchen good-bye, like I've been doing since our first date. Then Piper seemed to want a good-bye kiss for herself, too. I wasn't ready to take the plunge right then and there, but she was pretty aggressive. And you gotta remember, Katie, I've just been in the middle of nowhere for like three months, so those damn kisses really hit the spot.

So what I'm saying is, it happened. Me, Gretchen, and Plover. I mean Piper. But then, it didn't happen. It started to happen, but then it stopped. You know what I mean? Maybe it was just a little too much action for Littlejack all at once, y'know? But for some reason, I just lost it. I've heard about other guys losing it, or not even getting it, but not me. I've never lost it before, Katie. I get it, and I keep it. But this time, I lost it. And I didn't just lose it with one woman. I lost it with two! Those same odds that double your pleasure tend to double your humiliation if you can't stand up to the challenge.

It wouldn't have been so bad if Gretchen and Piper had been a little more understanding, a little more patient maybe. But you would have thought those two had a bus to catch or something. And that's the worst part of it. Those women only wanted me for one thing! I felt totally objectified.

I just spent three months in the rain forest and the mountains many, many miles away from plumbing and modern conveniences, but I never once felt as dirty as they made me feel last night. Why the hell did I ever leave the Amazon in the first place? It's a jungle out here!

Jackson

CHAPTER 7

✈

In Big Sur

Date: August 21
From: KateBogart
To: JackMacTavish
Subject: RE: Double Trouble

Jack: Didn't mean to ditch you. Hard to find a place anywhere in Big Sur in summer, but lucked into a cancellation at Deetjen's at the last minute. Couldn't pass it up. Do you know it? Going to unwind here for a few days. It'll make a great sidebar on the San Francisco piece.

Sorry to hear that your big adventure didn't work out. It sounds like you had your first run-in with the new class of male-ego-guzzling, sex-driven women who treat men, well, the way men tend to treat women. Members of this new breed are as common as cell phones, SUVs, the corner Starbucks, and all the other stuff you've been missing out on in the mountains and the jungles.

And since you raised the subject, can I ask why men take their erections so darned seriously? Even you, Jack. Have to admit I'm a little surprised. You just never seemed quite so hung up on all those trite masculine issues. C'mon, I'm sure it will come back to you. It just sounds like this particular situation wasn't especially inspiring, or the timing wasn't right or something. Somewhere out there, I'm sure, there's a woman for you. Maybe even two.

Wish You Were Here,
Kate

Date: August 21
From: JackMacTavish
To: KateBogart
Subject: RE: RE: Double Trouble

Katie: Of course I know Deetjen's. Been going there since I was a kid. I wish I was there, too. I really need to put this disaster behind me. Stay put. I'll come down and show you the kelp beds. They're amazing! Be there in three hours, if the old Volvo hasn't gone the way of Littlejack.

Jackson

Date: August 21
From: KateBogart
To: JackMacTavish
Subject: RE: RE: RE: Double Trouble

Jack, do any of your housemates speak even a smidgen of English? Tried to call you, but got a woman speaking what I think was Polish or Finnish, then she handed me over to someone who was speaking Tagalog, as best I could tell, who then passed me on to the only Walloon in the world who isn't multilingual. It took the three of them fifteen minutes to collaborate on "no Jack." Did you leave already? If not, don't.

I really don't think it's a good idea, Jackson. I want to catch up with some writing and I'm not crazy about the deep sea up close. And aren't there great white sharks out there, and currents that whisk you off to China with alarming efficiency? Also, there's only one bed, which could be very problematic.

Wish You Would Reconsider,
Kate

Date: August 23
From: KateBogart
To: VioletMorgan
Subject: To Big Sur with Love

Hi, Violet: Here I am in glorious Big Sur. Too beautiful to leave. Since you seem dead set on abandoning Truman and me, I was hoping you might consider looking after him for a few more days before I become a stay-at-home mom forever.

Jack is here, too. Just when he thought things were going swimmingly with his pole-climbing girlfriend, he had a disastrous experience. Poor Jack, he does have a hard time negotiating with the civilized world sometime. So he came here uninvited and against my futile protests to lick his wounds. Happy to say that he has been very well behaved, sleeping on a rollaway cot in my room by night, educating me re: the flora and fauna of Big Sur and the Monterey Peninsula by day. It's like having your own personal nature guide. While I work, he goes snorkeling around in the kelp beds.

I am helping him through his first romantic episode since our divorce. It's all very mature and civilized and mutually supportive. None of the usual drama. What a relief!

Wish You Were Here,
Kate

Date: August 24
From: VioletMorgan
To: KateBogart
Subject: RE: To Big Sur with Love

Bogie: I once heard tell that Gandhi, in preparation for nonviolent
battle with the oppressive colonial powers-that-were, used to sleep
with a virgin by his side just to test his mettle. It makes me wonder
about the fate of the modern world if he had shared a motel room
with the irresistible Jack MacTavish dozing on a rollaway cot just a
few feet away. How could he not pounce? Jack is made for pouncing!
More to the point, how can you not pounce? It defies human nature.

The only thing that seemed "right" in that whole e-mail was the
request to extend my watch over your worthless cat. That, I could see
coming since you left. Of course I'll do it. But I won't like it.

V

Date: August 24
From: Manowar
To: KateBogart
Subject: Up 'n Running

Dear Ms. Bogart: (Gday, Miss!) You will be pleased to know that I am
heeling niceley, tho I am still forced to rely on Mynah the Terribull to
assist me through my convolessence. (The cheek!)

Hired a college chap to type up my article on Speyside without a
single era Mynah and i fired it off to Ted yesterday. I have not heard
from our beloved editor yet, but iamb eagerley anticipating his response. The article is to run this wek, so do keep an I out, as I would
preciate your knowledgible opinion as well.

Fondley,
Mill s (and Mynah)

Date: August 25
From: TedConcannon
To: KateBogart
Subject: Two Headaches and an Ulcer

Kate: Where are you? Still in San Francisco? Can't wait to see your pages. Right now I'm going over Miles' piece on bicycling in Scotland. He didn't seem to enjoy himself one bit or meet a single kind or helpful person on the entire trip. He found no fault with the whiskey, though. He's putting a lot of miles on my red pencil and I'm not looking forward to the resistance I'm going to get from him when I suggest that expressions like "bosomy" and "hypospastic" aren't quite appropriate for the style and tenor of "WYWH."

Work is hell, but on the sunny side, it does provide a handy excuse for shirking all those exploratory committee meetings my wife has been trying to coerce me into attending. She and her campaign consultant are already the best of pals, and when Lorraine is elected she's going to rescue social security, provide free health care on demand, cure cancer, put an end to racism once and for all, and have all those irreconcilable Israelis and Palestinians over to our place for eggnog next Christmas. What's really crazy is that she'll probably succeed.

Save me from these people, Kate!

Ted

Date: August 26
From: Manowar
To: KateBogart
Subject: Movie Rights

Dear Ms. Bogart: Bandages have been removed from my right hand, so I shan't be quite as dependent on the merciless Mynah as before. Blessed freedom! You never know just how much you appreciate things like proper punctuation until you have had to rely on Mynah for your correspondences.

Just off the telephone with my agent, Jane Plank, who has arranged a series of meetings for me with some Hollywood demigods. It seems that there is some "real interest" in my trials and travails as fodder for the movies. Imagine that.

I'm not very well acquainted with Los Angeles and was hoping you might suggest a place where one could do some business comfortably and stylishly, if it is not too much trouble.

Yours,
Miles Maxwell

Date: August 27
From: KateBogart
To: Manowar
Subject: RE: Movie Rights

Maxwell: If you're going to impress those "demigods" you should book yourself a room at the Regent Beverly Wilshire, which is about as stately as LA gets. You will also be taken very seriously indeed if you choose to stay at the posh Bel-Air or the Beverly Hills Hotel, even if it is pink. (In LA, pink is in the range of "neutral" shades.)

Self-anointed mavericks and would-be auteurs, however, will feel an instant kinship to you if you go for the Chateau Marmont. It represents mythical Hollywood with more tarnished atmosphere than all the others. You'll even save a few dollars, though not so many that you won't be taken seriously.

Also, be sure to smile more than you would ever dream of doing in London, drink nothing stronger than white wine at your lunch meetings, and rent nothing less expensive than a Lexus, or all of your time and trouble will have been a waste.

Knock 'em Dead, Kid!
Kate

Date: August 28
From: TedConcannon
To: KateBogart
Subject: Slacking Off

Kate: You can't hide behind the fog forever. What is going on there?
You and George of the Jungle aren't playing treehouse again, are
you? I expect at least one piece out of this trip. I'm running out of
pinch-hitters and actually considered asking the coffee cart guy to
write a piece about Canarsie in autumn. While you're on the West
Coast, why don't you do a piece on Los Angeles, too? Kill two birds
with one airfare. Just a thought.

     TC

Date: August 29
From: KateBogart
To: TedConcannon
Subject: RE: Slacking Off

For your information, Ted, Jack and I are being very well behaved.
Model divorcees, really. We took a refreshing little side trip to Big
Sur, but now we're back in the city. He is trying to line up some work
for himself and showing me around San Francisco's neighborhoods.
Meanwhile, I am writing it all down and will send you the feature and
sidebar by week's end.

    I would love to skip down to LA for a week or so. However, Violet's
going on the road with her husband's band and there's no one to look
after my cat, so I'm afraid I'll only be doing local pieces from here on
in, or until I can find a reliable cat-sitter. Since Canarsie in autumn
seems taken, howzabout Ronkonkoma in the off-season? Just a
thought.

     Wish I Could Help,
     Kate

Date: August 29
From: TedConcannon
To: KateBogart
Subject: RE: RE: Slacking Off

Kate, that last e-mail is tantamount to a two-week notice. How could you do this to me? I'm running out of material here, and now I have to go looking for a writer who can afford to work for peanuts. And all because of a damned cat! This is dark news, deep dark news indeed. Why, if I had the money and the energy I'd cut out early and go on a whiskey-and-whore bender. That's how bad this is. Oh well, send me whatever you have.

   Achingly,
   TC

Date: August 30
From: Manowar
To: KateBogart
Subject: Worldly Advice

Dear Ms. Bogart: Took your expert advice and will be lodging at the Chateau Marmont next week. Very much looking forward to my trip. For transportation, I have also reserved a silver-green Jaguar at a most shocking daily rate, but do you think it will be too much?

   Yours,
   Miles

Date: August 30
From: KateBogart
To: Manowar
Subject: RE: Worldly Advice

Maxwell: There is no such thing as "too much" in LA, especially when it comes to automobiles. While the model is perfect, silver-green does in fact seem a bit subdued to me. There's the danger that it could go unnoticed. Maybe you should try to upgrade to red, or a pure silver that will reflect the low-riding late summer sun. That oughta blind 'em!

By the way, no matter how much they offer you for your life story, you want more. Once again, you want to be taken seriously, and accepting the first offer, no matter how exorbitant it may seem, will mark you as a lightweight. You might not get more, but you will at least have demanded more, and that's all that counts.

If you wonder how I come by this knowledge, I used to date a screenwriter, a living cliché who drank through his bitterness and drowned in a motel swimming pool. Still, he had his hard-boiled charm. And by the way, that's another thing you need to know about Hollywood: What we call a cliché, they call "reality."

Have a ball, Maxwell! You're about to get the education of your life!

Wish I Could Go with You,
Kate

Date: August 30
From: KateBogart
To: VioletMorgan
Subject: Abandonment Issues

Violet, my dearest, sweetest friend: Today, I dialed up the airline to put me on a standby flight for New York, and the reality of my grim situation hit me. How can you be rejecting me, your best friend since first grade, in favor of those noisy boys. Do they bring you fancy hand-milled soaps from Paris, or handmade chocolates every time they pass through Brussels? No indeedy.

And you have no idea what it's done to my poor editor. Now he has to audition writers and put on a social face and all that. He doesn't come by his social face easily.

Are you really going to make me pass up an assignment in kooky, nutty Los Angeles and force me to come back to New York, where I have no idea how I will make a living? Oh, Vi, please, please, please tell me that you've changed your mind before I book the flight.

Wish This Was All Just a Bad Dream,
Kate

Date: August 31
From: VioletMorgan
To: KateBogart
Subject: RE: Abandonment Issues

Wake up and smell the kitty litter, Bogie! I am out of here the day after tomorrow. After that, your cat is going to have to feed on his own stored body fat. That should give you at least a few more months on the road.

As for me, I am almost excited about this adventure. I am actually eager to watch Shane and the boys finally enjoy some success, and I will be very happy to share it with them. Say what you want about the Killers, but they are genuinely dedicated to their music and they work as hard as they rock. Wish Me Luck, O Selfish and Needy One.

V

Date: August 31
From: KateBogart
To: VioletMorgan
Subject: RE: RE: Abandonment Issues

Vi, you know I want nothing but the best for the Killer Abs, but I maintain that this isn't the best move for you. Or me. Or Truman. Okay, so I'm selfish and needy. There! I admit it! Nevertheless, I am afraid that once again you are going to be the put-upon woman behind the successful man, or men, or boys, or whatever they are. And speaking from experience, I can tell you that life on the road is not nearly as romantic as it seems. You need high tolerance for stress, frustration, rootlessness, and a shortage of creature comforts. But since you have made your decision, I stand behind you supportively (but in protest).

I hope that the Killer Abs know what a kickass manager they are getting and that they have the decency to thank you before they thank God when they win their first Grammy. Kiss Shane for me, promise you'll e-mail, and I will somehow figure out some way to get Truman fed and pampered while I try to make my meager living. I'll be home in time for Truman's afternoon feeding the day after tomorrow.

Wish You Luck and Love,
Kate

PS: You'll let me know if you change your mind at the last minute, right?

Date: September 1
From: TedConcannon
To: KateBogart
Subject: Flop Housing

Kate: What do you know about cheap extended-stay hotels in New York? Do they still exist? Are there waiting lists? Let me explain . . .

Lorraine Schultz-Concannon, the next US Congresswoman repre-
senting the 18th District, has asked me to take leave of our home, or
her home, I should say. I could never afford such a sumptuous pile of
bricks in Larchmont on my salary, a point she stressed with the ut-
most diplomacy, as she directed her "domestic assistant" to hand over
my neatly prepacked bags and reclaim my house keys.

It turns out that wifey and the woman who heads her exploratory
committee, one Roxanne Rexroth, have been exploring a bit more than
Lorraine's political chances in a tight race, if you get my drift. As
Lorraine put it, Roxanne has "rocked [her] world" and made her "see
and feel things" she always took to be "poetic exaggerations of human passion." Oh well, we'll always have Paris.

Honestly, it's a great relief, as Lorraine and I seem to have been
growing apart since the moment we dug into the wedding cake thirty
decades ago. Unfortunately, her sudden foray into Sapphic bliss has
caught me off guard and left me up the creek without the all-important
paddle. Any suggestions as to where a gentleman pushing sixty might
spend his Willy Loman years of obsolescence in affordable peace and
quiet?

The Happy Cuckold

Date:	September 1
From:	KateBogart
To:	TedConcannon
Subject:	RE: Flop Housing

Dear Happy Cuckold: I'm so sorry to hear of your split with Lorraine,
and you are *not* obsolete. I, for one, couldn't live without you. If it's
any comfort to you, if I lived in the 18th District I'd break party ranks
to vote for the other guy.

As to extended-stay accommodations, here's that "paddle" you so
desperately need to navigate that most unenviable creek. It's affordable, it's private, it's relatively quiet for New York, and it's much more
convenient to the office than Larchmont. It's my apartment at 246 Mott

St., #18! You can have it all to yourself, and I can scooch down to LA and write you a nice piece for "WYWH." It's all yours as of tomorrow, if you want. All you have to do is take care of Truman.

My condolences, or congratulations, whichever you choose.

Kate

Date:	September 1
From:	TedConcannon
To:	KateBogart
Subject:	RE: RE: Flop Housing

Kate, you're a lifesaver! Your generous offer would solve two of my problems: filling a "WYWH" slot and saving me from the indignities of the YMCA. Go, go, go to LA now!

Wee-hoo! My own bachelor pad in the city! Just tell me how I get the keys.

Gratefully,
Ted

Date:	September 1
From:	KateBogart
To:	TedConcannon
Subject:	The House Rules

Ted: Just off the phone with Violet. I gave her all the info and she will run the keys up to the office for you before six.

Now, there are a few things you have to know: Truman likes to have his litter changed every two days, and you might want to filter the box daily. There's a slotted spoon for this right next to the box. He likes to eat canned food in the morning (½ can) and dry food in the evening (½ cup). He prefers his drinking water cold, so if the weather is warm you might want to chill it with a couple of ice cubes. You should also freshen it up before bedtime. Since it's shedding season you might want to brush him every day. He likes it best and it's usually easiest to do while he's sunning himself in the late afternoon in the living room, or early morning in the kitchen. He has hairball medicine and urinary tract medicine above the kitchen sink. He needs these once a day in the morning. There's also a small claw-clipper right next to them, in case his claws get too long. (Important: You just want to snip the pointy little ends off; don't cut to the quick or you'll have a real mess on your hands.) Medicine and clipping can meet with some strong resistance, so I keep some steel mesh gloves by the sink just in case. I hope they fit.

The orchids and bonsai have their own care regimen, but that's a foreign language to me, really. Violet is writing up instructions for those.

You and Truman are going to have so much fun together, Ted, I almost wish I was there. But I'm off to LA!

Kate

Date:	September 2
From:	KateBogart
To:	Manowar
Subject:	Synchronicity

Maxwell! A happy coincidence: At the last minute I was able to take Ted up on an assignment in LA. I can show you the town, or what I know of it.

By the way, the Speyside piece was very interesting. Too bad you didn't much care for the bicycle, the hills, the food, the weather, the architecture, or the accommodations, but a lot of useful information on whiskey. I'm keeping it on file for future reference.

I'll be checking into the Beverly Laurel tomorrow.

Best,
Kate

Date: September 3
From: Manowar
To: KateBogart
Subject: RE: Synchronicity

Ah, Ms Bogart! A happy coincidence, indeed! As it turns out, I too will be taking notes on Los Angeles for *Home & Abroad*, when I am not trying to sell my soul to Satan's Hollywood representatives. Bless that agent of mine!

Glad to hear you found the Speyside piece so interesting and useful. Ted thought it a bit "edgy" and "testy," but it was watered down considerably by the time it went to print. Bawdlerized, in fact. So much for America's vaunted "freedom of the press." Ah well, lesson learned. Looking forward to sun, sin, silliness, and you.

Fondly,
Miles

CHAPTER 8

✈

In Los Angeles

Date: September 4
From: KateBogart
To: TedConcannon
Subject: Hooray for Hollywood

Hi Ted: Made it to LA. I'm at the Beverly Laurel Motel with a German TV documentary crew; a pair of contentious animators arguing
over whether their character should be a dung beetle or a slug; a wig-
gly, giggly Brazilian gay couple; some raucous frat boys who couldn't
get a room at The Standard; a few more slinky, inscrutable types I have
yet to figure out; and one average American family looking very much
perplexed by it all. You see, LA was built on the idea of American
suburban exclusionism and all these cultures were never supposed to
clash, which is one of the things that makes it so interesting.

Wonder how you are doing with your new freedom and my old
cat. Hope everything's okay.

Kate

Date: September 4
From: TedConcannon
To: KateBogart
Subject: Take My Wife, Please

Kate: Thanks so much for the hospitality. It's very thoughtful and gracious of you. I wish you'd told me that it's a five-flight walk-up, though, just to prepare me for the initial shock. But it's okay. The way I see it, there are schmucks who pay good money for a Stairmaster, and your place has one built-in. I just pace myself and pull over for fast-moving traffic. It's far more bearable than the indignities and humiliations of Larchmont, and who knows, I might finally get back in shape.

I wasn't prepared for the bathtub in the kitchen either, but I've really come to see the logic and convenience in it. Now I can watch the Mets while enjoying a good, relaxing soak. When I want a cold one, I just reach over to the fridge and grab it, upsetting nary a soap bubble nor missing a single play. All I need now are a couple of dancing girls and I can die happy.

I bet you have me pegged for one of those cranky urban types who don't like cats. Well, that's where you're wrong, Kate. I have nothing but respect for organisms that are basically lazy, antisocial, and meat-driven. Besides, the thing sleeps twenty-three hours a day, so it's a whole lot less trouble than my wife's pain-in-the-ass cockapoo and its delusions of Rottweiler grandeur.

Oh, I'm having a great time, Kate! I haven't felt this good since college. I even think there's a noticeable spring in my step. Where the hell has Roxanne Rexroth been all these years? Feel so good, I might even vote for Lorraine myself.

You just keep writing and traveling anywhere you want to go. Make your own schedule, have a ball, and rest assured I'll take good care of Truman.

The New and Improved,
Ted Concannon

PS: I intend to replace all your bubble bath, by the way. But where do you find that stuff? My skin is so soft, I can't keep my hands off myself.

Date: September 4
From: Manowar
To: KateBogart
Subject: The Big Sleep

Ms. Bogart: Thanks so much for your inspired recommendation. I am savouring the mise-en-scène at the Chateau Marmont most heartily. The place is a marvelous pile of contradictions, at once tatty and elegant, inconspicuous and striking, shadowy and bright. The venetian blinds and potted palms provide the perfect cover for making a deal, a tryst, or a sordid plot. It is easy to imagine that at this very moment, behind the curtains in one of those sweet poolside bungalows, some red-lipped femme fatale is planting the seeds of her husband's untimely demise in the impressionable mind of some hapless dupe named Joe. Ah yes, it sets the mood brilliantly for my conquest of this uncivilized wilderness they call "Hollywood."

In keeping with said conquest, Jane Plank has me following an obscenely ambitious schedule, with breakfast, lunch, and cocktail meetings almost every day. The cool desert evenings, however, are mine alone, and I am very eager to share them with you.

Do ring me up when you get the chance.

Fondly,
Miles

Date: September 5
From: VioletMorgan
To: KateBogart
Subject: I'm with the Band

Bogie: Here I am with the Killers in Providence, RI, just in time for all the back-to-school hubbub. Yipee. You should see what happened to Providence since my days at Brown. The place has been spiffed up, and there are all these schmancy restaurants with esoteric ingredients on their menus. There are even bodies of water that I didn't know existed. One of these, a river or a canal or something, features this weird public art installation where they light torches in the middle of the water and play a mish-mash of instrumental music while a bunch of art student volunteers in rowboats go through the motions of some performance art/new age ritual (for extra credit, I hope).

Anyway, the popularity of this spectacle was not lost on the Killer Abs. They were so inspired by it that I am now looking into pyrotechnics (cost, precedents, safety factors, state-to-state fire laws, etc.) to fire up their show, so to speak. As if the sight of five grown men in vinyl microminis, sequined diapers, tassled pasties, Day-glo wigs, mesh teddies, and body sparkle is not enough to get the attention of the audience. Backup bands have to work harder, don't you know.

Hope you are not suffering acute withdrawal from Big Sur, Jack, and other natural wonders of California.

Love,
Vi

Date:	September 5
From:	KateBogart
To:	VioletMorgan
Subject:	LA Confidential

Dear Vi: I'm in LA at a funky budget place, worrying that I might have outgrown funky budget places.

Anyway, I was just thinking about how Ted's wife discovered lesbianism just in time, and how many people are better off for it. Ted is getting very cozy with my bathtub, and he actually *likes* Truman. I get to drive around Los Angeles for a week singing along to Steely Dan, The Eagles, and other classic California rock of the 70s. (Discovered that if you cue Joni Mitchell's "Car on a Hill" at Crescent Heights, then cross Sunset up to Laurel Canyon, it's as if you are actually *inside* the song.) And of course, you get to fulfill your girlhood dream of running away with the circus. Providence, indeed!

You'll be pleased to know that Jack and I behaved like the good friends that we are, right up to the very last moment when the Super-

Shuttle van came to whisk me away. I can't say that it was easy, of course. It's hard to resist Jack, and not just because he's so nicely put together, superficial Violet, but because he's Jack, and he's earnest and sweet and thoughtful and sensitive. But we both managed to control ourselves and respect each other's differences. We really are friends. Sigh.

I had such a great time with Jack that I took a memento. It's this blue shirt that he let me borrow on our hike at Point Lobos. Even though it's big on me, it's very comforting. He bought it when we were married, and it reminds me of him so vividly. It's about two shades darker than his eyes, and it smells a little like pine and a little like sage and a little like the ocean. Just so fresh and Jacky, y'know?

But I have to admit I feel a little guilty. I mean, Jack will never miss it; he just doesn't pay attention to things like that, but I'm still having pangs of conscience. Do you think that I'm some kind of kleptomaniac?

Must go. Drinks with Miles Maxwell, who's trying to make a movie deal here.

Wish You Were Here,
Kate

Date: September 5
From: VioletMorgan
To: KateBogart
Subject: RE: LA Confidential

Dearest Bogie: Yes, you are a klepper. You have stolen Jack's blue shirt, just like you stole my pink cashmere sweater in college, my irreplaceable vintage Swiss dot sundress that I got at that church thrift store in Provincetown, and that giant-brimmed black straw hat that I found on the Lower East Side, when things were still cheap there.

What is intriguing about this theft, however, is the way in which it differs from all the others. Your previous crimes were all based on the presumption that those items looked better on you than they did on me. In "The Case of the Blue Shirt," however, you seem to have been purely motivated by male musk.

You should of course feel guilty. You are a thief, a shameless manipulator of the truth, and a public menace. Not only did you steal your ex-husband's shirt, you lied to your best friend when you told her you were over him (as the stealing of the ex-husband's shirt would clearly indicate otherwise). Shame, shame, shame on you!

Judge Violet

PS: Cut me a swatch!

Date:	September 5
From:	JackMacTavish
To:	KateBogart
Subject:	A Hole in My Life

Hey Katie: It was great having you in San Francisco, and so much fun showing you around Big Sur for the first time. I remember something that Sharmi told me about human relationships: "The world is richer seen through four eyes, rather than two." Or something like that. I don't think she was talking about eyeglasses, either.

Still trying to drum up some work; maybe that skiing expedition in the Rockies, or maybe back to the jungle. Someone suggested trying out for one of those TV "reality" adventure shows. I sure could use the million bucks, but I'm kind of attached to my pride too, so don't think I'll be going that route.

Have to admit I've been a little blue and lonesome since you left. You're still the best friend I've ever had. Speaking of blue, I can't find that blue shirt I let you borrow at Point Lobos. Do you still have it? I bought it in New York when we were married. Remember? It really reminds me of you. Oh well, it might be in the mess around here somewhere, or maybe one of the roomies borrowed it. We're going to have to have a council about that kinda stuff.

How's LA? Any ozone left? Don't know how you can stand that place. Wish I could see it through your eyes.

Missing You,
Jackson

Date: September 6
From: KateBogart
To: JackMacTavish
Subject: RE: A Hole in My Life

Oh, Jack, your provincial Northern California seams are showing. LA just isn't the pit of doom and evil you make it out to be. That's just a culturally ingrained prejudice that comes from an old geographic rivalry. Silly.

I'm both flattered and sorry that you're feeling sad, but as soon as you get your next adventure rolling, I'm sure your spirit will return. Sorry, I don't have any information regarding the whereabouts of the blue shirt. I'm pretty sure I gave it back to you.

Wish You Were Here,
Kate

Date: September 6
From: KateBogart
To: VioletMorgan
Subject: I'm No Angel

Oh, Vi! What a crazy day! First I deflected an e-mail from Jack who is missing me *and* the blue shirt. But you would be very proud of me, Vi. I did what any healthy, red-blooded, sexually vigorous female would do: I lied and told him I know nothing about that blue shirt. I'm just not ready to part with it yet.

Afterward, was planning to take my smarting conscience and the blue shirt to the Huntington Library Gardens for a walk when I got a phone call from Maxwell, who was arrested for jaywalking after a breakfast meeting at the Peninsula. Well, he didn't get arrested for jaywalking per se. He got a ticket for that. The arrest came because he got a little uppity with the cop and even started chanting Rodney King's name over and over again, trying to rile up some sympathy with the populace in the streets. In Beverly Hills, mind you. So he was actually taken in for disorderly conduct.

Anyway, I had to rescue him. Turned up the charm to "high" and engaged the none-too-bright cop in an extended comparison of pedestrian customs in London (where the pedestrian is king) vs. those in LA (where the pedestrian is revenue target if lucky; roadkill if not). You could tell this sort of argument wasn't mixing well with Officer Sky Widmeyer's quasi-military training or his steroid combination. Finally just told him that Maxwell forgot to take his medication today. Charges were dropped on the spot and he was released on his own recognizance.

Drove Maxwell back to the Chateau Marmont, where we had a decompressing cocktail in the lobby, then saw him back to his room, where I totally jumped him. That's right. Me. And Maxwell. Again.

I didn't mean to jump Maxwell at all. In fact, it was the furthest thing from my mind, but it's like this uncontrollable animal lust just came over me. Poor Maxwell, I don't think he knew what hit him. But he caught on pretty quick. It sure took his mind off the unpleasantness of the LAPD, I'll tellya.

Maybe there's something to this Miles Maxwell character, or maybe it's all that control I had to exert when I was with Jack, but my hormones are way out of whack. I know this is going to sound crazy, but I think it's the blue shirt. There's no aphrodisiac like it.

The most troubling thing is I'm not sure if I was jumping Maxwell because he's Maxwell, or if I was jumping Maxwell because it's safer than jumping Jack. Either way, the sex was even better this time.

Still, I'm feeling confused and maybe even a little guilty. After all, I have only been in LA for three days and already I have become a thief, a liar, and a fornicator. What's next?

Wish You Were Here,
Kate

Date: September 7
From: VioletMorgan
To: KateBogart
Subject: The Scent of a Man

Dear Bogie: While I do indeed think you're crazy and unconscionable, there's something to the whole male musk issue. Just recently I read of a scientific study that attested to the powerful role of scent in sexual attraction between humans. The same article even mentioned that in the past men used to dance with handkerchiefs tucked in their armpits. At the end of the evening, the handkerchiefs were then proferred to their prospective mates as tokens of affection. So you're not as crazy as you think.

Nonetheless, your situation poses some very intriguing questions as to just whose musk you were responding to so lasciviously at the Chateau Marmont. Was it Maxwell's? Or was it Jack's?

As I see it, there's only one way to clear up the matter, and I know that you're not going to like it: You have to wash the blue shirt right away. That's right. Once it has been thoroughly de-Jacked, you can then schedule a casual meeting with Maxwell. If you still have the urge to jump him, then you are free to do so. If you have been suddenly cured of the urge to jump him, however, then you will know that you were really jumping Jack the other night, and you might think twice about using poor Maxwell to satisfy your animal needs again.

In the name of science, please report back to me with results.

May the Best-Smelling Man Win,
Dr. Violet Morgan, LLD, Ph.D., M.S., B.S., etc.

Date: September 7
From: Manowar
To: KateBogart
Subject: Close Encounters

Dear Ms. Bogart: I am not sure how to interpret the events of last evening. As I might remind you, it was you in point of fact who instituted our mutual hands-off policy in Positano. Since that time I have managed to contain my feelings for you and accept your platonic wishes. However, I cannot pretend that last night was anything less than powerful for me, and I maintain that I was not giving in to cheap regional jest when I mistook our finale for an actual earthquake. Sadly, in light of past experience, it is impossible for me to tell whether I should be celebrating yesterday's brilliant finish, or lamenting it.

As you know, it is very difficult for me to discuss matters of the heart. I don't share that American habit of gushing out my emotions until everyone is soaked in tears of sympathy. Be that as it may, I am more than willing to put aside my discomfort so that we might explore our situation face-to-face, leaving no room for misinterpretation or misunderstanding. Do give me a few hours of your time, Ms. Bogart, so that we might sort out our feelings and intentions once and for all. Dinner perhaps?

Yours,
Miles

Date:	September 7
From:	KateBogart
To:	Manowar
Subject:	RE: Close Encounters

Oh, Maxwell! I'm so sorry about last night. Not that I have any regrets, mind you. I just don't know what came over me, but I agree that we need to talk.

Lost an entire day of work yesterday. Much catching up to do, along with some urgent laundry, but I will be free in time for dinner. I will call you at the Chateau Marmont in the afternoon.

Kate

Date: September 8
From: KateBogart
To: VioletMorgan
Subject: Action!

Violet: There's no arguing with your advice. It's very good advice, but I just can't seem to bring myself to launder that shirt. Every time I go near it I fall into a swoon that renders me powerless. Besides, I love that shirt and all of its Jackyness.

But what am I going to do? Maxwell wants to talk about "things" over dinner tonight, and I don't think I can hold him off for very long. Any other ideas?

Wish You Were Here,
Kate

Date: September 8
From: VioletMorgan
To: KateBogart
Subject: RE: Action!

Bogie: Does the Betty Ford Center accept people who are addicted to male-scented articles of clothing? I don't think so, and you couldn't afford it even if they did. That leaves you no choice but to wash that man right out of his shirt, and send him on his way!

I know you can do it. I have all the faith in the world in you. You just hold your nose, and you toss that baby into that purifying sudsy bath. You might want to send it through the wash twice, just to be on the safe side. And no taking any deep whiffs at the last second, either! You have to treat this with the same sharp decisive action you would use for tearing off a Band-Aid, injecting a hypodermic needle, or yanking a knife out of someone's back.

Go! Do it now! Before you get yourself in more trouble! Trust

me. You'll be happy once you're free of that shirt's evil influence. Go!
Go! Go!

Your Motivational Trainer,
Violet

Date:	September 8
From:	KateBogart
To:	VioletMorgan
Subject:	City of Angels

Well Vi, I did it! I washed the shirt. Or, I should say, the shirt got
washed.

I went to the Laundromat and put my coins in the slot and filled up
the washing machine, but when it came time to immerse the item in
question, I just burst into tears. A very kind woman named Marilla
came over to make sure I was all right, but all I could babble through
my sobs was something about my "husband." She took this to mean
that I was widowed and told me how her husband fell off a billboard
platform, broke his neck, and died at 32. I felt so sorry for her, I didn't
have the heart to tell her that I'm willfully and unhappily divorced
from my own sweet-smelling spouse and that I'm really just a big
whiner and a baby.

Anyway, Marilla just took charge and she tossed that shirt right
into the Maytag, which sent me into a prolonged wail. But Marilla
was very sweet, and she held my hand and patted my back just the
way you do sometimes. She also dried, sorted, and folded all my
things, and offered to drive me back to my motel, but I had gotten a
grip by then.

So, what had to be done got done, and now the shirt just smells
like Fab. What a come-down. But I think my senses have been restored, and it's off to dinner and damage control with Maxwell.

I can't imagine the world without people like you and Marilla.

Wish You Were Here,
Kate

Date: September 9
From: KateBogart
To: VioletMorgan
Subject: Car Culture

Dear Violet: Met Maxwell for dinner last night. Freed from the spell of Jack's blue shirt, I could finally think clearly. I apologized to Maxwell for my uncontrollable urges and for taking advantage of him. Maxwell, always the gentleman, said that the advantage was all his.

Then he asked me if I had any feelings for him beyond the carnal, and I said that of course I do. I told Maxwell that he's weird and funny and interesting and very fine company. I also told him that he's an exceptional kisser and great in bed, and he looked very, very flattered and very, very proud.

Maxwell asked once again if I thought we could possibly ever make a go of it. Since he is dead set on living in London, and I am dead set on living in New York, and we are both dead set on traveling as much as possible, I told him that it seems unlikely. I have already been that route with another perfectly lovable man and it didn't work out. Maxwell is on the rebound from a woman who is just as dedicated to travel as I am, so he saw my reasoning, and we spent the rest of the dinner in more or less uncomfortable silence.

Neither one of us wanted to leave it on this note, so afterward, Maxwell took me for a spin in the ridiculously rich silver Jaguar he has rented. I have never been in a Jaguar before. It has creamy leather upholstery. There's not a single chair that's that comfortable in my entire apartment.

We drove along Mulholland and found a spot to park where we could look out over the sparkling city. I wondered if Maxwell would work this into his piece on LA, and I wondered if I would, too. I think we both felt sad about our predicament, and we sat there quietly for a very long while, just breathing.

Then we did it. Right there in the car. Like a couple of teenagers. Only much better. It was just as good as the other night, proving once and for all that it wasn't the shirt that made me want Maxwell. I wasn't jumping Jack; I was jumping Maxwell!

Wish You Were Here,
Kate

Date: September 10
From: VioletMorgan
To: KateBogart
Subject: RE: Car Culture

Aha! So the blue shirt wasn't acting alone! Then there is apparently more to this Maxwell character than you have been letting on. Especially if he can rival Jackson MacTavish for raw animal appeal. Don't know where this is going, or if I even approve, but as long as you mind the stick-shift and keep the emergency brake employed, I can't see the harm in it.

Then again, I'm severely myopic . . .

V

Date: September 11
From: Manowar
To: KateBogart
Subject: In My Room

Dear Ms. Bogart: While staring into my grapefruit this morning, it occurred to me that it is silly for us to carry on in our current fashion, renting two separate hotel rooms. After all we are mature adults.

Won't you move over to the Marmont with me? There is plenty of room for the both of us here. During the day, while I am suffering through *dejeuners* with movie executives who are constantly making gestures over my shoulder to more important people at better tables, you can be working on your next article. In the evening, when we are both free, well, I leave that to your very frisky imagination . . .

Do say yes. And please do not go rushing back to New York, leaving me here with all these insincere people and their frighteningly white teeth.

Warmly Yours,
Maxwell

Date: September 11
From: KateBogart
To: Manowar
Subject: RE: In My Room

Dear Maxwell: I am so, so fond of you and it is such a good feeling, really, but it seems far sillier to me to have the both of us in the same room. After all, we are mature adults and we should both know that we'll get a lot more work done if we keep separate lodgings.

I do, however, agree that I should not go "rushing back to New York" as long as you are here and we are having fun. Therefore, I have a message in to Ted, telling him that I need more time to look into some mid-range properties. Waiting to hear back from him any minute. Tick-tock, tick-tock, tick-tock . . .

Friskily Yours,
Kate

Date: September 11
From: TedConcannon
To: KateBogart
Subject: 21st Century Fox

Kate: So you found a good corporate rate, huh? You and Maxwell must be having a heck of a time in LA. Knock yourself out! I just want everyone to have as much fun as I'm having, and I'm not ready to give your place up yet.

And yes, I'm brushing Truman every day and leaving the radio on for him while I'm at work. Don't worry!

TC

Date: September 12
From: JackMacTavish
To: KateBogart
Subject: LA Is Not My Lady

Katie! Guess where I am! I'm in LA for an outfitters' convention. A last-minute decision. I want to get together, but you're not at that motel. I hope you haven't gone back to New York already. I want you to show me what's so great about this overgrown parking lot.

Jackson

Date: September 12
From: KateBogart
To: JackMacTavish
Subject: RE: LA Is Not My Lady

Jackson: Everywhere I go, there you are. I have changed hotels, in that way of mine. Now I'm at the Avalon, in glitzy old Beverly Hills, but much nicer than last motel.

I'm much busier than I ever expected to be, but would love to see you. I'm sure you've got a busy schedule too with the convention, but let me know where you're staying and I'll come to your hotel. Maybe I can include it in my piece.

Glad You Are Here,
Kate

Date: September 12
From: KateBogart
To: VioletMorgan
Subject: A Peaceful, Uneasy Feelin'

Violet: Have stayed on in LA a few days longer. Not sure if that was wise, but Ted doesn't seem willing to give up my apartment. Besides, things are still sort of electric between Maxwell and me, and we have agreed not to fight it, or to push it.

I have moved over to the Avalon. Palm Springs moderne without being campy. Quite chic, in fact. The people are so good-looking it hurts. Everyone is very well dressed in Jil Sander and Prada, and who shows up in the lobby today but Jack MacTavish in his best droopy cargo shorts and dirty hiking boots. A bellman actually tripped over a cute little mid-century modern end table while ogling him and upset the whole supercool vibe.

Turns out Jack decided to take part in some outfitters' convention downtown, even though he hates LA. I wasn't expecting him so soon, and the first thing he noticed when he came back to my room was the blue shirt. He was so happy to see it, he put it right on. I pretended like it had been buried at the bottom of my suitcase, and then I got him out of the hotel before I lost my willpower.

So, spent the warm sunlit afternoon with Jack (he finds the vegetation here fascinating, or says so to please me, anyway) and the cool evening messing up Maxwell's perfect hair. It's almost more fun than I can handle. Don't know how much more I can take, or when I'll ever catch up with work. It's all making me a little anxious, naturally.

Wish You Were Here,
Kate

Date: September 13
From: VioletMorgan
To: KateBogart
Subject: Life in the Fast Lane

Kate, sounds like you're running yourself ragged, but at least you're doing it glamorously.

From the You-Think-You've-Got-Problems Dept: The stage lights have been hotter than the boys are used to and it's hard to get those pasties to stay on Damien's nipples. He's the one who plays the bass, and he *has* to have his pasties. Have spent most of my day combing stores in Portland, Maine, for a better adhesive. I wonder if denture cream will work.

Sick of Cheap Motels Already and Wish I Was There, Too,
Violet

Date: September 13
From: Manowar
To: KateBogart
Subject: The Last Tycoon

Dear Ms. Bogart: Just confirming our rendezvous at the Bar Marmont at 8:00. I'll probably arrive first, so I'll ask the barkeep to have your martini at the ready. Movie prospects looking quite dim. You are the only good reason to be in Los Angeles.

Eagerly,
Miles

Date:	September 13
From:	JackMacTavish
To:	KateBogart
Subject:	A Great Big Freeway

Katie: Thanks for lunch today. What's up? Are you in DND mode? I'm skipping the lecture tonight. It's just another French guy who nearly died trying to sail around the world solo. Killer sharks. Killer waves. Ho hum. Let's go for Mexican. Don't even bother trying to reach me. Busy with convention stuff. I'll come by to pick you up at 8:00.

Jackson

Date:	September 14
From:	KateBogart
To:	VioletMorgan
Subject:	LA Proved Too Much for the Man

Vi: After an afternoon lunch with Jackson at the Farmer's Market, went to keep my dinner date with Maxwell. Later, he invited me back to the Marmont, but it was already midnight and I desperately needed my sleep. Good thing too, because as I was shuffling wearily past the desk at the Avalon, the clerk arched an eyebrow toward the lobby where Jack MacTavish was dozing peacefully on a George Nelson sofa. Or maybe it's a Heywood-Wakefield.

Anyway, roused him and brought him back to my room. He had some questions as to my whereabouts, as if we were married. I didn't answer them. Then he confessed that he wasn't attending the outfitters' convention at all. In fact, there is no outfitters' convention in LA this week.

Turns out that Jack wasn't ready to commit to any of the job offers that have come up because he missed me and didn't want us to be apart again. Admitted that when he hasn't been with me in LA, he's been driving around the freeways like some alienated, anxiety-ridden character in a Joan Didion novel, waiting for the right time to approach the dreaded subject of "us." I was at once touched and furious, but it didn't matter, because as soon as Jack made his confession, he fell right back to sleep on my bed, where he has been ever since. I spent the night on the floor.

Jack didn't even wake up for the room service guy, who was clearly drawing all sorts of conclusions about the strapping Adonis in the single guest's bed. As soon as he does, I'm shipping him back up north where he belongs. He's a fish out of water here.

Wish You Were Here to Help,
Kate

Date: September 14
From: Manowar
To: KateBogart
Subject: The Final Act

Dear Ms. Bogart: Ah well, the Hollywood Satan does not seem interested in my meagre soul. I feel at once relieved and insulted, like the only girl in the secretarial pool passed over by the office wolf.

What's most sad about it all is that it brings our time together here to a close all too rapidly. I appreciate and admire your devotion to your old friend, but I have to curse her timing just the same. I'd be happy to meet her, of course, but please set some time aside for me before I leave, with or without your friend.

Impatiently,
Miles

Date: September 14
From: KateBogart
To: VioletMorgan
Subject: Hollywood Swingin'

Vi: Where are you when I need you? Jack finally woke up, full of apologies, and I told him that he's got to go back to San Francisco and get on with his life. He agreed, but reminded me that I had promised to take him on a hike up to the Hollywood sign, where neither of us had ever been before.

A good hike with incredible views over the city. Even Jack had to admit it was lovely and inspiring. So inspiring that he asked me to give things another chance. Then he suddenly embraced me, and I have to admit, it felt great. And did I mention that he was wearing the blue shirt?

There it was, Vi: sage and pine and ocean air, and I think there's a little lemon in it, with a bit of freshly mowed grass, too. The next thing I knew, I was intoxicated and we were getting biblical, right there on top of the world. Of course, it was transcendent.

Afterward, taking advantage of the natural truth serum that seems to be released in afterglow, Jack got me to admit that I stole the blue shirt because I missed him. Then he asked me if I felt that we were throwing away something really special, something really rare. And I had to admit that I have always felt that way. Jack started yelling "yipee-ee-ee" and "she loves me" over the hills to all the "shallow, water-stealing, environment-murdering robber barons." I didn't actually say the "L" word, but there's no convincing Jack of that. But just between me and you, it's a little hard to deny it.

Jack was more excited than a little boy with a new puppy. I haven't seem him so full of life in ages. We stayed until dusk, and all of a sudden LA's not looking so bad to him. He's in the shower right now, singing "Hotel California."

Meanwhile, Maxwell has left about six messages on my voicemail expecting our nightly tryst. I have to cancel on him, and I feel terrible about it. And yet I feel great, too.

Wish You Were Here,
Kate

Date: September 14
From: VioletMorgan
To: KateBogart
Subject: RE: Hollywood Swingin'

Who put the "Ho" in "Hollywood"? Kate Bogart, that's who!

Boy do you work fast, and in public no less! My first instinct was to tell you to get a room, but you already have a very nice one, apparently. You're obviously the more outdoorsy type. So, don't get arrested, watch out for poison oak, and have a ball. (So to speak.)

Enviously,
Violet

PS: Shane and the boys say: "Rock on, gold dust woman!"

Date: September 15
From: KateBogart
To: GamblinRose
Subject: Double Indemnity

Dear Mom: I'm in a fix and I need your advice. You remember the English journalist Miles Maxwell, Ted Concannon's old friend? Well, he's been in LA the whole time I've been here, and once again, we've had a very nice time together, much to my surprise. But things got complicated because I had a good time with Jack in San Francisco too, and he sort of added to the surprise by showing up here looking for an extension of those good times.

I know everyone warned me about Jack, but please don't say I told you so. The thing is, I really love Jack, and always have, but I've been through such torment with him. And yet, I'm genuinely fond of Maxwell, too. And who knows? It could even lead to something serious. Neither one knows about the other, but all the juggling is getting hard, with both of them here, and with Jack now installed in my room.

Do I tell Jack that we've had our run and we tried to be friends but it didn't work out, thus jeopardizing the greatest love this girl has ever known? Or do I tell Maxwell that I'm sorry the timing just wasn't right for us once again, jeopardizing the possibility of a relationship that just might bloom into something serious? Or, for the sake of simplicity, do I just send them both out of my life forever and start all over?

I kind of need an answer soon. Maxwell's waiting for a call back and Jack's smiling sweetly at me right now.

Wish You Were Here,
Kate

Date:	September 15
From:	GamblinRose
To:	KateBogart
Subject:	Play It as It Lays

Dear Kate: You're so smart about everything except men. Oh well, even Achilles had a bum heel, and I'm not as good at the slots as I am at cards, but I don't let that stop me from playing them just the same.

It seems to me that you're looking at this situation all wrong. You see it as an either/or setup, and I'd call it a strong, all-around maybe. Therefore, I wouldn't mess it up going for a flush or a full house. You see what I'm saying? You've been dealt a pretty good hand, Kate. Two "Jacks" are better than one, right? So I say, keep them both.

Okay, it might involve a little calculation and some deceit, but artful deception, a cool head, and a reasonable sense of the odds are what pays the winnings at the end of the game. C'mon, you obviously like this Maxwell guy in some substantial way. And since you've asked for my opinion, I think you and Jack threw in the towel much too soon in the first place. So take your time to figure things out. Get to know them both a little more, and most of all, have fun! Life's too short to pass up the kind of situation you're in. Remember what Mama taught you: Play to win!

Love,
Mom

Date: September 16
From: KateBogart
To: GamblinRose
Subject: Daily Variety!

Oh, Mom, you're absolutely right! Who says a woman can't have two
lovers? Where's it written?

I took your advice and told Maxwell that I had to spend the rest of
yesterday with my "friend" from San Francisco. He was very understanding, especially when I told him that I would spend his last day
with him at the Chateau Marmont.

So, yesterday Jack and I went to stroll on the beach in Santa Monica
and to explore the freaky scene at Venice. This morning, I sent him
off to San Francisco with lots of tears and hugs and kisses that didn't
feel nearly as bittersweet as all the other parting tears and hugs and
kisses we have lavished upon each other over the past few years.
Since I've got to fly back from San Francisco anyway, I'll spend another night or so there with Jack before returning to New York.

But right now I am at the Chateau Marmont with Maxwell, who
is getting ready for our big day together. We're going to the Getty
Center, then to dinner at Spago in Beverly Hills. You are a genius and
the best mother and friend anybody ever had.

Wish You Were Here (So I Could Give You a Big Fat Kiss),
Kate

CHAPTER 9

✈

In New York

Date: September 18
From: JackMacTavish
To: KateBogart
Subject: The New Order

Katie: That visit was much too short, but sweet, sweet, sweet, and I'm grateful for every nanosecond I get to share with you. You're probably just touching down in New York right now, but wanted to let you know that I've given some further thought to our conversation at the café last night.

I'm happy to hear that you agree being together feels so much more natural than being apart. I know that it will be difficult for us to stay together in one place, but with time and patience and maturity, we might want to settle down. In the meantime, I'll do my best to meet you halfway in your travels. Really feel like I've grown up a lot since our last reconciliation and will also try to keep the jealousy in check this time. I'm totally open to being open, to being together when we're together, and to giving you as much time and space as you need, even if it takes forever. I'm not putting any pressure on you and I appreciate that you are willing to do the same for me.

I think the new arrangement will help me not to feel so crushed by the impossibility of us, and that miserable feeling that I have no one in the world who loves me whenever we're apart. I would still like to see more of you, though, to meet on common ground more often than we have been doing since the Big D, y'know? That's my one condition, but I promise not to put too much pressure on it.

If, along the way, either of us meets someone else and it develops into something serious, then we need to tackle that situation with the same openness. But honestly, Katie, I can't imagine ever feeling that way about anyone else. Who else is there in the world but you?

Love Always,
Jackson

Date:	September 18
From:	Manowar
To:	KateBogart
Subject:	The Long Good-bye

Dear Ms. Bogart: You are probably just touching down in New York now, if my calculations are accurate. Unfortunately, my sense of time has been thrown into shock after crossing so many time zones.

I do wish that I could say I am happy to be back in London, but I miss you lustily. As I review my notes on my experiences in Los Angeles, my mind inevitably wanders over to you. In a generous attempt to lure me back to the here and now, Mynah has been indulging my every fancy. She prepared a gooey spotted dick for me, but even my favorite childhood pudding is not narcotic enough to ease the symptoms of withdrawal.

You rushed off to San Francisco before we could discuss what is to become of us, and that is perhaps the most burdensome part of our separation. If your attraction to me is purely physical, then I am flattered and humbled, and more than willing to be your slave, I might add. But how much sweeter my life would be, if I knew that you were also feeling some deeper connection.

Do call as soon as you arrive in New York, and please don't leave me twisting in the wind.

Yours,
Maxwell

Date: September 18
From: KateBogart
To: JackMacTavish
Subject: RE: The New Order

Dear Jackson: Missing you, too. Just back and I am already having serious travel withdrawal. This always happens after a trip, but it's so much more acute because I had such a lovely time with you. Imagine us rekindling the fire in LA, of all places.

I agree that we need to make an effort to see each other more than we have since the "Big D" and now that the pressure is off, we can do so without such agony. As for "getting serious" with other people, how serious is serious? Maybe we should talk about this. Soon.

Ted has some substitutes working on "WYWH" and I am planning to spend a couple of weeks in New York, reorganizing closets, paying bills, taking Truman for his six-month check-up, and of course, planning next escape. It's looking like off-season Europe, culture at discount rates, and a Parisian Noël. Maybe you'll want to join me.

Wish You Were Here,
Kate

Date: September 18
From: KateBogart
To: Manowar
Subject: RE: The Long Good-bye

Maxwell: How touching to know that you are missing me and so sorry if you are feeling tortured. Not at all my intention. I suppose that we do have to talk. You can now reach me at home in New York.

In the meantime, if it's any consolation, of course I appreciate you for your mind as well as your body. The whole package that is Miles Maxwell is really quite agreeable. I also miss you quite strongly and find my mind wandering back to our time spent in LA as well. But I must be frank: I have very recently been seeing someone else who I am also very fond of. Unfortunately, the situation is very similar, a long-distance matter with someone who travels for a living.

I don't know what is going to happen between us, Maxwell, and I don't plan to string you along against your will. We had a lovely time in Rome and Positano and LA, and I would love to keep things open, to give us some more time to become better friends, or more if that's meant to be. But I wouldn't want to snare you into any of the binds for which I'm famous, Maxwell; I couldn't bear the thought of you suffering on my account. I know that your relationship with Odette was torturous and I can't promise that I'm any less difficult. I must warn you up front that I'm a woman who needs time, space, and patience, but I am very, very fond of you and would love to see more of you, too.

Wish You Were Here,
Kate

Date:	September 19
From:	Manowar
To:	KateBogart
Subject:	Ready and Willing

Dear Ms. Bogart: Snare me, torture me, and string me along! I could not imagine a fate more tantalizing than to be caught in one of your "famous binds."

I appreciate your honesty, and I am naturally disappointed to hear that there is a rival for your affections. But I am surprised, and grateful, that there is only one. I so long to hear your voice and will call you this evening, when I am free and clear of Mynah's guileless eavesdropping. Until then . . .

I Think Only of You,
Miles

PS Odette? Odette who?

Date: September 19
From: KateBogart
To: VioletMorgan
Subject: Balls in the Air

Oh, Vi! Got back to NY yesterday and so much to talk about, but have no idea where you are. Anyway, at Mom's advice decided it is better to have two of a kind than a bum hand and have decided to keep things open with both Jack *and* Maxwell.

That's right. I'm playing the field, with my ex-husband and my editor's drinking buddy. Haven't figured out exactly how this is going to work yet, or really how to juggle them, but not at all willing to throw either one away. There were e-mails waiting from both of them when I got home, and I have to admit, it feels kind of great, though also scary, as both are a bit intense.

The biggest surprise is that Ted was still here when I got in last night. Turns out he didn't get my message at work because he took the day off to go to a spa. Can you imagine it? I've never seen him looking so happy or relaxed. Didn't have the heart to send him off to a hotel. He has been sleeping in the tub, even though I think a chair would be more comfortable.

Does any of this sound crazy to you?

Wish You Were Here,
Kate

Date: September 20
From: VioletMorgan
To: KateBogart
Subject: RE: Balls in the Air

Kate: Still working the college circuit, taking advantage of all the impressionable students. Not glamorous at all. I'm not sure where I am either, but it's somewhere in Massachusetts. Trees and steeples and lots of Dunkin' Donuts. It all looks the same to me. Pretty as it is, I'm just not a country girl.

To answer your question: Your current situation sounds crazy, as usual. And yet, there's a perfect logic to it. If I understand you correctly, you have never fallen out of love with Jack, and you're apparently pretty hot for Maxwell, too. So you're dating your ex-husband and your lover doesn't know. Hey, if that sort of thing can work for all those Ricki Lake guests, I don't see why it can't work for you.

Have a feeling I'll be playing some part in this as your advisor. I hope so, as it sounds pretty juicy, and the Killers and I are pretty much surviving on Pringles, Yoohoo, and news of your adventures, so keep us posted.

As for Ted in the tub, *that's crazy*! Why, there's not enough room in your apartment to swing a cat, though the temptation is always strong.

V

Date:	September 20
From:	JackMacTavish
To:	KateBogart
Subject:	Open Season

Katie! What's up? I called you last night and some gruff dude answered the phone. Who's that? Are you seeing someone else already? Is this guy living with you? Why didn't you tell me that when you were here? I know we agreed to keep our minds and hearts open, but how open is open? And why haven't you returned my call? Katie, you're killing me. Can we talk about things? I love you!

Jackson

Date: September 20
From: KateBogart
To: JackMacTavish
Subject: RE: Open Season

Jackson: That "gruff dude" was Ted Concannon, the travel editor from the *Standard*. Remember? The guy who fell asleep at our wedding? His wife is Lorraine—skinny, google eyes, nervous energy like an over-bred dog. Well, she discovered politics and lesbianism and threw him out on his duff.

Ted's staying here while he's searching for options, which aren't materializing fast enough for me. You'll have to forgive him as he's still getting used to those conventional roommate customs like writing down phone messages. I had no idea you called.

Feeling silly? You should. Jumping to jealous conclusions seems to go against the new openness we agreed on back in San Francisco, Jackson. We do indeed need to talk about things. I'll call you tonight. By the way, I love you, too!

Wish You Were Here (But There's Not Enough Room),
Kate

Date: September 21
From: KateBogart
To: TedConcannon
Subject: Boxing Day

Ted: Twelve boxes came to the apartment today in your name. Heavy ones. Luckily, the UPS guy helped me carry them up the stairs, but I think his long-standing crush on me is officially kaput.

I didn't know twelve heavy boxes were on the way, Ted. Did you? It's a lot of boxes for such a small apartment. Truman is deeply intrigued by them, but frankly, it's feeling a little tight in here.

Wish You'd Been Here,
Kate

Date: September 21
From: TedConcannon
To: KateBogart
Subject: RE: Boxing Day

Kate: Meant to send you a heads-up on the boxes. Slipped my mind, what with the pressure of the apartment search and all that. Lorraine decided it would be better if all signs of me were erased from Larchmont to accommodate the new Rexroth regime. It's all just stuff like my high school baseball trophies, my bowling balls, and those six-packs of Billy Beer and the New Coke I've been holding on to. Sorry about the inconvenience. I'll deal with them when I get home tonight.

It seems like we're getting a little low on milk, so I'll pick some up. Let me know if we need anything else and think about what we should do for dinner tonight. I've got some apartments to look at, so I should be home around 8:00.

Ted

PS: Forgot to tell you, your ex-husband called for you the night before last.

Date: September 21
From: KateBogart
To: VioletMorgan
Subject: So Many Men

Vi: Hit the first real trouble spot in my rich new love life. Told Maxwell that I was still involved with someone else who means a lot to me. He was pretty understanding about it, though asked a lot of competitive questions, which I refused to answer. Still, he agreed that we've really just met and said that he was willing to give us some time.

Feeling emboldened by that, tried the same thing with Jack, who wasn't so understanding. When he learned that Maxwell lives on the other side of the Atlantic, he didn't seem quite as threatened, but I could tell he wasn't terribly happy about it, either.

Finally, got him to agree that if we do see other people, we do so discreetly, without a lot of details, unless of course we fall in love with someone else completely. Then it's time to fess up. Otherwise, no need hurting each other's feelings and putting each other through a lot of jealous snits.

The far bigger problem is Ted, who seems to be slowly assuming my living quarters. I'm afraid that pretty soon he's going to start borrowing my sweaters. It is a very tight squeeze, as I'm sure you know, and negotiating our morning toilettes with the tub inconveniently in the middle of the kitchen takes some delicate maneuvering indeed. Let's just say that you never really know your editor until you've seen him schmearing his morning bagel wearing nothing but a skimpy bath towel.

Wish You Were Here,
Kate

Date: September 22
From   GamblinRose
To: KateBogart
Subject: Pajama Games

Kate: Thinking about your predicament, I decided this would be the perfect time to have a sleepover. Why don't you come home to Brooklyn for the weekend? I'll call the Sisters and we can have a potluck pajama party, play cards, eat like crazy, and rent a stack of movies. Althea bakes a chocolate sheet cake that can make your heart race. Whadaya say? Just the girls. It's been so long since we've had a pajama party and you're in the city so rarely. It would make the Sisters and me so happy. They want to hear all about your travels and your romances. And bring some pictures!

Love,
Mom

Date: September 22
From: KateBogart
To: GamblinRose
Subject: RE: Pajama Games

Mom: Thanks for the invitation. That sleepover would be hard to pass up even if there weren't a portly, hirsute, and immodest gentleman celebrating his newfound bachelorhood in my tiny apartment. But I most certainly am not playing cards for money with you and the Sisters of Perpetual Bingo. If you'll recall, I wasn't born yesterday. Is tonight too soon? I can taste that sheet cake already!

   xx
   Kate

Date: September 23
From: TedConcannon
To: KateBogart
Subject: I Want to Be a Part of It

Gee, Kate, I didn't mean to drive you out of your own place. I hope I'm not intruding too much, or that I seem like an ingrate. Words can't express how much I appreciate your hospitality and patience. You're really up there in the pantheon of great pals, you know.

I've forgotten how exciting it is to live right smack dab in Manhattan, and I've fallen in love with the city all over again. Your neighborhood! I remember when it was just a bunch of mooks hanging around outside their social clubs. Now it's so many young, good-looking people rushing around in their crazy-looking shoes and speaking French and German on their cell phones. What do all these young people have to do that's so important?

The truth is, Kate, the apartment search isn't going real well. I don't have to tell you how tough the real estate game is in New York, and it demands someone who is either a lot younger than I am, or a lot richer. Ah well, I suppose I'm going to have to start looking out in the boroughs where us old guys belong.

But here's my deal in the meantime: Why don't you give me a couple of weeks more to keep looking. I'll pay your rent for the month, which would buy you at least a couple of nights in a swell hotel. No? Plus, you can write about it for "WYWH," so you'll get a budget on top of that, too. Stretch your stay even longer. It'll be a piece of cake for a hometown girl like you, and they'll love it in the suburbs.

Take some time to think it over, and thanks again from the bottom of my recently rediscovered heart.

Ted

Date: September 24
From: KateBogart
To: TedConcannon
Subject: RE: I Want to Be a Part of It

Ted: That's the best idea you ever had. If I stay with my mother and her friends much longer I'm either going to end up broke, fat, or both. I'm checking into hotel rates now. However, I must be able to visit with Truman every now and then when you're at the office. Good luck with the apartment search.

Kate

Date: September 25
From: JackMacTavish
To: KateBogart
Subject: The Jealous Kind

Katie: Feel like such a hammerhead about the other day. Getting jealous over Ted Concannon, and then giving you the third degree about the other guy. So uncool. So retrograde. I apologize. Had to go up to talk to Sharmi and she set me straight. All I really want for you is happiness. Do you forgive me?

    Your Big, Dumb, Ever-Loving,
    Jackson

Date: September 25
From: KateBogart
To: JackMacTavish
Subject: RE: The Jealous Kind

Dear Big, Dumb, Ever-Loving Jackson: Apology accepted. Speaking of my happiness, I have gone on assignment in New York, largely to accommodate Ted's homelessness. An exhilarating itinerary of different hotels every two nights, so if you want to lower the risk of Ted's poor telephone manners, stick to e-mail until further notice.

    Wish You Were Here,
    Kate

Date: September 25
From: Manowar
To: KateBogart
Subject: The London Blues

Dear Ms. Bogart: Imagine my surprise when I called your apartment today and dear old Ted Concannon picked up. At first, I thought I had dialed him mistakenly, but he explained the situation. How altruistic of you to surrender your flat to him in his time of need.

    Must say old Ted sounds chipper, a virtual spokesman for the rejuvenating wonders of marital separation, actually. He is very much my opposite in that respect, Ms. B, as I am positively forlorn without you. Since my return, London just seems crowded and colorless. Part theme park, part concentration camp.

    I would very much like to see you again, the sooner the better.

Deadlines be damned. How welcome or unwelcome would I be, were I to show up at whichever NY hotel has been lucky enough to claim you as its temporary resident? Do let me know.

Achingly Yours,
Maxwell

Date: September 26
From: . KateBogart
To: Manowar
Subject: RE: The London Blues

Dear Maxwell: It's e-mails like that one that make you so hard to re-sist. You'd be quite welcome to stay with me at whichever NY hotel I happen to be in. I'm sampling a bunch over the next week.

Right now I happen to be at a charming and strange little place called the Chelsea Star. It's an old flophouse and the one-time resi-dence of the struggling Madonna, the pop singer, not the deity. But it's been refurbished as a place for hip, young, European budget trav-elers. Décor is on the wacky side, like the very large mural of Uhura in my Star Trek room. The median age is about 21 and a half. Also, there's no elevator and only shared baths and showers. Sound like something you'd be interested in? C'mon, Maxwell. It will make you feel young again.

Wish You Were Here,
Kate

Date: September 26
From: Manowar
To: KateBogart
Subject: The British Are Coming!

Ms. Bogart: The Chelsea Star? It sounds so poetic! Even I am sur-prised at the effect your invitation has had on me. I feel as if I have had a transfusion. Why, instantly my heart began pounding and I began speaking much too fast for Mynah to follow my train of thought and the next thing I knew I had booked a flight to New York and Mynah was subduing my overstuffed luggage with her ample hindquarters.

You've made me so very happy, Ms. Bogart. I can't wait to see you. I shall find my way to the Chelsea Star by late afternoon, and follow you anywhere that you lead.

Yours,
Maxwell

Date: September 27
From: JackMacTavish
To: KateBogart
Subject: Outward Bound

Katie: Just letting you know that I have finally settled on a plan for the upcoming season. Sharmi says some outward-directed energy would do me good at this point. She thinks I've been way too self-absorbed recently. Going to lead a group of incarcerated teens and their counselors on a hike in the Sierras next week. That should give me some balance. Then, I'm going off to teach at that climbing school on Mt. Rainier for a while. One of the other instructors broke her leg and I need the money. But I should be done in time for the holidays and would love to have you show me around Paris.

Missing You,
Jackson

Date: September 28
From: KateBogart
To: JackMacTavish
Subject: RE: Outward Bound

Jackson: How lucky for those incarcerated teens. Still working out my itinerary for the fall myself, but Mom wants to spend Thanksgiving in New Orleans. She's never been and has been pestering me to take her for years.

    Congratulations on landing the class, by the way. Call me when you're back from your climb. And please remember, no matter how cute those kids are, each one is a potential homicidal maniac. Watch your back.

    Wish You Were Here,
    Kate

Date: September 28
From: KateBogart
To: GamblinRose
Subject: Lady Liberty

Mom: Feeling a little guilty. Got an e-mail from Jack asking when we'd see each other again. I was vague and didn't commit to anything. Nor did I mention that Maxwell is with me and we are having a positively romantic turn in New York, hotel hopping, drifting through the blissfully empty Chelsea galleries, riding the Circle Line, and living on swell prix-fixe lunches and sinfully cheap street food, all in the glorious early autumn air and the golden September light.

    Advice? Comfort?

    Wish You Were Here—and You Are!
    Kate

Date: September 28
From: GamblinRose
To: KateBogart
Subject: RE: Lady Liberty

Kate: There's nothing worse than a sore winner. Here you are having a ball of a time in the greatest city in the world with a man you like, while on the other side of the country, there's a peach of a guy waiting for you anytime you're ready. What's to feel bad about? Jack knows about Maxwell, but that doesn't mean he has to know every little thing you and Maxwell do together.

Of course, if you would introduce me to this Maxwell character, I could speak with more expertise on the subject. But that's okay. I understand if you're not ready to take that step yet. I did take the liberty of researching him on the Internet, though, and even fresh from a kidnapping he cuts a dashing figure.

So just remember that you and Jack aren't married now. You have an open arrangement, and what he doesn't know can't hurt him. If anybody gives you any flak about this situation, just tell them your mother gave you permission to have two lovers.

Love,
Mom

Date: September 29
From: TedConcannon
To: KateBogart
Subject: Urgent!

Kate: Which hotel are you at now? Tried you at 60 Thompson, but they said you haven't checked in yet and you're not at the Hudson, either. I don't want to send you into a panic, but I couldn't find Truman this morning. I even rattled his food dish like a maraca player, and nothing. I like to sleep with the window open, especially when the air turns cool like it's been, and I think he broke the screen and went out on the fire escape. Must have seen a tasty-looking bird.

I'm really sorry, Kate, but I'm sure he's okay. Somebody probably just saw him and took him home. I left the window open in case he comes back the way he went out, and I'll do whatever else I can to help. I'll canvass the neighborhood, and post flyers everywhere. I'll even cover the reward.

Ted

Date: September 29
From: KateBogart
To: GamblinRose
Subject: Mean Streets

Oh, Mom! How awful! Truman has run away from home. He has never been out of the apartment before except for trips to the vet and I'm very worried about him. I have brought a picture of him to the *Standard* and Ted is running off some copies. Maxwell, doll that he is, has agreed to help me post them all over Little Italy. Here's your chance to meet him if you want. Will be at my apartment by 3:00. Meet me there after school or leave a message. And bring your staple gun.

Kate

Date: September 29
From: KateBogart
To: VioletMorgan
Subject: Cats!

Well, Vi. You finally got your wish. Truman has run away from home. I'm bereft. Spent the afternoon with Rose, Maxwell, and Ted pasting reward notices all over the neighborhood. Maxwell and I covered the area from Houston to Canal between Mott and Bowery, and Ted and Rose took care of Mulberry and Lafayette. Then we all went to Lombardi's for pizza. Ate four slices just out of nervousness. Everybody tried their best to comfort me and convince me that he just got taken in by some lonely European Nolita shopgirl. Don't know why I'm even telling you. You're probably the one behind his abduction, but I just can't sleep with all the worrying, even with Maxwell all warm and peaceful. Maybe I'll wake him up and make him go to a diner with me.

Wish You Were Here,
Kate

Date: September 30
From: VioletMorgan
To: KateBogart
Subject: RE: Cats!

Picked up by a European Nolita shopgirl! How horrible! If the second-hand smoke doesn't kill him, the attitude will. We've got to rescue him! Have you tried the shelters?

I don't know how you could ever think this news would make me happy. The Killer Abs can do quite well without me. I'm hopping the bus into New York tomorrow to help. Or maybe that so-called high-speed train from Boston is faster. Tell me where you are! This is an emergency!

V

Date: October 1
From: KateBogart
To: VioletMorgan
Subject: RE: RE: Cats!

Aha! So you do love Truman! Well, I'm glad to know that you do have a heart, but you're a little late coming around.

No sign of Truman at the shelters, and two days without a meow.

Don't know how much you can help, but I have moved downtown to 60 Thompson St. so that I can be nearer to the neighborhood. Very stylish and cool and sybaritic and all that, but I just can't get into it. Every time I talk to the concierge or a bellhop, he just seems to be wearing a big cat head.

Wish You and Truman Were Here,
Kate

Date: October 2
From: KateBogart
To: GamblinRose
Subject: When the Cat's Away

Hi, Mom. Today Maxwell and I went to the Rose Planetarium and even though it's great, I couldn't help but think about Truman when I saw the constellation of Leo. I'm trying to enjoy New York in its prime season, and Maxwell's doing his darndest to cheer me up. Last night he even did an uncanny Eartha Kitt impression after her show at the Carlyle, but then I remembered that she played Catwoman on TV, and then, well, you know, on went the faucets full force.

Wish Truman Were Here,
Kate

Date: October 2
From: GamblinRose
To: KateBogart
Subject: RE: When the Cat's Away

Oh, Kate! Don't be such a gloombucket. You have to believe that no harm has come to Truman until you have some solid reason to believe otherwise. You just go about your business. Enjoy your time with Maxwell and keep thinking warm thoughts for Truman and he'll turn up.

If it's any comfort, Ted Concannon feels even worse than you do, poor man. After pizza last night I told him that I'd help him comb the shelters again today. I think it will help you both feel better.

Love,
Mom

Date: October 2
From: VioletMorgan
To: KateBogart
Subject: On the Case

Bogie, I have arrived. It's 1 AM and I am heading over to your neighborhood now. After all, cats are nocturnal. So are European shopgirls, for that matter, so I might catch all of them while they're out on the prowl. Besides, still on a rock 'n' roll schedule and right about this time would be hauling instruments to the bus anyway.

Tomorrow I would like to visit the scene of Truman's disappearance, so I can put myself in his little white boots. I turned my keys over to Ted, however, so I'll need access. I'll come by your hotel in the morning.

Vi

Date: October 3
From: TedConcannon
To: KateBogart
Subject: Bide-a-Wee

Dear Kate: Don't know how to tell you how sorry I am about Truman. Here you are being the pal of all pals helping me out in my time of need, and I go and muck it up by letting your damn cat out the window. And to top it all off, you haven't even laid any guilt on me. You're a stand-up guy, Bogart. I don't know how to make it up to you, but believe me, I will.

I also have to tell you, Kate, your mom is a great lady. She's really behind you 100 percent, and she helped me out, too. Last night she took me to the Bide-a-Wee Home. We didn't find Truman, but we saw some adorable kittens and some other poor unfortunate cats who really deserve a good home. Afterward, we came back downtown and had dinner at Joe's Shanghai. The sight of all those rabbits and chickens strung up in the windows in Chinatown got me to thinking about Truman, though, and I kind of lost my appetite. Still, I really enjoyed your mother's company.

Anyway, you really should go look at those kittens at the Bide-a-Wee, Kate. I know none of them is Truman, but they're pretty hard to resist.

Sorry Again,
Ted

Date: October 3
From: KateBogart
To: TedConcannon
Subject: RE: Bide-a-Wee

Ted: So I suppose you think Truman ended up on a menu in a Chinatown restaurant! Well, thanks a lot! That's comforting!

Maxwell and I went to the Bide-a-Wee home today too, and the people there are getting a little tired of us. Yes, the kittens are adorable, and the other animals are quite touching too, but I am just not ready to replace Truman at this point. Sadly, my hope wears thin by the day.

I know you didn't mean to lose Truman, so there's really no need to apologize. But I do think it's time for me to reclaim my shelter. I'll do everying I can to help you find another place, but this just isn't working out, Ted.

Wish Truman Were Here,
Kate

Date: October 3
From: VioletMorgan
To: KateBogart
Subject: Nine Lives

Bogie: Left messages on hotel voice mail, but in case you check e-mail first: Truman has been found. Turns out he was right under our noses all along. All I had to do was put myself in Truman's position the night of his disappearance to figure out what was going on in his pea-sized brain. He couldn't have been on a bird hunt at night, as they are all asleep, as are all the squirrels. So, at a loss, I ventured out onto the fire escape itself and did some investigating. And what did I discover?

Mrs. D'Anunzziatta, the old shut-in two stories down, has five cats of her own. And when I peered into her window, who did I see sunning himself on the sill but one Truman Capote Bogart, looking fatter and lazier than ever. He bolted under her sofa as soon as he saw me, of course, and it took a hell of a lot of catnip to get him out of there.

I am lucky that Mrs. D'Anunzziatta didn't shoot me on sight. She's not exactly a friendly old woman. She hasn't been out of the building since 1988. Not because she's disabled, but because she's hostile and paranoid. Anyway, how could she know there were missing cat notices all over the neighborhood? Her good-for-nothin' son doesn't tell her a damn thing. She shoulda given him up for adoption when he was born, yadda, yadda, yadda . . .

So, I hefted the old bag of fleas (Truman, not Mrs. D'Anunzziatta) back to your apartment, fed him, brushed him, and locked him in tight. Ted Concannon will probably have a heart attack when he sees him, so you might want to warn him. You can thank me with dinner.

Smugly,
Violet Morgan, Pet Detective

Date: October 3
From: KateBogart
To: VioletMorgan
Subject: RE: Nine Lives

Vi! You're the greatest! Thank you so much for rescuing Truman from
that crazy cat lady. I've never even met her before, but I've heard her
through the airshaft. What a true and brave friend you are. I have already spoken to Ted and he insists that you take the reward. Meanwhile,
we're planning a party at my place tonight to welcome Truman home
and send Ted off to points unknown. Please come.

Don't know what got into Truman. I think he was probably pun-
ishing me for leaving him alone with Ted for so long. I had no idea he
was craving the company of other cats so badly. Maybe I should go
back to the shelter and get him a companion.

Wish You Would Stay,
Kate

Date: October 4
From: KateBogart
To: VioletMorgan
Subject: New York Sex Shocker!

Vi: I know you probably haven't even arrived in Boston yet, but this
is important. Did you notice that my mother and Ted were acting a little odd last night at Truman's party? Well, I did. And when I went to
look in on Truman this morning, who did I find in my very own bed
but *my mother* and *Ted Concannon.* Together. Like a couple.

Violet, my mother was in my bed with my editor! And I think they
might even have been naked! I was speechless. After all, what's the
proper etiquette in a situation like that? I pretended to be looking for
a pair of shoes I left behind, then flew out of that apartment like a tor-
nado. I think I told them to have a nice day on my way out, too.

I don't know what to think, or how to feel, even. I'm still reeling

from the shock of it. I didn't tell Maxwell, though he has was quite
concerned about my strange and distant behavior. He thinks it's because he's leaving in the morning. Oh, Vi, this is just weird.

Wish You Were Here,
Kate

Date: October 4
From: VioletMorgan
To: KateBogart
Subject: RE: New York Sex Shocker!

Wow! Rose and Ted? It's not the prettiest picture, but it sort of makes
sense. They're the same age more or less, both unattached, and a
matching pair of down-to-earth, native New York, brook-no-bullshit
types. It's kind of sweet when you think about it. Nevertheless, she is
your mother, and he is your associate and the closest thing to a father
figure you've ever had. You should probably get yourself to a trauma
center.

Looks like I left for Boston a day too soon. Can't wait to tell the
Killers. Maybe they'll write a song about it.

Vi

Date: October 5
From: GamblinRose
To: KateBogart
Subject: The Facts of Life

Dear Kate: Obviously we have things to talk about. I should have told
you sooner, but there was all the agida over your cat and the distractions of Miles Maxwell and your assignment. One minute you're riding the Circle Line, the next you're at the planetarium, then you're
crying your head off in an animal shelter, then you're oohing and ahh-

ing over the tapestries at the Cloisters. Not to mention the schlepping from hotel to hotel. I just couldn't find the right moment.

Ted and I really hit it off the first night that we were posting those flyers all around your neighborhood, but you were eating so much pizza you didn't seem to notice. He's like a changed man since his separation, one with a lot more life in him than I ever saw in our very brief meetings before. After you and Maxwell went uptown that night, Ted saw me to the cab and we made our date to visit the animal shelter. Seeing Ted so touched by all the helpless unwanted animals was so sweet and so moving, and I have to tell you that we both felt a powerful, beautiful connection right there on the spot.

After Truman was found and we all had dinner together at your place, we were so happy that I stayed behind so Ted and I could celebrate in our own private way. And I don't mind telling you it was the best nookie of my life, Kate. It's been so long, I've forgotten how good it can be. Everyone says it's like riding a bike, but it's so much better. I think if I got on a bike I'd have a coronary.

Anyway, I didn't think you'd be returning home, especially on Maxwell's last day, and I am very sorry for not thinking about you. To tell you the truth, my heart ran away with me. Please don't go giving me the cold shoulder, Kate. That wouldn't be fair. After all, Ted and I are two extremely mature people with enough life experience between us to know what we are doing. Let's talk about this.

Love,
Mom

Date:	October 5
From:	KateBogart
To:	GamblinRose
Subject:	RE: The Facts of Life

Dear Mom: No need to explain. It was awkward and sort of mortifying actually, but these things happen. We were just the victims of bad timing. That's all. We'll just pretend it never happened. Said a sad

good-bye to Maxwell and home working all day. Call me when you
get the chance.

Love,
Kate

PS Can we make this the last time we use the word "nookie" in
our e-mails?

Date: October 5
From: TedConcannon
To: KateBogart
Subject: All in the Family

Dear Kate: First I take over your apartment, then I sleep through your
cat's great escape, then you catch me in bed with your mother. I'll understand if you don't want to have anything to do with me anymore, but I
hope that this won't be the end of our friendship or change things between us professionally.

The thing is, I tried to tell you how I felt about Rose, but I just
couldn't find the opportune moment what with all the agonizing over
the cat. Let's just say I'm crazy about her, Kate. Haven't felt that way
in the company of a woman in many, many, many years. I love her
spirit and her good sense and those beautiful dark eyes.

I hope that this isn't too upsetting for you, but if there's anything I
can do to soften the impact, I'm more than willing to help.

Ted

Date: October 6
From: KateBogart
To: TedConcannon
Subject: RE: All in the Family

Thanks for that e-mail, Ted. Spoke to Mom last night and she told me
all about her feelings for you too, and that you have even moved in
with her temporarily. Wow. I'm happy that you're both happy, of course,
but it will take me some time to adjust to the whole idea, as there's a
certain Freudian whiff to it all. After all, you're my mentor and she's
my mother and it's all so sudden.

   There is one thing you can do to help, however. Thinking of going
to Provincetown to write up the New York pages. Think I can get a
"WYWH" piece on it? Call me.

   Kate

Date: October 7
From: KateBogart
To: Violet Morgan
Subject: I Vant to Be Alone

Vi: Going to Provincetown for some much-needed peace and solitude. After discovering Rose and Ted together, can't seem to sleep in
my own bed. Big surprise. Truman is boarding with my mother, as is
Ted. Even bigger surprise. Planning to avoid it all in Cape Cod.

   Wish This Was All a Dream,
   Kate

✈

CHAPTER 10

In Old Cape Cod

Date: October 8
From: Manowar
To: KateBogart
Subject: Such Sweet Sorrow

Ms. Bogart: Thank you so much for that lovely week in New York. I am so pleased that it came to a happy conclusion and that Truman was eventually rescued. How I envy that creature your fanatical devotion to him. I was also very pleased to meet your mother and the delightful Violet.

Everything about your world seems so charmed to me, somehow. Even your quaint neighborhood with its countless little handbag boutiques and your funny flat with the old-fashioned tub in the kitchen are precious to me. Your life seems so full of character and noise and whimsy and passion. I realized in New York what I'd been missing all those years tromping from one desperate battle zone to the next with Odette—that wonderful sense of warmth and safety and connection. How could you ever feel lonely with people like Rose and Ted and Violet so devoted to you? Although Mynah does provide some diversion occasionally, of course, my daily existence seems hollow and dull compared to yours—an extended exercise in ennui.

How I miss you already, Ms. Bogart! I am thinking of you looking lovely and heroic at the prow of that tourist boat pointing out the neighborhood where you grew up, and the way you squealed when the salty spray of the East River caught us by surprise. Do tell me that I will see you again soon. A week with you is simply not enough.

Yours,
Miles

Date: October 9
From: KateBogart
To: Manowar
Subject: RE: Such Sweet Sorrow

Maxwell: Just arrived in Provincetown, after stopping in Boston on the way to hear Violet's husband's band perform. Settling in for a week of solitude, writing, and long walks on the beach.

You were a sweetheart to put up with me in New York. I'm sure that your plans didn't involve so many trips to the Bide-a-Wee Home or posting notices all over Little Italy in the middle of the night. As anguished as I might have been at the time, I think I will always look back on it as one of my favorite times in the city ever.

I miss you too, Maxwell, but let's not get carried away. I know it's difficult, but we should try not to overwhelm each other. Let's give ourselves a little breathing space, a little time to catch up with our work, a little time to get to know each other better, and a little more time to enjoy this mutual infatuation. Shall we? In the meantime, I'll be savoring the memory of your Eartha Kitt. It was just per-r-r-fect, Maxwell.

Wish You Were Here,
Kate

Date: October 10
From: JackMacTavish
To: KateBogart
Subject: Desolation Wilderness

Wow, Katie! Amaaazing experience up in the Desolation Wilderness! Great backcountry up near Tahoe. Not desolate at all, either. Really connected with those kids and think the experience really affected them. There's nothing to get through a kid's hardened shell like a nighttime visit from a hungry bear, y'know? You should have heard them screaming. Scared the hell out of the poor bear, too.

The kids also had to do a lot of survival stuff and learn some trust issues that they never picked up on the street, and by the time they came down from that mountain they seemed so much more like regular kids than the thugs-in-training we first picked up in the minivan. You should have seen their faces when they saw all the stars at night. It was so gratifying.

One of the kids says that he wants to learn to be a mountain guide just like me when he gets out. Maybe it's corny, but I can't tell you how proud it made me feel, and it reminded me how much I really want to have my own kids someday. Of course, I would only want to have them with you. Thoughts? Feelings?

Where are you, by the way? Sick of talking to your machine.

Love,
Jackson

Date: October 10
From: KateBogart
To: JackMacTavish
Subject: RE: Desolation Wilderness

Dear Jack: A crazy week in New York. While I was visiting hotels, Truman ran away, then Violet found him, then I found my mother and Ted Concannon in bed together. Ted has actually moved in with my mother in Brooklyn, and I have sought refuge in Provincetown.

The Desolation Wilderness sounds like a life-changing experience for you. Flattered that you want to have children with me someday, Jack, but you know I don't see myself as the maternal type. Certainly can't imagine forgoing things like wine or airplane travel during pregnancy. In case you haven't noticed, I absolutely live for wine and airplane travel! In fact, I'm enjoying a nice ripe Burgundy right now.

Rest assured, however, that if I change my ramblin', wine-drinkin' ways someday and find myself yearning for sleepless nights, soiled diapers, and bankrupting tuition bills, you'll be the first man I run to.

Wish You Were Here,
Kate

Date: October 11
From: JackMacTavish
To: KateBogart
Subject: RE: RE: Desolation Wilderness

Whoa! Rose and that cranky Concannon guy? That's a real walk on the wild side, Katie.

Totally disappointed that you still have that cynical New York view of children being nothing but drudgery and sacrifice. I know that you and you alone have the right to choose what you do with your body, but if we adopt, you don't have to worry about trimester flight restrictions and you can drink yourself under the table every night if you want. I'll take care of the kids. I promise. I can't wait!

Love,
The Future Father of Your Five Children, Jackson MacTavish

Date: October 12
From: GamblinRose
To: KateBogart
Subject: Rose's Turn

Oh, Kate! What a gorgeous autumn we're having. Maybe it's because Ted and I are hitting it off so well. The night before last, we rode the Staten Island Ferry at sunset, just for the fun of it. Last night, he took me to a wonderful restaurant on the Upper East Side called Kings' Carriage House. Very romantic. I want to make it up to him and take him out for a nice, romantic dinner this week. Any suggestions for a place that will get him in the mood for love?

Love,
Lady Peaceful, Lady Happy

Date: October 12
From: KateBogart
To: GamblinRose
Subject: RE: Rose's Turn

Dear LPLH: Are you telling me that Ted Concannon took you to Kings' Carriage House? And he paid? The same Ted Concannon who finds Gray's Papaya stuffy and pricey? Boy I wish I was a fly on that flocked wallpaper. And the Staten Island Ferry, too? Mom, it's like you're living in an Edna St. Vincent Millay poem.

I'm still not sure how I feel about this whole thing, and frankly, I think that asking me for courting tips is almost like asking a death row inmate to pitch in for the electric bill. But the Ted I know would probably be happy with a family-sized bucket o' chicken from The Colonel.

Wish You Were Here, Too,
Kate

Date: October 12
From: GamblinRose
To: KateBogart
Subject: RE: RE: Rose's Turn

Katherine Alison Bogart! In all your running around the globe, have I ever been anything less than supportive of your love life? I have not. Not when you were involved with that Portuguese toreador or whatever he was, or that crazy flamenco dancer last year, or that poor screenwriter, or that gondolier in Venice, or that Irish terrorist, or your lovely ex-husband. Did I once ever dampen your joy with a snide, disapproving attitude? I did not, though I was presented with many opportunities to do so. I would very much appreciate the same treatment, but instead you have run off on some impromptu trip in that way of yours so that you can avoid dealing with a difficult situation. Then you send me smarty-pants comments from the comfort of your high horse.

For your information, being with Ted makes me realize how much I have just been settling for a good life instead of enjoying a rich one. Right now, I am choosing to put my heart on the line for the first kind, gentle, and attentive man I have been involved with in many years. Frankly, it's a bit scary, but I have to say I'm happier than I've been in years. Maybe it's something you'll come to appreciate with maturity. If you can't share in my happiness, then I am very concerned that I have failed you as a parent.

Sorry, that's just my opinion, and I can say these things because I'm your mother and I love you.

Wish You Were Here (So I Could Ground You),
Mom

Date: October 13
From: KateBogart
To: GamblinRose
Subject: RE: RE: RE: Rose's Turn

Mom, the Irish guy was a tenor, not a terrorist, and when you add him
up with that Portuguese bullfighter and that screenwriter and that flamenco dancer and that gondolier and all the others, what you get is a
very worrisome daughter when it comes to affairs of the heart. I know
how treacherous and wearying and discouraging they can be. Just the
same, I can't say I regret any one of these experiences. In fact, I treasure each one in its own way, so of course I'm happy for you and I'm
truly sorry if I purged on your party dress.

But you might send a little sympathy my way, too. After all, I have
never actually had to deal with having a father, real or step, and you
happen to be shacking up with a man I rely on for my bread and
butter. It raises all sorts of discomforting issues of conflict of interest
for me. I would also like to remind you that I did not exactly invent
Freudian dynamics or the squeamishness that any daughter feels when
confronted with her parent's love life.

As for travel as "avoidance," I would like to say a few more words
in my defense. I maintain that travel is not at all running away from
life. Indeed, when we are traveling, we are closer to our fundamental
selves than when we are going about our humdrum everyday lives. It
is when we are most alive, most open to new ideas, new experiences,
and new people. No, I have not been running away from life; I have
been living it to its fullest and trying to be the best person I can possibly be. I am glad that you and Ted are too, but I would like a little
time to absorb the shock in the way that I know the best. My apologies again.

Wish You Were Here,
Kate

Date: October 14
From: JackMacTavish
To: KateBogart
Subject: Conjugal Visits

Katie: Heading up to Rainier to substitute at that climbing school. Got people signing up for it already. Will you come here before I go, or maybe meet me in Seattle? I'm aching for you, Katie. Everywhere.

    Love,
    Your Jackson

Date: October 14
From: KateBogart
To: JackMacTavish
Subject: RE: Conjugal Visits

Oh, Jackson, I'm aching for you too, but don't think I can make it West right now. Have so much work to catch up with and I know I'm going to have to go back to New York to make peace with the Rose and Ted situation. Sorry. It hurts me as much as it hurts you, but we'll be together again soon, I'm sure.

    Really Wish You Were Here,
    Kate

Date: October 14
From: Manowar
To: KateBogart
Subject: Love Is the Drug

Dear Ms. Bogart: Once again I find myself burning for you. You are like a delicious and powerful opiate to me. How long must I endure this torture? Don't make me join the French Foreign Legion, or go back to suicidal daredevil reporting. Make me whole and happy, Ms. B. Free me from the indignities and banalities of the everyday world, as only you can do.

Fervently Yours,
Maxwell

Date:	October 14
From:	KateBogart
To:	Manowar
Subject:	RE: Love Is the Drug

Oh, Maxwell. I miss you, too. Just as fervently. Still trying to catch up with work without the distractions of my mother, Ted, or my plump little Truman. Have also been thinking about you being just across the Atlantic the whole time. Maybe we can talk about a London visit when I get back to New York.

Wish You Were Here,
Kate

Date:	October 15
From:	Manowar
To:	KateBogart
Subject:	RE: RE: Love Is the Drug

A smashing idea, Ms. B! Do come to London. And don't just stay a week. You and I have not been together for more than ten days at a time. How can we get to know each other in such short visits? For that matter, when was the last time you were in any one place for more than a few weeks?

I am extending an invitation for you to come for as long as you like. You can make this your base and come up with countless articles for Ted's little newspaper, so you won't have to give up your precious work. I would prefer it if you would stay forever, of course, but I leave that entirely up to you. I will take as much of you as you are willing to give.

Anxiously,
Miles

Date:	October 15
From:	KateBogart
To:	VioletMorgan
Subject:	Playing House

Yikes, Vi! Maxwell has asked me to stay with him in London for as long as I want. Even if it means indefinitely. The scary thing is, it's tempting. I like London, and I could produce a bunch of articles to sell here, so I wouldn't have to give up my work. And yet, I'm not sure if I like *Maxwell* quite that much. I really don't know him that well. And isn't moving in with someone essentially saying that you're ready to go exclusive? Kind of like being married? Don't think I'm ready to take that step yet, but then how can you tell? It's always a risk, isn't it? All I know is that I've jumped into these things in the past and always messed it up. This time I want to do it right. What do you think?

WYWH,
Kate

Date:	October 15
From:	VioletMorgan
To:	KateBogart
Subject:	RE: Playing House

Bogie: Essentially, Maxwell just asked you to marry him. Now, you might go to London for a while, just to see if you and Maxwell are meant to be, but I wouldn't promise him the world at this point, as it sounds as if he is very sure how he feels about you. And you're right;

you do tend to jump into these things and mess them up, which is why it's so entertaining being your friend.

Great show in NY last night. The Killers got a bigger ovation than Potty Mouth. Unheard of for an opening act. "Pulaski Skyway" brought down the house. On to Philly this weekend. Can't believe there are two more months of this madness. Say hello to the seagulls and the drag queens for me.

Vi

Date: October 16
From: KateBogart
To: VioletMorgan
Subject: Tall Ships

Dear Vi: I think you're right about Maxwell, and told him over the phone last night that I would mull over the invite while I'm here. Now hear this: I came to Provincetown for some solitude and off-season quiet, but little did I know the town is gearing up for its annual transvestite convention.

So, this morning, tired of the sound of machinists in high heels pounding heavily down the hallways of my guesthouse, decided to go for a ride on the bike trails through the Beech Forest. Figured no one would be there this time of year. Much to my surprise, I had to share the trails with an armada of suburban accountants in their stiff wigs, Tootsie glasses, and stretch denim jeans. You should have seen them pumping away at their rented girls' bikes, all with little flowers woven through the plastic baskets, which held their weekend-in-the-country straw handbags, naturally.

Feeling a little crowded, locked my bike up and took to the dunes, where I'd decided to hike to the ocean to see if the seals had arrived yet for winter. I'd forgotten how otherworldly the landscape can be here, like a cross between the surface of the moon, the desert, and the seaside. I had it all to myself, except for one lone figure I could see cresting the dunes behind me. Stopped to have my picnic in a warm sun-filled hollow, when the lone figure walked right up to me and helped himself to a couple of carrot sticks. And who should that lone carrot-stealing dune-walker be? Why, Jack MacTavish of course.

He couldn't bear the thought of us being apart for so long and figured it would be romantic if he surprised me in Provincetown, scene of our last honeymoon. It is indeed romantic and he promises he won't get in the way of my work, but I have to wonder how far I must travel to enjoy some solitude.

Wish You Were Here,
Kate

Date: October 16
From: Manowar
To: KateBogart
Subject: Anticipation

My Dearest Ms. B: Have you decided my fate yet? Will you be coming to stay with me in London? Mynah and I are both going mad with suspense. She has convinced me that my flat is not proper for a "lady," and she has been going about placing little bowls of dried flowers in the bath in preparation for your arrival. She calls it "pot paree," in that quaint way of hers. She is not very well educated, the poor thing, but she really is a faithful old dog.

If you are having difficulty making up your mind, perhaps I should hop over to Boston to guide you through your deliberations. There must be flights from there to Provincetown, or perhaps a ferry service. I am utterly available, Ms. Bogart, and even more than willing. Do tell me where you are staying and I shall be there in an instant.

Yours,
Maxwell

Date:	October 16
From:	KateBogart
To:	Manowar
Subject:	RE: Anticipation

Maxwell! Don't you *dare* come to Provincetown. It just wouldn't be wise at this point. This is a very personal and private time for me. I have to be alone to catch up with my work, remember.

Even though I am quite grateful that you and Mynah are so eager to show me your hospitality, I really haven't made my mind up one way or another about London, and I wish you wouldn't put so much pressure on me. I have hardly had the time to consider it.

I think that you should try to drum up another assignment, or maybe get to work on those memoirs of yours. I will let you know whether I can come to London, and for how long, at the end of the week. In the meantime, I desperately need this hard-earned time and space to myself. Is it too much to ask?

Yours,
Kate

Date:	October 16
From:	KateBogart
To:	VioletMorgan
Subject:	Old Cape Cod

Vi: Having a great time with Jack in Provincetown and a hard time keeping Maxwell at bay. Got an e-mail from him today, with Jack practically reading over my shoulder. Haven't told Jack yet that I am considering going to London for a while. Nor have I told Maxwell that I am having a second honeymoon with my ex-husband in Provincetown.

You think it's easy having two lovers? You try it. I'm not getting a damn thing done, but I've been getting some really great back rubs, foot massages, and anxious e-mails from across the Atlantic. Still, they don't pay the rent.

Wish You Were Here,
Kate

Date: October 17
From: VioletMorgan
To: KateBogart
Subject: RE: Old Cape Cod

Bogie: I am so full of myself today. Yesterday, the Killers and I met with this really slick record producer, Akbar Barhan. You must have heard of him. The guy with the funny turban, the fancy car collection, and the record company. He was totally trying to sell my Killers a bridge, trying to squeeze some crazy percentages out of the contract he was offering as a "gift" to them. He went on and on about how they're so much older than all the other bands he's been signing, and how the company isn't even signing bands right now, etc. etc. etc. Essentially, he was telling them they weren't all that hot, so that he could get them to take whatever he offered. But I, Violet Morgan, queen of the universe, kicked his pseudo-soulful ass.

I went right into hardball mode, setting limits on song approval, number of albums due over five years, royalty percentages, and concert restrictions. Told him not to even think about a contract with the boys if he couldn't deliver the goods, and reminded him we have a whole week of meetings ahead of us. He totally caved and agreed to every one of my demands on the spot, all the time making it seem like he was doing the band a huge favor. You see, I learned something working as an assistant to crazy people over the past five years. Take that, Sharon Osbourne!

I'm sorry, did you have a problem?

Violet

Date: October 17
From: KateBogart
To: GamblinRose
Subject: Falling in Love Again

Hi, Mom. Guess who found me in Provincetown. Hint: He was once your son-in-law.

Supposed to be getting work done, but not very successful so far. Very pretty here, though. Nothing like the sea air in autumn. So many stars at night. We're staying at a little place called the Dinghy Dock, about a foot away from the beach. You can hear the foghorn all night, the lapping of waves on the beach, and the seagulls singing across the harbor from Long Point. Sort of heavenly.

There's also a transvestite convention going on. It's an annual event called Fantasia Fair. Sometimes Jack seems to be the only man in Provincetown who actually shops in the men's department. Lots of fun though, and it'll be great for the article. Since there's really not a lot to do here at night in the off-season, we've been attending all the functions so far, and the guys, gals, whatever, have been very sweet, as have their wives. We've been to the Town n' Gown spaghetti supper, and last night they asked Jack to stand in for a missing judge at their talent contest. The winner was an ophthalmologist from Tenafly who did a surprisingly good version of "Falling in Love Again" in his own voice. No lip-synching or channeling Marlene Dietrich. Very impressive. Made the gown himself, too.

Jack is such a great sport and it's actually touching to see him be his regular, chivalrous self with all these foofed-up dockworkers. I know this sounds funny, but more than anything else that's happened these past few months, it has reminded me why I love him so much and have had such a hard time going on without him since our divorce.

Afterward, I just couldn't get that Marlene Dietrich song out of my head. It made me think of you too, and even though you don't believe me, I really am happy for you and Ted. So is Jack.

Wish You Were Here,
Kate

Date: October 17
From: GamblinRose
To: KateBogart
Subject: RE: Falling in Love Again

Dear Kate: How nice to hear that you're enjoying Provincetown with Jack so much. I've never been there this time of year, but I bet it's romantic. Maybe Ted and I will rent a cottage with a fireplace this winter and just mark off a whole weekend for snuggling.

I know what you mean about those little unpredictable things that men do that can just make your heart swell up like a bad knee. For me it's when Ted is sleeping on his side and he tucks his hands between his thighs like a little boy. It's one of the sweetest things I've ever seen, and it reminds me that inside this big, old, world-weary New Yorker is really just a tenderhearted little boy craving warmth and comfort.

Glad to hear you're happy for me and Ted too, because I've invited him to spend Thanksgiving with us in New Orleans. Why don't you bring Jack? Or Miles. Or whoever it is you're favoring next month.

Love,
Mom

Date: October 18
From: KateBogart
To: Manowar
Subject: Ms. Bogart Regrets

Dear Maxwell: Have seriously considered the invite to London, but really don't think it's wise this week. I have to be honest with you at this point and tell you that the other man that I've been seeing recently is actually my ex-husband. I don't know what the future holds, but I must tell you that my heart has been split between the two of you for the past month and it feels like it's going to burst.

Frankly, your eagerness to have me join you is terribly tempting, but it gives me great reason to pause, too. I'm just not ready to do it right now. I don't want either of us to get hurt, Maxwell, and I truly feel that I need more time. I know that I'm asking for a lot of patience from you, and I don't blame you if you can't muster it, but please know that I appreciate your kindness and perseverance and I am truly and deeply fond of you.

Wish You Were Here,
Kate

Date: October 19
From: Manowar
To: KateBogart
Subject: RE: Ms. Bogart Regrets

Dear Ms. Bogart: Your ex-husband is it? If I recall correctly, he is some sort of latter-day Hemingway adventurer with a California sensibility and the looks of Adonis. I saw those pictures of the two of you in your flat. Foolishly, I thought it was a matter of oversight on the part of a preoccupied and peripatetic divorcée who simply hadn't the chance to update her surroundings, but suddenly I see all too clearly where it is that I stand. I have been snared into the web of a woman who is still in love with her ex-husband, but does not want to admit it. Suddenly, all the waffling, the half-heartedness, the advances, and especially the retreats, make perfect sense to me.

I have been in countless war zones, Ms. Bogart. I know an impossible situation when one is in my sights and I know all too well the acrid smell of defeat. I shan't complicate the matter for you any further. I suggest that you go back to your husband, work through all your difficulties, forgive him whatever his shortcomings or incompatibilities may be, and let yourself be happy.

As for me, things are quite hot again in the Middle East. The Near East is tempting, too. Indeed, new conflicts seem to be bubbling up in distant lands every day. It seems that unrest is the only true love I'll ever know.

Adieu,
Maxwell

Date: October 19
From: KateBogart
To: Manowar
Subject: RE: RE: Ms. Bogart Regrets

Just what I need—another drama queen, when the streets of Province-town are teeming with them. Please don't be so fatalistic, Maxwell. I really think that we need to talk, but Mynah told me that you left on very short notice and she doesn't know where to reach you. For God's sake, Maxwell, don't jump to conclusions about a situation you don't really understand, and don't do anything rash! Now where the heck are you? I'm concerned and very eager to talk.

    Wish You Would Be Reasonable,
    Kate

Date: October 19
From: KateBogart
To: VioletMorgan
Subject: Back Street

Oh, Vi, whatta week! Just saw Jack off to the Provincetown airport, which always reminds me of those tiny little airports in 1950s melo-dramas, the ones where a Susan Hayward type is always waiting for a John Gavin type to disembark and appear through the fog on the run-way, if she's not actually kissing him good-bye through the chain link fence while the propellers whirr. Anyway, the role of John Gavin was played by Jack MacTavish, and I was Susan Hayward, and we even kissed good-bye through the chain link fence.

    Needless to say, we had a great time here. Hikes in the dunes and along the breakwater, long walks on deserted beaches, lobster every night, but I won't sicken you with the details. I just hope our story doesn't end as tragically as a Susan Hayward movie.

    Also, had a disastrous exchange with Maxwell. Decided to tell him about Jack, for the sake of total honesty, but he jumped to all sorts of conclusions and assumed that I was just toying with him while resisting my own unconditional love for Jack. Well, Jack and I *did* have a wonderful few days here, but I had a lovely time with Maxwell in New York, too. I mean, I'm trying to be polygamous here! But these guys sure don't make it easy. Maxwell has run off to points unknown, but Ted and Mynah are both on the lookout.

Congratulations on kicking executive butt on the Killers' behalf, by the way. Saw a transvestite lip-synching "I Am Woman" and thought of you. You are strong, you are invincible, you are my Violet!

Wish You Were Here,
Kate

Date:	October 20
From:	JackMacTavish
To:	KateBogart
Subject:	Sand in My Shoes

Katie! Arrived in SF last night. Still had sand in my shoes! Stars in my eyes, too. Thanks so much for Provincetown. What a great time! Figured out why I feel so at home there: It's those sunsets over the ocean like you only see on the West Coast. Figured out that the tilt of the earth and the width of Cape Cod Bay must allow for just enough of the earth's curve to create the illusion. (The sun doesn't really sink into the ocean every day, babe.)

Wouldn't it be a great place to raise our kids? Maybe I could get a job working for the National Seashore as a nature guide or doing some work to reforest the dunes, and you could write just as easily there as anywhere else. Think about it.

Flying up to Seattle now. Time to go up the mountain, Katie. Will meet the students and the leader I'm assisting at the base, then lead the charge on to Rainier. "Why?" you ask. "Why, because it's there," said the Bodhisattva.

Very excited, but I know I'm going to miss you, too. I'll think about you every moment. In fact, I'm dedicating this climb to you. If you really loved me, you'd be waiting for me at the base when I come

back down. But no pressure! You're free to follow your own path, my
little dune bunny.

Yow, I love you so much!

Kisses All Over,
Yr Jackson

Date:	October 20
From:	KateBogart
To:	TedConcannon
Subject:	Miles Away

Hi, Ted. Or should I call you "Pop"? Any word on Maxwell? I spoke to
Mynah again. She doesn't know where he is, and she's quite concerned.

I know you don't want to triangulate and I don't blame you one
bit, but frankly, I'm a little worried about him. You don't have to di-
vulge his whereabouts, just let me know that he's okay, and maybe tell
him that I'm sincerely sorry about things and would love the chance
to tell him this in person. I'm home tomorrow, by the way.

Love,
Kate

Date:	October 20
From:	TedConcannon
To:	KateBogart
Subject:	RE: Miles Away

Kate: Don't you dare call me "Pop." I really don't know where Miles
has gone to, but in my experience the rule of thumb has always been
where there's danger, there's Miles Maxwell. Of course, if you've sent
him into a really dark funk, he might have gone off to his family's
place in Madeira to brood. Or he just might be on one very long
pub crawl. It has happened. London's great for that sort of thing. My

advice: Leave him alone and he'll come home, wagging his tail behind him.

Now leave me alone! I'm busy loving your mother up.

TC

Date: October 21
From: KateBogart
To: GamblinRose
Subject: The Prodigal Daughter

Well, Mom, I'm heading home today. I didn't get so much accomplished with Jack by my side, but I got to see a lot of the Provincelands and the ocean, and it was lovely. Now he is across the country, dizzy with love and naming "our five children" as he prepares to teach a mountain-climbing class on Mt. Rainier. When Maxwell found out about Jack and me, he flew the coop, and even his housekeeper and your new boy-toy don't seem to know where he has gone. I feel terrible about it. So much for having two lovers.

I know that you think I ran away from you and Ted, and you're sort of right, but I think I've absorbed the shock by now, thanks in part to your frequent graphic e-mails and phone calls. I love the both of you very much and whatever makes you happy, makes me happy. Let's all have dinner this week. But first, promise me you won't smooch in between courses. Hope Truman wasn't too much trouble.

Love,
Kate

CHAPTER 11

In Thin Air

Date: October 22
From: JackMacTavish
To: KateBogart
Subject: Small World

Katie? Do you know some English dude named Miles Maxwell? 'Cause he's here at the climbing school, and he claims to know you. What's the scoop on this guy? Good thing they're keeping us busy, cause I'm missing you like crazy.

XOXO,
Jackson

Date: October 23
From: KateBogart
To: JackMacTavish
Subject: RE: Small World

Dear Jackson: Do you remember when I told you I had met another man recently? Not the Portuguese bullfighter, but the other guy? Well, meet the other guy.

Miles Maxwell is an old friend of Ted's. We were both in Rome at the same time, and we became friends. Then we started seeing each other, off and on, over these very bumpy months. He went missing recently because I told him that I was still involved with you. And look where he turned up!

I never intended for things to get quite so complicated, and now I'm very sorry I didn't tell you all about him sooner. I'm afraid I've gotten all of us into an awkward situation. A sticky one, huh? Since you obviously can't back out of your gig, maybe Maxwell will be gracious enough to enroll in another class. He's very much a gentleman about things like that.

Why do I have the feeling we're going to have a lot to talk about soon?

Wish He Weren't There,
Kate

Date:	October 23
From:	KateBogart
To:	Manowar
Subject:	Rocky Mountain Low

Okay, Maxwell, I know where you are and I know you have e-mail access. Just because I wouldn't join you in London, you go off stalking my ex-husband? How could you do that, Maxwell? It's something I'd expect from a high school student or an obsessive villain out of a Hollywood thriller. Tell me that you aren't planning to cut Jack's rope at the summit, or push him into a crevasse or something like that. It's so beneath you, Maxwell.

I'm waiting for an explanation.

Kate

Date: October 23
From: Manowar
To: KateBogart
Subject: RE: Rocky Mountain Low

My Dear Ms. Bogart: It is only with great reluctance and in the name of self-defense that I am breaking my silence. When I received your rejection of my offer, I fought very hard to resist running off to a hot zone in search of a thrill, and decided instead to indulge a long-held desire to investigate the world of mountaineers. It seemed to me the best way to get away from that which I obviously cannot have and a new way to boost my adrenaline. Also, there seemed an article in it that I might sell to one of the adventure travel magazines.

At the time, I had no idea that the man who would be leading this course of instruction would in fact be the very rival to whom I owe my sad love luck. I can assure you I did not venture here in order to terrorize or eliminate him, and in fact I resent your distrustful suspicions quite powerfully. I might say that *they* are quite beneath *you.*

It is indeed an awkward bind we three are in, and I realized it as soon as I met our instructors. Truthfully, I had anticipated retreating to a more hospitable altitude as soon as I made the connection, but I could not reasonably dissuade myself from having traveled so far and at such expense to forgo something I had thought about for so long, all because I had made the mistake of falling for another fickle woman.

Instead, I decided to discreetly make the matter known to your MacTavish, without breaching any levels of tact, since I did not know how much he knew of our relationship at the time. You, however, have beat me to the punch, as it were—and I now have a handsome shiner to show for it. Quite a strong wallop that MacTavish throws. Luckily, there's lots of ice handy to reduce the swelling and numb the pain.

Regretfully,
Miles

Date: October 24
From: KateBogart
To: JackMacTavish
Subject: Fire in the Belly

Jack MacTavish! You gave Miles Maxwell a black eye? How thin is the air up there? What happened to Mr. Sensitive? Mr. Pacifist? Mr. Nonviolence? Mr. Feelings? Mr. Communication? Mr. Centered? Mr. Acoustic? Mr. Yin-Yang? I am thoroughly disappointed in you, and really think that you should apologize to poor Maxwell.

   Wish You Would Be Reasonable,
   Kate

Date: October 24
From: JackMacTavish
To: KateBogart
Subject: RE: Fire in the Belly

Katie: I am just as disappointed in my own bad self. After I got your e-mail telling me about Miles, I was just furious that this guy was on my mountain and didn't tell me about your connection. I went totally alpha. When I saw what I did, I felt like such an ass. I volunteered to leave the mountain, but Miles proved totally cool and talked me out of it. I offered him two free shots at me, but he declined in a way that was so decent, it was almost sweet.

Instead, we split a flask of brandy and had a completely open man-to-man. Miles understands that you and I are really made to be together, and he doesn't hold it against me at all. He's an interesting guy, Katie. I really dig that he seems all Tori (sp?) and proper and everything, but that he has also done all those completely courageous and fundamentally correct things. You know I have enormous respect for that. He even covered for me and told the other people in the class that he was injured practicing some rappelling techniques.

Tell you the truth, I can't wait to go up the mountain with him. Even though he's got a couple of years on most of the other students,

I think he's going to be the strongest link in the chain. You sure do have good taste in men, baby.

Love,
Jackson

Date: October 24
From: KateBogart
To: JackMacTavish
Subject: RE: RE: Fire in the Belly

So, you and Maxwell are hitting it off. Well isn't that just ducky! Also, a little insane. Are you really planning to climb a mountain with a man I've been seeing for the last few months? This doesn't make you uncomfortable in any way? It sure is making me uncomfortable 3,000 miles away and at a sensible altitude.

But maybe this is just one of those peculiar things that men like to do together—like Greco-Roman wrestling, peeing in the woods, and that old adolescent chestnut, the circle jerk. I'm not going to try to figure it out. I just thank God I'm not there. I have enough problems watching my mother and Ted Concannon billing and cooing over dinner like a couple of plump pigeons.

Wish You Were Here,
Kate

Date: October 25
From: VioletMorgan
To: KateBogart
Subject: Warts and All

Dear Bogie: Here I am in the City of Brotherly Love and cream cheese. Rollicking show last night, but wonder when I'm ever going to get any sleep. Have to take Ivan to the hospital today to have a painful plantar wart excised. You think it's easy jumping up and down on stage like that and landing on a plantar wart? I told him months ago he should try wearing shoes every now and then.

Sorry I missed you in New York, but how's every little thing? Have you found Miles Maxwell? Have you and Jack gotten remarried? Or are you planning your next escape? Send me news from home.

Love,
Violet in Exile

Date: October 25
From: KateBogart
To: VioletMorgan
Subject: RE: Warts and All

Vi: Laying low in Manhattan. In my very own apartment. Just Truman and me for a change. But that doesn't mean that my life has become manageable or sensible in any way.

I found Maxwell all right. As luck would have it, he decided to pursue a lifelong desire to learn mountain-climbing techniques and enrolled in a class taught by none other than Jackson MacTavish. They're both on Mt. Rainier at this moment. Fancy that.

Meanwhile, took Rose and Ted to dinner last night at Florent. They promised not to smooch at the table, but that didn't stop Ted from scooping juicy little mussels out of their shells and feeding them to my mother. It was appalling, but I held my tongue. Mother dear is insisting on Thanksgiving in New Orleans this year, forcing me to break one of my strictest travel rules: Never travel anywhere domestically over Thanksgiving. Oh, well, at least I'm getting some work done.

Wish You Were Here,
Kate

Date: October 26
From: TedConcannon
To: KateBogart
Subject: Fixer Upper

Thanks for dinner the other night. By the way, got an e-mail from Miles. What a pickle! But he and Nanook MacTavish seem to be getting along famously. I know you think it's all over between you and Miles, but I know the guy pretty well and I think he's still a little crazy for you. I know he's a little cracked, Kate, but I've never known him to go climbing a damn mountain before. I sure wish the two of you would give it another chance, and not just for the sake of his physical safety. You both looked so happy together when he was in New York.

   TC

Date: October 26
From: KateBogart
To: TedConcannon
Subject: RE: Fixer Upper

You just worry about keeping my mother safe and happy, Ted. And as I told you the other night, it was Maxwell's choice to run off to the mountain. I was seriously considering joining him in London to give us some more time together. I can't be responsible for his rash decisions. If Maxwell wants me, he knows where and how to find me. Oh, and just because you're shacking up with my mother, doesn't mean you can butt in on my affairs. Interloper!

   Kate

Date: October 27
From: KateBogart
To: JackMacTavish
Subject: Talking Turkey

Jack: I'm not sure of your plans for Thanksgiving, but Rose and Ted and I will be in New Orleans and I was wondering if you would like to join us. Let me know soon, as Mom and I are in the process of squabbling over arrangements. She of course wants to go on a gambling cruise, but I refuse. Please say you'll come. I'd love to show you New Orleans, and I can't stand the thought of spending the weekend in such a romantic place alone with Abelard and Heloise.

By the way, how is Maxwell doing?

WYWH,
Kate

Date: October 27
From: JackMacTavish
To: KateBogart
Subject: RE: Talking Turkey

Katie, I'm there! Class will be over by Thanksgiving and it sounds like fun. But I'm not getting in any card games with your mom. She's a hustler. Can't wait!

Love,
Your High and Mighty Jackson

PS: Miles is at the head of the class for sheer nerve, though the altitude's not agreeing with him. Still, he works right through the pain and the nausea, and I'm sure he'll adjust. Dude's a trooper.

Date: October 27
From: Manowar
To: KateBogart
Subject: Headaches

Dear Ms. Bogart: Jack tells me that you inquired of me lately. I am flattered and touched by your interest. You may be pleased to know that I have traded in my heartaches for headaches, brought on by the celestial altitudes. Indeed, my brain pan feels as if it has been scoured clean by the frigid gusts that rattle our camp throughout the day. Despite the pain, it has helped me enormously to accept the impossibility of our situation with resolve, clarity, and even something akin to peace.

Who might have guessed that we would have gotten as tangled up as we have, now that your ex-husband and I have also become fast friends? I must say I admire the man for his strength, his knowledge, and his discipline, as well as his inextinguishable devotion to you. We even had a great laugh over his impetuous assault on me! I could not pick a better partner for a woman I hold so dearly.

I do hope that you and Jack are able to reconcile your differences, Ms. Bogart, and to find some mutually happy approach to coupledom. It would be a shame to have to forfeit such a rare chance at a true and lasting love. As for me, my journey begins anew as I prepare to make my ascent up this fearsome pile of rocks called Rainier . . .

Always,
Miles

Date: October 28
From: KateBogart
To: Manowar
Subject: RE: Headaches

Oh, Maxwell, that's all very noble and gentlemanly of you, but I really don't like the idea of you climbing some gargantuan mountain with altitude sickness, a black eye, and a stiff upper lip any more than

I like the idea of you trying to sell me on my ex-husband's winning qualities. I wish you hadn't run off so impulsively without letting me explain my feelings, but things have certainly gotten more complicated, haven't they?

Come what may, Maxwell, I hope that we can continue to be friends forever. Do be careful, and do everything that Jack tells you to do. As always . . .

Wish You Were Here,
Kate

Date: October 29
From: JackMacTavish
To: KateBogart
Subject: Up We Go

Dear Katie: We start the climb to the summit today. Me, Miles, and the three others in our party. After Denali and the Himalayas, it should be a piece of cake. I'll be in touch as long as the satellite connections hold and I'll think of you the whole time I'm up there. Also, all the delicious food and sex we're going to have in New Orleans. *Oo-oo-wee!* I'll keep an eye on Miles, too. Don't you worry.

Love,
Jackson

Date: October 30
From: TedConcannon
To: KateBogart
Subject: The Wicked Sisters

Kate, I finally met the gang you call the Sisters of Perpetual Bingo. I was a special guest at their weekly poker night. I am now out exactly $237.53. Those women are merciless! And I think your mother's the fiercest of them all. I know I should have heeded your warning, but I thought you were exaggerating. Have to admit, my ego suffered even more damage than my wallet.

They've invited me to join them next week too, the vultures. I accepted in the name of sportsmanship, but I don't think I can afford it. Do you think your mother will be hurt if I decline?

Ted

Date: October 30
From: KateBogart
To: TedConcannon
Subject: RE: The Wicked Sisters

Dear Ted: I hate to say I told you so, but . . .

Of course my mother will mind if you back out, but unless you want to spend the rest of your life ducking loan sharks, I'd recommend it. One thing you have to understand about Rose is that she lives to win. When the impulse to play seizes her, it's pretty hard to stop it. My approach to this problem has always been to insist on games like Scrabble and Old Maid, the kind where I won't actually lose my shirt when I lose the game. If I'm in a particularly bratty mood, I play to lose. Nothing makes her more irate.

But never, ever get involved in any wagering game with the woman, unless you are prepared to take a financial loss. If, however, you do decide to give in to her entreaties, taunts, and come-ons, and you find yourself being hustled right out of your own good sense, look at it this way: You're bound to get your money back in the form of a nice meal, a really well-made sweater, a gift certificate for a full body massage, or something extravagantly thoughtful, because my mother is also extremely generous with her winnings.

Good Luck,
Kate

Date: October 30
From: Manowar, Jack MacTavish
To: KateBogart
Subject: 9,500 ft high

katie! isn't this wild? maxwell brought this cool satellite gizmo in case we get caught in an avalanche or something. cutting edge! tiny keyboard, but there's a special s.o.s. button. talk about being prepared! he's letting me use it to e-mail you. love this guy!

made it to inter glacier, where we'll pitch a camp for the night and try to sleep. miles and i will be sharing a tent. hope he doesn't snore.

the world is white and blue here. amazing, pure and pristine. you should have seen some of the crevasses we had to jump on the way up. fissures like dark open jaws waiting to swallow you whole like a little peanut. don't tell him I said so, but miles looked terrified. still, he held up, even though I had to yank the rope a couple of times.

at midnight we charge the summit, as fast as any five men roped together can charge a summit one step at a time with 300 lbs of gear between them and half their breath. as with every climb i've ever made, thoughts of you are getting me through the pain, the fear, and the fatigue. i love you, baby, and can't wait to be with you again.

i wish you were here,
jackson

Date: October 31
From: KateBogart
To: Manowar, JackMacTavish
Subject: RE: 9,500 ft high

Maxwell and Jack: Good to know that you boys are sharing your toys, and how convenient for me having to fire off only one e-mail instead of two. I hope you two are enjoying your little challenge against nature and the elements, and I'm sure things are quite cozy in your two-man tent. Hope that Maxwell's habit of grinding his teeth isn't keeping Jack awake, and that Jack isn't flailing in his sleep.

I know you told me that Rainier isn't as risky as most summits, but I've been doing a little research and learned that it's not exactly a kiddie park, either. Avalanches, whiteouts, bottomless crevasses, and massive rolling blocks of ice are just a few of its more charming features. Also, discovered that you're up there past the normal climbing season, something you didn't mention before you set out. Why didn't you?

Every single time you take a climb I get the hives, and since there's two of you flirting with disaster, the itching is particularly acute. But, as my mother says, "Boys will be boys," or, as Violet says, "Men are sheep." I still don't know what she means by that, but please, please be careful and please let me know as soon as you are off that stupid mountain so I can tell you both how exceedingly dumb and maddening you are.

Wish You Were Here (So the damn itching would stop),
Kate

Date: October 31
From: Manowar, JackMacTavish
To: KateBogart
Subject: 14,410 ft high

katie! sorry you're so worried, babe. but everything is better than best. made columbia crest in just over eight hours. great timing. You wouldn't believe what the world is like from here.

the native americans called this mountain tahoma, and she is a wise and benevolent goddess. it's like you're above the clouds, and you can see beyond the widest horizons you've ever seen before. if you lie down in the snow and look straight up at the sky you can actually feel the earth turning. there's no better way to get a sense of your place in the universe. no church, no symphony, nothing can compare to this! man, how I wish you could see it!

you can stop worrying too, katie. the hard part is over. the descent only takes a few hours, cause you spend much of it sliding down on your ass. weeeeeeeeeeeee!

gotta go. fingers numb. my love for you is big as a mountain. gonna shout it out right now for all the world to hear. oh. better not. avalanche. here's miles.

　　xoxo,
　　jackson

dear ms. b: everything jack says is true. it really is quite transporting. moving beyond words. the bracing cold air, the clarity of the light, the sheer sweep of the landscape, and that giddy, delirious feeling that you can reach the sky simply by stretching your arms. it's absolutely intoxicating.

of course, that could be the lack of oxygen or the excruciating signals of pain and fatigue that are constantly being sent to my brain from parts of my body i never even knew existed. must say, however, the most powerful part of the experience has been knowing that even in my attempted escape from you, in this desperate and foolhardy hejira, you are still somewhere down there in the grey workaday world, going about your quotidian affairs and caring quite so much about me. i am deeply, deeply touched, ms. b.

　　your friend,
　　miles

Date:	October 31
From:	KateBogart
To:	Manowar, JackMacTavish
Subject:	RE: 14,410 ft high

Wow! Duelling epiphanies. Imagine that. Sounds great, and I can't wait to see the pictures. I won't be happy, however, till I know you're both safe in Seattle sharing a half-caf venti mocha latte, okay? So just as soon as you're done sliding down the mountain on your two adorable asses, please call or e-mail me. Thanks. WYWH.

　　Love,
　　Kate

Date: November 1
From: Manowar, JackMacTavish
To: KateBogart
Subject: squall!

katie: having a great time on the descent, but maxwell and i got separated from the rest. caught in a little squall. no biggie. it's just going
to take us a little longer to get back to the base camp. but don't you
worry one bit. we'll be at the camp in two hours.

   xoxo,
   jack

   ps: miles says cheerio.

Date: November 1
From: KateBogart
To: Manowar, JackMacTavish
Subject: RE: squall!

Just how little is that little squall and why haven't I heard from you in
three hours if you were only two hours away from your camp? And
how the heck did you get separated from the rest of your party in the
first place? Maybe it's time to press that SOS button?

   WYWH,
   Kate

Date: November 1
From: Manowar, JackMacTavish
To: KateBogart
Subject: RE: RE: squall!

katie: squall is now a whiteout. not sure where we are. have notified
base camp. they advised us to wait it out. sending help when it clears.

m and i have pitched a tent and are keeping each other warm. please know that i love you. so does m. everyone loves you. you are so lovely. everything sure is white around here. and coldcoldcold.

   j (and m)

Date: November 2
From: KateBogart
To: Manowar, JackMacTavish
Subject: Mountain Do's

Please please please tell me that you are still receiving e-mails. I have called Rainier Ranger Service and located your outfitter, too. They will send out choppers and a search party as soon as the storm passes. Are you okay? Has the snow subsided near you? Do you have flares? The greatest danger is hypothermia. The two of you should take off all of your clothes and get inside your doubled-up sleeping bags. Skin-to-skin contact is the best way to get optimal body heat. I know you know that already, but don't let your silly masculine pride keep you from *doing it*, forgodsake. Also, rub each others' hands and feet if they start to go numb. Oh God. Do you have water? Do you have food? If you can e-mail me, I am waiting by my computer. Maybe it will help to keep you alert. I love you, and more than ever before, I wish you were here.

   Kate

Date: November 2
From: Manowar, JackMacTavish
To: KateBogart
Subject: RE: Mountain Do's

1 step ahead of you, k. very cold up here, but m is nice and toasty. cute bum 2. water almost out. 2 pieces of fruit leather, a fistful of

trailmix, and three toffies (sp?). but don't worry. everything will be ok. been through worse. married you. (kidding!) thanks for standing by. very supportive. very wifey. when you wrote i love you did you mean me or m? we have a bet. gotta go. my turn to massage m's earlobes. here he is.

xxx,
yr jaxon

ms. b: i am writing you from the life-sustaining comfort of j's iron embrace and i can assure you that he is quite hale, indeed. not feeling too poorly myself, given the circumstances. so kind of you to tend to us in this most indecorous and awkward situation. so, how are your travels?

fondly,
m

Date:	November 3
From:	KateBogart
To:	Manowar, JackMacTavish
Subject:	RE: RE: Mountain Do's

My travels? Well, I'm home right now. Planning a trip to New Orleans for Thanksgiving with my mom. Trying to book a cottage at the Maison de Ville. It's already tough getting dinner reservations, but hoping there's a cancellation at the Commander's Palace for the holiday. Still the best restaurant in the city, and that's saying something. Also looking into some good, informative bayou excursions and plantation tours, as these can be sugarcoated for the tourists and I want to make sure my mother sees something beyond the casino. And this is absurd! I'm carrying on about New Orleans while the two of you are naked and freezing on some mountaintop in the middle of a blizzard! I know that you need something to keep your minds alert and distracted, but please tell me that you're both okay. I'm just distraught with worry here.

WYWH,
Kate

Date: November 3
From: Manowar, JackMacTavish
To: KateBogart
Subject: k-k-k-katie

evvverythinggg okkkayy. bbbbut aaaa litttttlle dizzzzyyy too. wherrre isssearch ppparrrttty???? mmmiles asleep. i tttthink. sssorrrry bbout the ssssshivversss. cccan't helllpp it. ttttime forrrrrr beddd. mmmm-milessis ssooooo warrrrmmm. niteynnnite.

lllllllllovvve yooouuujjjjjjjjjjjjjjjjjjjjjj

Date: November 3
From: KateBogart
To: Manowar, JackMacTavish
Subject: RE: k-k-k-katie

Jack, no! You can't both go to sleep at the same time! You can't afford to lower two body temperatures at once. You know that one of you has to stay awake to keep the other one warm. I'm calling those damn rangers again, and the outfitters. Then I'm getting on the phone with the airlines and coming to Rainier myself. Hold on, boys!

Date: November 4
From: KateBogart
To: GamblinRose
Subject: Rescue Mission

Mom: I'm afraid something terrible has happened to Jack and Max-well. They were e-mailing me regularly from their tent on Mt. Rainier, and now the messages have just stopped. Called the ranger service, but they have not been able to find them. They're afraid that maybe their tent has been completely buried in the snow. How awful!

I know that there's not much I can do, but I can't bear doing noth-ing so far away either, so I'm on my way to Seattle now. Can you or Ted see to Truman's needs while I'm away? I'll call you as soon as I land and keep you posted on further developments.

Love,
Kate

Date: November 4
From: GamblinRose
To: KateBogart
Subject: RE: Rescue Mission

Oh, Kate, I'm concerned for Jack and Miles too, but promise me that you won't do anything foolish like climbing any mountains to go look for them.

By the way, Ted has been acting strange ever since he met the Sisters, and all of a sudden he's begging out of poker night. Do you think he can possibly be threatened by strong female bonds of friend-ship? I made it clear that the Sisters come with the territory, but men are so strange sometimes. Well, I guess I don't have to tell you that. I'll keep praying for Jack and Miles, and don't worry about your cat. Promise me you'll be careful. I'm very concerned.

Love,
Mom

CHAPTER 12

✈

In Seattle

Date:	November 5
From:	KateBogart
To:	VioletMorgan
Subject:	High Anxiety

Vi: I don't know where you are right now, but I'm in Seattle, on my way to Mt. Rainier. Not an impromptu travel article, unfortunately. Maxwell and Jack got caught in a whiteout on their descent and ended up trapped on the mountain. We were e-mailing back and forth and I was trying to keep them alert so they wouldn't succumb to hypothermia, but then their e-mails just stopped coming.

Oh Vi, it's so scary, but the ranger reminded me that if anyone could survive this situation it was Jack, and that their rescue services usually have great luck. Turns out that Mt. Rainier has its own microclimate and can even brew its own storms. One more reason not to climb a mountain, if you ask me.

Wish I knew where you were, cause I sure could use a friend right now. I'll keep you posted.

WYWH,
Kate

Date: November 5
From: VioletMorgan
To: KateBogart
Subject: Charm City

Bogie: Terrible news about your guys. What can I do to help? I'm
stalled in Baltimore right now. Damien is in Fells Point having a tattoo
artist morph the name of his last girlfriend, but "Dagmar" is proving
tricky to work with and it's taking forever. Don't think the relationship
itself lasted this long. If you want me to come to Seattle, just let me
know.

　　Vi

Date: November 5
From: KateBogart
To: Violet Morgan
Subject: ALIVE!

Vi! They're alive! Both of them! And they have all their fingers and
toes and everything! Which is good, because as soon as they recover,
I plan to break every bone in their bodies.

By the time I got to the ranger's station, the rescue party had found
them. Jack was all bundled up in his fleecy blanket, hunkered over a
bowl of chicken soup, which he was devouring with big manly gulps.
He was so involved with his soup that it actually took him a few sec-
onds to notice me. But as soon as Jack looked up at me with those
eyes bright as ever, I lost it. I jumped into his arms and the two of us
fell into a sort of sobbing tango.

Then somewhere outside of Jack's embrace, I heard someone mut-
ter an uncomfortable "Right, then" and moving some chairs around
nervously. That's when I realized that Maxwell was in the room. Jack
and I both ran to him, and the three of us got caught in a big, slobber-
ing, embarrassing group hug, until the elation gave way to awkwardness. It proved too much for Maxwell, who politely excused himself

and retreated to his room. Looked in on him just now, but he's lost in a very deep sleep.

We're all at a rustic little inn called The Paradise—what else. Even though Jack generally thinks lodges are for "weenies" and "city slickers," he seems to be appreciating the fireplace, the comforter, and the feather bed quite a bit.

WYWH,
Kate

Date: November 6
From: KateBogart
To: GamblinRose
Subject: The Life in My Men

Hi, Mom. Jack and Maxwell alive and well, you'll be happy to know. Mostly they were weak from hunger and very exhausted. They've been sleeping close to twelve hours. All three of us are staying at a nice little inn on Mt. Rainier.

Not a heck of a lot to do on the mountain alone, but grateful for the lull after so much worrying, and it sure is pretty. Even in the rain. It gives me plenty of time to consider what to do when Jack and Maxwell wake up.

I hadn't anticipated how I'd deal with my two lovers if they were both alive and well once I'd found them. I can't go on seeing both of them now that they've bonded on their own. Can't decide if I'm the luckiest woman alive, or the unluckiest, but fate seems to be forcing me to make a very tough choice here. I'll keep you posted.

Wish You Were Here,
Kate

Date: November 6
From: GamblinRose
To: KateBogart
Subject: RE: The Life in My Men

Dear Kate: So glad to hear Jack and Miles are okay. I didn't want to add to your sense of panic, but boy my nerves were shot. It totally threw me off my game. Please give them both my love and tell them not to do anything foolish like that again.

I know you have a very tough choice to make, and only you can make it, but it's the kind of dilemma most women would kill to have. Whatever you decide, I support you 100 percent.

On the home front, a little concerned about Ted and me, too. Over dinner the other night, he was strangely silent and whenever we made eye contact, he gave me these nervous little halfhearted smiles which, in the male nonverbal language, means that there's something he'd like to talk about but he doesn't know how to approach the subject.

Finally, I broke the ice, and he admitted that he feels a little funny about joining the Sisters and me for poker night, but blamed it all on his male pride. I could tell that he was looking for me to adopt the standard woman's role, expecting me to skip poker night myself and spend it with him. I informed him that I would never skip poker night with the Sisters as long as we were all physically able to make it to the table.

He said he understood, but he was concerned because his friend Smitty ended up in divorce court when he gambled away his wife's fanny-tuck fund. Then I told him I wasn't playing fast and loose with anyone's fanny-tuck, and if I was, my luck is so good they'd probably have the most well-proportioned fanny in the world. Then he said I was being a little too defensive, and then I said he was being a little too patronizing, and on and on and on.

While Ted didn't exactly sleep on the couch last night, he might as well have. And tonight, he's staying at your apartment with Truman, claiming that he has a lot of work to do. All of a sudden, I think we might be just three in New Orleans.

Love,
Mom

Date: November 6
From: KateBogart
To: GamblinRose
Subject: Break Up to Make Up

Mom: Congratulations! You and Ted just had your first fight, so you're about to have a really great time making up.

Look, it's difficult for me to deal with your little "hobby," and it's probably going to be difficult for Ted, too. Still, that doesn't mean you can't work through it somehow. Give Ted some time. I'd hate to see the two of you split up just when I'm starting to live with the idea of the two of you together.

I know that getting advice from me on relationships is probably like getting tips on etiquette from Attila the Hun; but trust me, I know what I'm talking about. Jack and I have been having the very same kind of tussles for a couple of years now, and boy oh boy the making-up can be sweet. In fact, he's in the shower right now. I think I'll go pick a fight about how his singing is driving me crazy.

WYWH,
Kate

Date: November 6
From: Manowar
To: KateBogart
Subject: Exit, Stage Left

Dear Ms. Bogart: How marvelous it was to see you after the harrowing experience of our descent, but seeing you in Jack's arms was as heartbreaking as it was heartwarming. He has made his feelings for you quite clear to me, and you are very lucky to have someone who burns quite so feverishly for you, Ms. Bogart. Odette, my former fiancé, refused to follow me out of the trenches, choosing the world's discord over me, and losing sight of the things that give life meaning, as I see it. I do hope that you don't make the same mistake and wait too long to devote yourself to someone. Living, after all, is really just a matter of personal habit, and speaking from experience, I can tell you that those habits become harder and harder to change the longer that they are indulged.

I do hope that you and Jack can overcome your differences and find some way to revive your marriage. It seems to me that you both need this time together, much as I need to be getting along in search of my own happiness. I am now heading up to Vancouver to investigate a story for *Jaunt*. Something along the lines of "What's So British About British Columbia?" Will be staying at the Pan Pacific. Do you know it?

I shan't bother you and Jack further, but please know that I count you both as dear and exceptional friends and do so look forward to crossing paths in the future.

Yours Always,
Miles

Date: November 6
From: KateBogart
To: Manowar
Subject: RE: Exit, Stage Left

Maxwell, what a touching message! How I wish you hadn't checked out without saying good-bye first. There's so much I wanted to say to you. But I understand just the same, and it's probably the most sensible thing either one of us has done in months.

I am so sorry for having dragged you into this mess. Never in my wildest dreams had I imagined that you and Jack would end up clinging to each other for dear life in a freak blizzard, and yet somehow I feel responsible. Maybe if I'd told you more about him, we all would have been able to avoid this situation. Please accept my deepest apologies.

Nice to hear that you're going to Vancouver. Such a lovely city, and much safer than the top of a mountain in a snowstorm. Wish I could go with you, but we're trying to make matters less complicated, aren't we? Words cannot express how relieved and happy I was to find you alive and safe. Now promise me that you'll also be happy. I miss you already, and . . .

Wish You Were Here,
Kate

Date: November 7
From: GamblinRose
To: KateBogart
Subject: This I Like

Dear Kate: You were absolutely right about making up. Last night, Ted and I finally had our talk about my so-called "problem." By the end of it, he was insisting on joining the Sisters and me on bingo night, and I was insisting I cut down my gambling nights and learn to like ESPN, and the next thing you know the two of us were rolling around like a pair of frisky puppies. No resolutions were reached, but what fun! It almost makes me want to start something, just so we can fix it up later.

What a smart daughter I raised!

Love,
Mom

Date: November 8
From: KateBogart
To: GamblinRose
Subject: I Can't Stand the Rain

Dear Mom: If only I could follow my own advice. Jack and I are in Seattle now and it's raining, raining, raining. Jack wanted to take the ferry over to Bainbridge Island so we could explore it on bicycle. My thighs still haven't recovered from trying this in San Francisco two months ago, and I recommended hiring a taxi, which is against his do-it-yourself thrifty ways. Instead, we wasted the whole day sulking at each other across the unbreachable chasm of our stubbornness.

Glad to hear that you and Ted have made it through your chilly phase, though could do without the frisky puppy reference. It sure does rain a lot here.

Wish It Would Stop,
Kate

Date:	November 9
From:	Manowar
To:	KateBogart
Subject:	I Smell a Story

Dear Ms. Bogart: Vancouver is brilliant. Quite cosmopolitan and diverse, with a very strong accent of the Far East. The weather is dreary and rainy, but not without its moody appeal. Today, the *Jaunt* photographer and I hired a taxi to drive us out to the Capilano River so we could cross its famous suspension bridge. Quite a marvel, really. Just a stringy bit of cobweb swaying 230 feet above the river rapids, all in a lush green rain forest. It brings to mind a scene in a Chinese scroll or a Japanese woodcut. Exhilarating and magical. How I wish you could have been there.

On the return, the taxi driver, a Korean college student and snowboarder named Kim, told me about the local marijuana trade and of the young hydroponic growers in the suburbs who are quickly becoming millionaires on the American market. I do believe there's a story in this, Ms. Bogart, perhaps even a book—a comprehensive history offering an extensive view of the contemporary international marijuana trade from dealer to user. Kim has agreed to introduce me to his personal supplier. As I will no doubt have to build up some trust with these outlaws, I will be staying on here a bit longer than I expected.

Isn't the world a fascinating place, Ms. Bogart?

Best,
Miles

Date: November 9
From: KateBogart
To: Manowar
Subject: RE: I Smell a Story

Dear Maxwell: The world is indeed a fascinating place. It's why I'm never very happy standing still for too long. Glad to hear you've found a lead to pursue and that you're not dwelling on our affair or the Rainier debacle. In fact, it sounds as if you've gotten right back on your horse, just as I knew you would. Good for you, Maxwell! Jack and I have stayed on in Seattle, which we're enjoying immensely.

  Wish You Were Here,
  Kate

Date: November 9
From: KateBogart
To: VioletMorgan
Subject: Northwest Passage

Dear Vi: After sleeping for about 20 hours, Jack spent his first day eating and soaking in the Jacuzzi. Meanwhile, poor Maxwell, feeling like a third wheel, tiptoed off the mountain in the middle of the night to go to Vancouver to do some research. Do feel so bad about the way things ended between us. Maxwell sent a spirited e-mail and seems to be doing just fine without me. Wish I could say the same.

  Jack escorted me through Seattle for a couple of days, but his be-havior has been very strange. He's been distant and moody and his speech patterns are a little odd, almost like those feeble British affec-tations that Madonna adopted when she married that English movie director.

  I'm wondering if Jack didn't suffer some serious exposure-related injuries or something, but when I suggested he see a doctor, he dis-missed it as my usual excessive worrying. He says he's just crashing from the mountain high, that it happens all the time, and also he's a little blue from all the rain here. Maybe he's right. We're both heading home tomorrow.

Wish You Were Here,
Kate

Date: November 9
From: VioletMorgan
To: KateBogart
Subject: RE: Northwest Passage

Seattle. Wow. Had a bad cup of coffee there once.

As far as I know, speaking in bad foreign accents isn't a symptom of hypothermia. I know Jack wasn't being held hostage, per se, but do you think he could be suffering from some variation of the Stockholm syndrome? Maybe he identified so strongly with Maxwell on that mountain that he picked up his mannerisms. Stranger things have happened. I once read about a Mexican migrant farm worker who suffered a head injury and started speaking perfect Polish, even though he'd never heard the language in his life.

I am in another Washington altogether. DC. Whoever says that power is an aphrodisiac never took a good long look at rep ties and blue suits. Instant neutering! These men have no asses. Now, there's a condition for the medical journals. I'm so glad I married a man who can pull off zebra-skin tights.

I can't wait to get back to New York. Call me parochial, but all these other cities just seem like cheap imitations. Missing you, too.

Love,
The Reluctant Wanderer

Date: November 10
From: JackMacTavish
To: KateBogart
Subject: Tally-ho!

Dearest Katherine: I have made my return to the city of St. Francis and already I find myself craving your pungent essence. It seems that life's banal circumstances are in cahoots against us so that we might only share our stingiest moments with each other. A shame that we cannot be affixed to each other permanently, as our syncopated hearts are permanently conjoined across vast voids.

But you are dedicated to sharing your wanton wanderings with your homely readers, and I have comprehended long ago and far away that you care for them about as much as you care for me. How thoroughly grateful I am then to have shared those paltry and aquaceous few days with you amidst the topographical pleasures of Seattle, despite all the gross and extraordinary excesses of the high-tech moguls who have made it so unbearably common. No urban transgressions or meteorological malaise can dilute your pulchritude, my love.

I will count every day this week, and also the weekend, until I see you again in the vibrant and musical crotch of our homeland's gulf.

Chop-chop!
Jackson

Date: November 10, 2001
From: KateBogart
To: JackMacTavish
Subject: RE: Tally-ho!

"Dearest Katherine"? "Chop-chop"? "The musical crotch of our homeland's gulf"? Are you okay, Jack? Did you sustain some head trauma or something when you were up on that mountain? Ever since Rainier, you just don't seem like yourself.

Frankly, you were talking a little funny in Seattle, and now you're writing even funnier. I'm concerned, Jackson. I'm leaving in a few hours for the airport, but I'm wondering if maybe I shouldn't come down to the "city of St. Francis" to check on you before I head East.

Wish You Were Sane,
Kate

Date: November 10
From: JackMacTavish
To: KateBogart
Subject: RE: RE: Tally-ho!

Wish you were sane! A mirthful missive, that. Have I reported to the gods on high that my lovely is also endowed with a prodigious wounding wit? I have not, but I am rectifying the oversight anon.

  Although I could barely stand the pleasure of your presence here in my provincial shangri-la, I don't deserve or require your kind attentions at this point in time. Rest assured that I am in a fine fettle. Indubitably so, and I will enjoy you fortnightly in the French Quarter and its environs.

Amorously,
Jackson

Date: November 10
From: Manowar
To: KateBogart
Subject: They Always Get Their Man

Dear Ms. Bogart: Don't know where you happen to be at the moment, but I have run into a spot of trouble. Kim introduced me to the suburban marijuana farmers just as the Canadian authorities were swooping down upon them, under pressure from your own zealous government, naturally. A bit of an inconvenience in the short-term, as I got swept up in their dragnet. But great for the story in the long-run, don't you think?

If it is not too much trouble, I am wondering if you wouldn't mind coming up to Vancouver to help. All of my papers are at the Pan Pacific, room 612. I am being held at the Georgia St. police station. Do believe these chaps would release me into your custody, if you could produce proof of my identity and the bail funds (wholly reimbursable, along with any additional airfare, of course).

If you have already flown back to New York, there's no need to bother. I could always try Jack, who might actually be closer. Frightfully sorry about all this. I would like to say that it is highly irregular, but we both know that's not true.

Always,
Miles

Date:	November 10
From:	KateBogart
To:	Manowar
Subject:	RE: They Always Get Their Man

Maxwell: I see the Vancouver police now allow you one e-mail. How progressive. Don't worry. I'll come to bail you out. I don't have anywhere else to be. Got your message at Sea-Tac, so I'll just hop on the next shuttle into Vancouver. Don't contact Jack. I think he suffered some brain damage on that mountain. Frankly, I'm worried about him, but let's take things one disaster at a time. Shall we?

Sit tight.
Kate

CHAPTER 13

✈

In Vancouver

Date: November 11
From: KateBogart
To: TedConcannon
Subject: North by Northwest

Hi, Ted: Won't be home today as expected. Maxwell ran into a bit of trouble with the Canadian authorities while researching a story about marijuana growers. I'm in Vancouver now, bearing witness to his character, scouting for attorneys, and batting my eyelashes at the Mounties. Not really the best way to see Vancouver, but it's pretty just the same. Staying at the Pan Pacific as Maxwell's guest. Very cushy, and lovely views, too. That Maxwell sure knows how to live. He's installed in a much less elegant room at the local holding pen downtown. Still, he could do worse. In fact, he has.

Maybe I can get a "WYWH" piece out of this? Can you look after Truman until I am done here? And tell my mother not to worry? And give her a kiss for me? (A *daughterly* kiss.)

Wish You Were Here,
Kate

Date: November 11
From: TedConcannon
To: KateBogart
Subject: RE: North by Northwest

So you and Miles are getting cozy in the Great Northwest, eh? How did
you of all people end up on that particular rescue mission? Poor Miles,
if he knew what was good for him, he'd stay in jail where it's safe.

  Tonight's your mother's night with the Sisters of Perpetual Bingo,
so I will gladly go to visit with Truman and have a nice long bath in
your kitchen tub, and pray for Miles.

  You're a special issue, Bogart.

  TC

Date: November 11
From: KateBogart
To: TedConcannon
Subject: RE: RE: North by Northwest

FYI, O Ye of Little Faith: I am not here to toy with Maxwell's heart. I
am here to save him from rotting away in a Canadian jail. It's an act of
friendship, and that's all. I'll also have you know that Maxwell asked
me to come here. How could I refuse him after all he's been through?
Very much resent your insinuation that I have any motives beyond
seeing our Maxwell to justice and freedom. Also, seeing what's doin'
in Vancouver, staying at a posh hotel, and enjoying the room service.
So there. Be good to my cat and my mother. Or else.

  WYWH,
  Kate

Date:	November 12
From:	JackMacTavish
To:	KateBogart
Subject:	Wherefore Art Thou?

Dearest Katherine: As my calls to your Gotham chambers have heretofore gone neglected, I am resorting to electronic transmissions. My perspicacity tells me that you have met with some rude obstacles in transit. I do so hope you are all in one vivacious piece. Please apprise me of your present whereabouts and condition.

    Your ex-husband, friend, amour, and kind benefactor,
    Jackson MacTavish, Esq., Ltd., 1st Duke of Monterey

Date:	November 12
From:	KateBogart
To:	JackMacTavish
Subject:	RE: Wherefore Art Thou?

My Dearest "Duke": I did indeed meet with some pretty "rude obstacles in transit." Miles got himself in a jam with the Canadian authorities and needed an advocate pronto. This guy is jinxed. Anyway, found him a fierce attorney with a tight hairdo and imposing shoulder pads, got Mynah to send some documents over from London, and have the British consulate trying to straighten things out. It's all over but for some legal red tape, and Maxwell should be sprung by tomorrow. Almost a shame, really, because I'm enjoying Vancouver quite a lot.

    I should be in my "Gotham chambers" soon, but still wondering if I should zip down to SF first to see if we can't get thee to a psychiatric professional before New Orleans. I'm getting worried.

    WYWH,
    Kate

Date: November 12
From: JackMacTavish
To: KateBogart
Subject: Forsooth!

Katherine: How distressing to hear of Miles' latest minuet with tragedy, and how noble of you to blow like a zephyr up to the nether provinces to succor him in his most pathetic hour. Although it may reflect shabbily upon my manhood, I must confess that I feel a bit left out of the equation. Why did Miles not summon me? After all, it was my effulgent body heat he usurped to survive the ordeal upon the mount called Rainier. And why did you not ask me to venture with you to that hostile territory where he is being detained? I do feel as if my personal sense of security has been breached and wish I were there, most egregiously.

I shan't be requiring the attentions of any psychiatric personnel as you recommend, but when you return to your domicile, please appease me with the knowledge that you are mine, and mine alone, once and for all perpetuity.

Heatedly Yours,
Jackson MacTavish III, Esq. Ltd. (Dropped the Duke bit.)

Date: November 13
From: KateBogart
To: JackMacTavish
Subject: RE: Forsooth!

Jack: I cannot tell you that I am yours and yours alone, because I belong to no one but myself. Ever. Let's get that right out of the way. Although you are front and center in my heart, I will not even lease it out to you, until you can assure me that you have not lost all your pretty marbles, as your recent e-mails would suggest.

Maxwell is out of the hoosegow, and I am now free to leave Vancouver, but I don't want to head back East until you can tell me what's going on or promise me that you'll see your doctor, or your guru, or Sharmi, or someone. Please, I pray you, milord!

Wish You Would Get Help,
Kate

Date: November 13
From: JackMacTavish
To: KateBogart
Subject: RE: RE: Forsooth!

Katie: I'm crazy all right. Crazy in love. When I was up on that mountain with Miles, he told me all about the two of you in Rome and Positano and New York, and in LA, by the way. (Slick, Katie.) When we both realized we were being two-timed in LA on a daily basis, we laughed ourselves silly. But afterward, when Miles finally gave in to exhaustion, I lay there listening to the howling wind and looking at him, 'cause there wasn't anything else to look at. And you know what? Even unshaven, worn-out, dehydrated, freezing, and on the brink of death, that guy looked as suave and composed as James Bond.

I can't compete with that, Katie. I don't have Miles' sophistication, or his knowledge of art and music and history. I don't dress just right, or have an expensive haircut, or read everything that's published. I don't speak perfectly and eloquently. I don't even know what goes in a damned martini. I'm just a big dumb American clod with knobby knuckles, scraped knees, and rough elbows.

When I looked at you and Miles together at the inn, you looked like you belong with him, and it was like my chest caved in. I felt like maybe I'm keeping you away from the guy who really deserves you, and getting in the way of your happiness. Like a fool, instead of just telling you that, I thought I'd try to cultivate some culture and some savwah fair (sp?). I even picked up a biography of Winston Churchill and the collected works of Shakespeare. Bought the Cliffs Notes too, 'cause I feel like I've got a lot of catching up to do.

Anyway, went to meet Sharmi to tell her about all my issues, and she laid right into me, in a way that was kind of disturbing the other patrons at Del Taco. Basically, she said to lose the phony English accent 'cause I sounded like an ass, and to stop trying to be someone that I'm not because it is so *not* the way of the Buddha. Or very sexy. So now I'm trying to get back to the clear path.

I wouldn't be surprised if you and Miles aren't up there rekindling the fire right now, laughing in the rain, looking great against the mountains, and discussing how to break the news to me that he'll be going to New Orleans in my place. I wouldn't really blame you, either. Whatever you are doing, please find a little time to forgive me for my foolishness. Love makes you do such dumb crap.

Always,
Jackson

Date: November 14
From: KateBogart
To: JackMacTavish
Subject: RE: RE: RE: Forsooth!

Oh, Jackson, why must men be so competitive with each other all the time? Of course you and Maxwell are very different people. And *vive la difference!*

So his hair holds up when he's suffering through an arctic blizzard. While that might be an enviable quality, it's not quite enough to recommend someone as a life partner. Why, Maxwell is so rarefied at times he could probably make the Queen of England herself feel like an uncouth, raucous yahoo, so don't let it get you down.

You'll be pleased to know that we're not laughing in the rain at all. It's all been work, work, work. I've hardly had a chance to see Maxwell except through a Plexiglas shield. He's finally out now, and I am heading off to New York tomorrow to get ready for New Orleans, and as long as you're feeling more like yourself, you'd better be there.

I do regret that I never got that English accent on tape, but I have

saved those bizarre e-mails, and I plan to open them up whenever I'm
feeling down and need a little laugh.

Wish You Were Here, but Glad You're Back,
Kate

Date: November 14
From: Manowar
To: KateBogart
Subject: Laughter in the Rain

My Dear Ms. Bogart: How sweet the rain felt this afternoon and
what a pleasure it was sharing my hard-won freedom with you, dodging in and out of the little boutiques in Yaletown. I do wish we
could stay on here a bit longer. Your mere company is more effective
against the dreary weather than any umbrella or raincoat Burberry
could devise. But we both must get on with our work and our lives,
mustn't we?

I can hardly tell you how much I appreciate the valiant rescue. Bit
of a sticky spot that, and I do apologize with all my heart for the inconvenience. Who would have imagined that the very same people
who keep the Queen's visage on their currency would have been so
inhospitable to an actual Englishman? Must say I was treated better
by my kidnappers in Beirut *and* Colombia.

One could not ask for a better or more gracious friend than you,
Ms. Bogart. How lucky you and Jack are to have each other. I feel
quite blessed to have been so intimate with such an exceptional pair
of people, and if you have not had your earlobes massaged by Jack, I
highly recommend it. He is such a strong, decent, and gentle man, the
kind that you really deserve.

It seems as if we are always saying good-bye to each other, and it
is something I am just not good at, so I look forward to our next hello.

Your Loving Friend,
Miles

Date: November 14
From: KateBogart
To: Manowar
Subject: RE: Laughter in the Rain

Dear Maxwell: I am now at Sea-Tac, once again trying to get home.
Very generous of you to keep me on as your guest, and very gentlemanly to insist on a separate room once you were sprung. I do regret
that I can't spend more time in Vancouver. I had a great time as well.
I especially liked drifting through the lovely Sun Yat-Sen Garden with
you in the gray afternoon. Calming and peaceful. Just what I needed.

It isn't any easier for me to say good-bye to you, Maxwell, but
now that you and Jack have become friends, I suppose it would be
impossible for us to go on the way we were. And so, until that next
hello . . .

Wish You Were Here,
Kate

Date: November 14
From: KateBogart
To: VioletMorgan
Subject: Lonely in Love

Hi, Vi. Here I am at the Seattle airport, headed for home. Finally!
Unless, of course, Maxwell gets arrested again. Wondering where in
the world you are.

Confession: I was having such a great time in Maxwell's hotel room,
I actually held on to some of his papers for an extra day, so I could enjoy it a little longer. Oh, Vi, sometimes I think I travel not because I
love to travel, but because I love hotels. I just wasn't ready to give up
that room. Do you think that's awful?

Also, Jack finally admitted that he was trying to impress me by being more like Maxwell. To assuage his insecurities, I told him that I
wasn't actually enjoying Vancouver with Maxwell, when in fact I was

doing just that. Even when I'm being true to Jack, I feel like I'm not being true to Jack. What do you make of that?

Here's the real kicker. The whole time I was with Jack in Seattle I was haunted by this vague, but powerful feeling I just couldn't put a name to. On our last day we stopped for lunch at a place with a view clear across Puget Sound. After our meals came, we sat there watching the water and the lashing rain and the big moody clouds sliding across the other big moody clouds, and I realized that we hadn't uttered a word to each other in those kind of bloated minutes that feel like hours. Then I looked around and noticed that all the people around us were talking and laughing and carrying on so unselfconsciously, and I realized that what I was feeling was loneliness. Have you ever known me to complain of loneliness, Vi? While I've certainly felt alone in my life, in a cozy, contented sort of way, I've never really felt lonely. I always thought I was immune or something.

Then, when I got to Vancouver to spring Maxwell, the lonely feeling was gone. Just like that. Same clouds, same rain, same ocean—no loneliness. Do you ever feel lonely with Shane? Is this something I should be concerned about? It's all so new.

Gotta go. Flight is being called. Home soon. Miss You.

Kate

Date: November 14
From: VioletMorgan
To: KateBogart
Subject: RE: Lonely in Love

Hey There, Lonely Girl: Pulling out of Atlanta soon and heading down to Gainesville, Florida, for final show in the East. Hallelujah! To address your questions:

1) I think it's truly wicked that you left Maxwell in some dank Canadian dungeon while you took advantage of his room service and

full cable. It may be the most unconscionable thing you've ever done, and I am so proud to call you my best friend.

2) It doesn't really matter that you were playing down your enjoyment of Vancouver for Jack, since you weren't really cheating on him. That's just tact. Unless, of course, you really were sleeping with Maxwell, but for some strange reason, I don't think you were.

3) As for loneliness, right now I am in a motel room where Shane and Mike are dyeing each other's hair and Ivan is trying to torture a stubborn song out of his Fender. Meanwhile, Joey and Damien are in the next room with Sasha, a doctoral candidate we acquired in Atlanta. She's researching her thesis on the "Anthropology of Rock." Essentially, she's a shameless groupie with strong GRE scores. Her "research" seems to involve an awful lot of tickling, and even some occasional light spanking. If you could bottle that lonely feeling, I'd buy it by the case.

But to answer your question, I have never felt lonely with my loving husband, even in the company of others. Lifelong companionship, after all, is sort of the whole point of marriage. Nor do I ever find myself envying the happiness of strange couples at the roadside diners where we tend to graze these days.

Maybe you just haven't gotten Maxwell out of your system yet, or maybe you're just a woman who needs to have at least a couple of lovers. Before you go any further with Jack, however, you might want to get your feelings for Maxwell straightened out. See you next week.

Love,
Vi

Date: November 15
From: KateBogart
To: VioletMorgan
Subject: RE: RE: Lonely in Love

Oh, Vi, you're so right! If I'd taken Maxwell up on the offer to go to London who knows how differently things might have turned out? I can't let Maxwell just decide that Jack and I belong together. I have to take control of my own love life. Don't get me wrong, I love Jack. I really do. But things have changed since Maxwell entered the equation and I can't get him out of my mind.

That's why I am on my way to London. Cashed in some miles and I am at JFK right now waiting for a flight so I can take this up with Maxwell in person. Haven't told Mom and Ted because I want to surprise him. You'll probably think it's crazy, but as soon as I made the decision, I felt better. Crazy, but better.

Love,
Kate

CHAPTER 14

✈

In London

Date: November 16
From: KateBogart
To: VioletMorgan
Subject: All in the Timing

Dear Vi: Made it to London this morning, so excited I didn't even notice my own jet lag and exhaustion. Found my way to Maxwell's loft in Southwark. So happy to see him at the door I jumped straight into his arms. The surprise was all mine, though, when a very pretty, very fit woman wearing one of Maxwell's Turnbull & Asser shirts, and nothing else, entered from the bedroom. She bounded right up to me, hand extended, and said in a husky, hard-edged French-Canadian accent, "I am Odette Francoeur, the fiancée." I said, "I am Kate Bogart, thethethethethe . . ." Luckily, Maxwell jumped in with his all-purpose "Right, then!" and reminded Odette that I am "that friend of Ted Concannon's who was so kind to help him out of that scrape in Vancouver." Odette looked unimpressed, if not actually unconvinced. My hand is still aching from her grip, which had the unmistakable firmness of territoriality behind it.

As if cued by a sitcom director, Mynah entered loaded down with shopping bags. She was "gobsmacked," as the Brits would say, and the next thing you know a dozen oranges were rolling across the floor. We were all grateful for the distraction as we raced to collect them, and ourselves. Next came the obligatory English invitation to tea, and though I tried my best to wriggle out of it, Odette insisted.

It turns out that Odette was waiting for Maxwell when he returned from Vancouver and proposed to him on the spot. That's right, she asked for his hand in marriage. As you'll recall, Maxwell tried to get her to settle down last year, but she refused to give up her profession at the time—a real deal-breaker that. As luck would have it, she has reconsidered now that her "biology clock is tickling," as she put it in her devil-may-care English. She wants very much to have a baby, or maybe two, with "her" Miles. Get this: Maxwell has even agreed to be a stay-at-home dad so that she can keep her career options open.

All during this cozy little meet 'n greet, Mynah bustled around the kitchen rolling her eyes and muttering doubtful asides in that rumbling burr of hers. These were lost on Odette, however, who was too busy scrutinizing me. She interrogated me as to my purpose in London and the length of my stay, like some humorless customs agent. I made up an excuse about a last-minute "WYWH" piece on London. Don't know if anyone really bought it, but who could challenge it under the circumstances?

Claiming a hectic itinerary, said a hasty good-bye before my tea went cold, congratulated the new fiancées, and politely promised to meet up with them later. Odette, who has no plans for the entire week, seemed especially eager to take me up on the promise, too. Maxwell just seemed nervous, and is probably grateful I got the hell out.

So here I am in London. Found a good room in Bloomsbury, but boy do I feel stupid. Why couldn't I just leave well enough alone? I'm a menace to myself! Now it's time to hit the streets and get working on that article I seem to be suddenly writing.

Wish I Weren't Here,
Kate

Date: November 16
From: Manowar
To: KateBogart
Subject: Reconcilable Differences

Dear Ms. Bogart: Imagine my surprise, my shock really, when you arrived at my door this morning. It is always pleasant to see you, but I do wish that we'd both had some time to prepare for the meeting and I apologize for any awkwardness.

It's just a few days since Odette marched back into my life in that impulsive way of hers. She is now determined for us to be married. I daresay that when Odette makes up her mind, she makes up her mind, and I am quite happy for this second chance with her. (Truth be told, it is really the fifth or sixth.) I do so admire her strength and intelligence and courage. It isn't at all easy being a woman in her profession, as you can imagine, especially not in some of the hostile countries she has covered, but I have seen her walk into situations while trained soldiers were running the other way. Her photos are famous, as you know, largely because she seems to know no fear, not even in the midst of pelting gunfire and carpet bombs. She is a wonderful woman and I do hope that you can be friends.

Having recently reunited with Jack yourself, I am sure you can appreciate how glad I am to have Odette back in my life. I feel quite blessed, and it has helped me to recover fully from our own short-lived affair. While Odette knows of our past connection, I have assured her that it is squarely in the past and that you have happily reconciled with your ex-husband. She seems mollified indeed and in fact is quite eager to get to know you better, as I have raved about you quite uncontrollably. To that end, do let us show you around London, as our guest.

Fondly,
Miles

Date: November 17
From: KateBogart
To: Manowar
Subject: RE: Reconcilable Differences

Maxwell: No need to explain. The apologies are all mine. How rude of me to come clomping up to your door yesterday without any advance warning. Americans abroad, y'know.

I am of course very happy that you and Odette were able to reconcile your differences and wish you all the best together. I was indeed caught by surprise, but I have your own mature and worldly example to follow, and look forward to years of friendship with you and your future wife.

I have checked into the Harlingford in Bloomsbury and can't wait to get to know Odette and London better. Call me.

Fondly Too,
Kate

Date: November 18
From: KateBogart
To: GamblinRose
Subject: No Sex Please, We're British

Dear Mom: Please don't be angry. I did something very, very foolish. After Vancouver, I skipped over to London, where I am right now. Found myself having powerful feelings for Maxwell and decided that I didn't want to let him just sashay out of my love life without a fight. Wanted to take this up with him in person. Thought he'd be happy to hear it, even, but when I got here, he had already gotten engaged to Odette Francoeur, war photographer extraordinaire. How's that for timing?

At first I was afraid I had sabotaged his engagement, but did some quick thinking and yesterday, for the sake of damage control, agreed to go on the town with them. We went on the overgrown ferris wheel called The London Eye, one of those things that makes you proud to call yourself a tourist. Quite thrilling, actually, as the weather was clear and you could see all the way past the city's sprawl. Still, it was hard to enjoy it completely, with Odette and Maxwell making sweet with each other the whole time. They extended their love scene through dinner at a nice little Italian place called Passione, of course. Funny, it doesn't seem like Maxwell at all. He was never like that with me, but if there was an Olympic event for public displays of affection, these two could really give you and Ted a stiff challenge.

Speaking of Ted, I haven't told him that I'm here yet, or why I came here in the first place, but since I am here, I might as well get a week's work out of it. Please do me a favor, Mama Rosa, and don't tell him that I came to try to patch things up with Maxwell. I feel lousy enough as it is. My pride is wounded and my heart is bruised and Ted's gloating just might drive me into the Thames.

Wish You Were Here,
Kate

Date: November 18
From: GamblinRose
To: KateBogart
Subject: RE: No Sex Please, We're British

Oh, Kate, I'm so sorry London is such a wet blanket, but if you had checked in with me, I could have warned you about the engagement, as Miles informed Ted right away. Miles was waiting for you to return to New York so he could tell you himself. But your heart is as hard to keep track of as your itinerary and I had no idea you'd switched gears again.

Since you're feeling so bad, I'm not going to take you to task for running off to another continent without telling me first. It's not my way, but please don't do it again. Also, you have no need to worry; I won't tell Ted why you went to London in the first place. I'm very sorry it didn't work out for you, sweetie. I just have one question: Does this mean Jack will or won't be joining us next week?

Curiously,
Mom

Date:	November 19
From:	KateBogart
To:	GamblinRose
Subject:	RE: RE: No Sex Please, We're British

Oh, Mom, I didn't switch gears ever. Maxwell jumped to a conclusion about Jack and me in Provincetown, and once they struck a friendship of their own, the thought of seeing both of them became untenable. But my feelings for Maxwell hadn't subsided at all; in fact, they seemed to be building by the time we ended up in Vancouver. But now Maxwell and Odette look so happy together, I don't want to get in the way.

I'm sorry again for not calling. This mission seemed so urgent at the time, but now I realize what a mistake I made. Of course Jack will still be joining us in New Orleans, unless he has "switched gears." And thanks for sparing the rod. You are a model mother.

Wish You Were Here,
Kate

Date:	November 19
From:	KateBogart
To:	TedConcannon
Subject:	This England

Hi, Ted: Guess where I am. Found myself at JFK last week with an extra week in my schedule and a bucket of frequent flyer miles, so I booked a last-minute flight to London. You know how whimsical I can be. Don't worry, I'm working very hard, going to the theater and museums and flea markets all day. A brutal schedule, really. You'll love it when I write it up.

By the way, met up with Maxwell. How 'bout that engagement? How lovely that things are going so swimmingly for Maxwell, who seems so happy with his future wife. Odette's quite a character, too. She asked me to help her pick out a wedding dress tomorrow. Great fun. It'll be good for the piece, too. Take good care of my mother and my cat and yourself.

WYWH,
K

Date:	November 20
From:	TedConcannon
To:	KateBogart
Subject:	RE: This England

Kate: You fly off to London with no notice at the same time that Maxwell is returning home from his mountain-climbing debacle with your ex and you tell me that you're happy that Maxwell is marrying that Canadian crackpot. There's something fishy going on here, but I'm not even going to try to figure it out. I just want to make it known that I'm on to you, Bogart.

In the meantime, I think the idea of shopping for a wedding dress in London's swanky department stores makes a very nice angle for a travel piece. Since it's for Odette, you might suggest one with a bullet-proof bodice.

Best of Luck,
Ted

Date: November 21
From: JackMacTavish
To: KateBogart
Subject: Remember Me?

Hey, Katie! Where you at? Sick of your machine, and trying to finalize plans for next week. New Orleans? Thanksgiving? Remember, babe? Can't wait.

> Love,
> Jackson

Date: November 21
From: KateBogart
To: JackMacTavish
Subject: RE: Remember Me?

Hi, Jackson: Here I am in London. A last-minute assignment. Didn't even have a chance to unpack in New York. You know how it is. Sorry I didn't let you know sooner, but I have been running myself ragged here. London's so bustling. So much to see.

By the way, Maxwell and his amour Odette have reunited and are even engaged. Sweet, isn't it? You might want to forward your best wishes to him. I've been helping his fiancée hunt for a wedding dress, which is not as much fun as you think it is. Yesterday, Harrods and Selfridges, today Liberty, Harvey Nichols, and three by-appointment bridal shops in Kensington and Chelsea. Why did I ever agree to this?

I'll see you next week. I can't wait, either.

> Wish You Were Here,
> Kate

Date: November 22
From: JackMacTavish
To: KateBogart
Subject: RE: RE: Remember Me?

Wow, Katie, righteous news for Miles! Just e-mailed him an Incan wedding chant. Not to heavy up on you, but I really wish you had told me sooner about going to London. I know it was a sensitive issue when we were married, but we're really going to have make some ground rules if we're going to make this relationship-without-borders thing fly. Let's put it on the table for New Orleans, along with all that delicious food we're going to eat and all that marathon sex we're going to have. Okay, my little frequent flyer? So happy for Miles and can't wait to go to the wedding. They always make me cry. (Which always makes you frisky! Lucky me!)

    Love,
    Jack

Date: November 22
From: OdetteFrancoeur
To: KateBogart
Subject: *Merci*

Dear Kate: Thank you a lot for helping to pick out the dress for my wedding just yesterday. I never have a brain for this sort of thing anyhow and I don't keep too many girlfriends to help me. I spend all my time with men. Mostly reporters, rebels, and the warlords. They are not so good as you at the fashions.

    It has been such a long time since I wear a dress. I prefer not to wear them at all. Too much like the burka. But I will do it for my Miles who I have liked to treat badly for too long past the years. Will you enjoy being my bridesmaid? Miles and I would enjoy it too much. You don't have to reply. It's only just to think about it for now. We are planning to make our wedding in Montreal on the 4th of May. Please throw it up on your calendar.

Your New Friend,
Odette

Date: November 23
From: VioletMorgan
To: KateBogart
Subject: RE: All in the Timing

Kate, I just got back to New York. Home, sweet blessed home! Just got your e-mail, too. Ouch! Very bad timing with the engagement. Guess it pretty much ruined your trip. I hope you're okay, and that I don't read about any famous photojournalists being pushed in front of any speeding double-deckers.

Vi

Date: November 24
From: KateBogart
To: VioletMorgan
Subject: RE: RE: All in the Timing

Dear Vi: My last night in London. Can't say I'm going to miss it this time, either. Not because of London, of course. It's more grand than ever. But to catch you up . . .

After Miles convinced Odette that there was nothing between us, she decided she wanted to be my friend. I spent most of the week watching them get reacquainted. When they weren't stealing kisses between every course and at every crosswalk, Odette and I were off shopping for her wedding dress. That's right, she asked me to help her pick out her dress. The woman has no fashion sense whatsoever. She kept rejecting one idealized dress after another because they have no pockets. I had a hard time convincing her that she wouldn't need extra rolls of film or pepper spray at the wedding.

I am trying to be happy for Miles, but frankly it's not easy when I'm feeling so sorry for myself. It all feels worse because they seem so right together. After all, what do I know about foxholes and Kalashnikovs? They spent an awful lot of time telling me their war stories in great detail. She even bragged about how determined she was to rescue Miles from his Colombian kidnappers, when all the military and government personnel had given up, and how "hot" the sex was afterward. She has never "enjoyed so many of the orgasms!" Miles and I nearly blushed ourselves to death.

All the talk of their experiences together in the war zones just made me feel more like an outsider, and made me realize how wrong Maxwell and I are for each other. It dawned on me, too, that the whole reason Maxwell stepped aside to give Jack and me another chance is because he so desperately wanted his own second chance with Odette.

This woman is heroic, and beautiful, and brave, and interesting, and I can't blame Maxwell one bit for falling in love with her. But she sure does make me feel like a fraud, Vi. Here I am telling myself that I'm this world-traveling adventurer, this irrepressible, independent free-loving spirit. But I've never faced down a ragtag band of drug-dealing kidnappers to rescue my lover, or beaten up an armed Taliban soldier with a rock because he was trying to steal my Leica, or rescued any Kosovo orphans from their house just before it was blown to dust.

But bitterness is so unattractive, I won't give in to it. Besides, I have my sweet, beautiful Jackson, who so sincerely wants to make things work this time. How could I take him for granted? Feel like such an ass. And to think how close I came to messing this up for Miles! I am many things, Vi, but I'm no homewrecker. He has no idea why I came to London in the first place, and now he'll never know.

To make up for all of this, took myself to tea at Claridge's. Very civilized. Almost restorative even. Home tomorrow, then off to New

Orleans for the holiday. Would you mind taking care of Truman while I'm there? Silly question, I know.

Wish You Were Here,
Kate

✈

CHAPTER 15

In New Orleans

Date: November 26
From: KateBogart
To: VioletMorgan
Subject: Voodoo

Vi: Mom and Ted and I have arrived at Maison de Ville. A nice splurge, if you ever get the chance: really swell, old French Quarter–style, beamed ceilings, French antiques, working fireplaces, port and sherry in the afternoon. I didn't want to leave at all, but Mother dear insisted on seeing some of the Quarter and having her fortune told. As it is the day before Thanksgiving, the Quarter is unusually quiet, even Bourbon Street. There's nothing more unsettling than the atmosphere of an abandoned honky-tonk.

We went to the Voodoo Museum, where the infant caskets and preserved housecats and alligators didn't help to settle our spirits any. The palm reader, Varina, told me that she saw an aura of red around me, and when I told her that might be my hair she gave me a smirk that said "Don't mess up my routine, sister." She also said that I was due to take a trip soon. When am I *not* due to take a trip? Finally, she said that I have already met the love of my life (Truman), and that music is about to play a big part in my "personal journey." Right. I'm in New Orleans, where music really does pour out of every other doorway. She also said that I am feeling very close to my father right now. What father?

She also told my mother that she saw the number 27 around her and something gold, or maybe something silver. Definitely something shiny. Again, I pointed out my mother's silver streak, but Varina wasn't amused. She couldn't tell if she saw one or two men in Mom's life, but she was sure that she'd be finding a husband soon. She also said that she saw my mother's sisters missing her, and something about Monte Carlo. Even I was impressed by that one.

Right now, I'm enjoying my afternoon port in the garden, and waiting for Jackson to arrive so we can play Stanley 'n Stella. Please don't forget to look in on Truman tomorrow and give him some turkey giblets. He looks forward to them every year.

Wish You Were Here,
Kate

Date:	November 27
From:	TedConcannon
To:	KateBogart and JackMacTavish
Subject:	Bananas Fosterfather

Dear Kate and Jack: Wanted to write this because I'm not always good at speaking what's in my heart. I'm sorry if I set things off to a bad start at dinner last night. I talked it over with Rose, and I just felt like a fat old nutria afterward. I didn't mean to upset Jack, and certainly didn't mean to suggest he's not good at his job. I understand that when you're dealing with nature, life is unpredictable in the extreme.

I like to think I'm pretty fair-minded, Jack. (Don't laugh at that, Kate; I can hear you across the courtyard.) But maybe I do feel a little resentful since Kate chose you over my pal. Rose has made me see that I just have to accept and respect Kate's choice and to take you on your own merits. I hope Kate can forgive me and that Jack and I can put it all behind us and learn to be friends.

Sorry Again,
Ted

Date: November 28
From: KateBogart
To: TedConcannon
Subject: RE: Bananas Fosterfather

Dear Ted: We both appreciate how difficult that e-mail was for you to send, as I know you never like to admit when you're wrong. (Note to self: Warn Mother about this.) It is encouraging, however, to see that she's having a positive effect on your usual obstinate ways. Here's Jack . . .

Ted: No problemo. You're a very gracious guy. And since I really appreciate the second chance I'm getting with Katie, happy to oblige someone else who screwed up big, too. Looking forward to years of good relations with you. Maybe we can go to a sweat lodge or something next time you're in Cali? Just a thought.

   Kate and Jack

Date: November 29
From: GamblinRose
To: KateBogart
Subject: Rollin' on the River

Kate, Ted and I are off to our riverboat cruise, and I don't want to wake you. I sure hope Jack isn't mad at Ted anymore. Sometimes Ted speaks without thinking, but I don't think he really meant it when he called Jack "a California flake."

   Anyway, Ted and I will be back in New Orleans in a couple of days. I hope you and Jack enjoy your time alone. Let's all try to have a civilized dinner again when we return. But somewhere convenient to Harrah's, okay? I'll leave the reservations up to you.

   Love,
   Mom

Date: November 29
From: KateBogart
To: VioletMorgan
Subject: Horn o' Plenty

Oh, Vi! What a Thanksgiving. It started out just fine. Jack and I slept late, while Mom dragged Ted to opening day at the Fair Grounds for the local holiday horse racing jamboree. Later, had an amazing dinner at the Commander's Palace, but Ted got a little surly with Jack, blaming him for nearly killing himself and Miles on Mt. Rainier. Jack got a little defensive, naturally, and even though the food was scrumptious, the whole evening was tainted by the tension between them. The next day, they made up, and Mom and Ted went off on their riverboat cruise while Jack and I moved over to more affordable digs at The Columns. That's where things got even stickier.

There's a really good combo that plays in the lounge there, and Jack was very eager for me to hear them. He was right. They sure were great, but imagine my shock when the piano player said, ". . . and Red Bogart on saxophone." It kept echoing over and over and over again, like in a 1940s melodrama. It finally stopped when sweet, clueless Jack said "Hey, Katie, that guy has the same name as you!" Poor Jack. I didn't mean to kick him so hard.

But really, Vi, of all the gin joints and jazz bars in New Orleans, we have to walk into his! I didn't feel comfortable staying there knowing that my long lost father is playing downstairs. Have moved over to Le Richelieu.

Mom and Ted are due back tomorrow. Still trying to think of how I'm going to drop the bomb on her. As you'll recall, the last time she saw Red was 27 years ago when he took off on that one-way Scandinavian tour with his band and just stopped returning her calls and letters. Eventually, Rose decided that he started a new family and retired to the fjords or something. So she worked like a demon to raise me—and the money for a divorce—and that was it. A clean break. She never felt sorry for herself, moved on with her life, and rarely mentioned Red again. I have no idea how she'll take the news. Very anxious about this.

Wish He Weren't Here,
Kate

Date: November 30
From: GamblinRose
To: KateBogart
Subject: Going to the Chapel of Love

Kate: Tried to call you, but they told me you checked out of The Columns early. Where have you and Jack gone to now? I have very important news and I want you to be prepared: Ted proposed to me on the cruise!

The air was nice and cool and the moon was shining over the Mississippi and he just surprised me with a beautiful, shining diamond ring. I was so surprised, I thought I'd fall overboard! That must have been what that fortune-teller was talking about when she said I'd find my husband soon and you were close to your father. She's good!

Of course, I said yes, but we haven't set a date or anything like that yet. Plus, I played number 27, just as the fortune-teller said, and I won! Just think about it: Since I've been in New Orleans, I'm up $957, a diamond ring, and a fiancé! Now where in the heck are you? We have to celebrate.

Love,
Rosa Maria Louisa Milanazzo Bogart Concannon-to-be

Date: November 30
From: KateBogart
To: GamblinRose
Subject: RE: Going to the Chapel of Love

Dear Mom: My sincerest congratulations. I am very, very happy for you and Ted, and we do indeed have to celebrate. I am calling around for reservations for dinner tonight. My treat. I am also assuming that you're not going to try to get married until Ted has actually obtained a divorce from Lorraine.

Speaking of divorces, before we celebrate, I seriously need to speak to you. Woman to woman, that is, daughter to mother. Very important. Maybe we can meet at Café du Monde? At 3:00? Jack and I have moved over to Le Richelieu. I'll explain. Call me.

        Love,
        Kate

Date: November 30
From: KateBogart
To: VioletMorgan
Subject: Red Alert

Dear Vi: My mother and Ted got back from their riverboat cruise engaged to be married. Can you believe it? She was so excited, I almost didn't have the heart to tell her that I stumbled upon her ex-husband, but what else could I do?

So, I brought her to the Café du Monde and after I gave her the news, we both just sat there like an oil painting, taking in the buskers and the tap dancers and the incessant Dixieland jazz and the whiny tourists yelling at their whiny kids on Decatur Street. Finally, Rose just burst into this little chuckle that eventually fulminated into a hearty belly laugh. I thought she might be losing it, but when she finally settled down, she just called the waiter over and asked for two more orders of beignets. After all, she told him, who knows when she'll be in New Orleans again.

Rose's whole attitude is "what the heck." She genuinely seems to be enjoying the twisted irony of it all. She's much more concerned with what I plan to do and how I feel about it. But for her, it's one of life's cracked jokes. As for me, I have no idea what to do, but I still have some time to worry it over. So you know how I'm spending the rest of my time in New Orleans.

Last night, Jack and I took Rose and Ted to dinner at Galatoire's to celebrate their engagement and their last night in New Orleans. It was a lovely dinner, and Ted and Jack even found some common ground in liberal politics. Grateful for that, and genuinely happy for Rose and Ted, but really, my mind was elsewhere.

Wish You Were Here,
Kate

Date: December 1
From: GamblinRose
To: KateBogart
Subject: Seeing Red

Dear Kate: Thanks so much to you and Jack for such a wonderful dinner last night. Boy, did I have a great time in New Orleans. Why did I wait so long to come here? I think the Sisters would love it, too.

After dinner, I got to thinking about Red, and how he left you all those years without a father and left me working so hard, and it finally hit me. For the first time in years, I felt myself getting ticked off. Well I'll be damned if I'm going to lose a good night's sleep being angry. So, while my Teddy bear slept off that delicious meal, I threw on my clothes, rubbed his big Buddha belly for good luck, and hopped a cab over to The Columns. After all, who knows when I'll be in New Orleans again?

When I got there, the combo was just finishing up their set. Red was in one of his musical trances and he didn't even notice me at the table. When it was over, I pulled up next to him at the bar and ordered a bourbon. Red just turned to me and asked me how I've been, as if

we hadn't seen each other for a couple of days. Just fine, I said, better than ever, and then I told him about teaching and raising you and my brand-new engagement. Red just nodded through it all, expressionless. When I asked him how he was doing, he said his chops were better than ever. That's it. His chops. It just all comes down to the music for Red.

I reminded him that he had a daughter, who's a terrific person. I also told him that I was never really angry at him for walking out on me. In fact, I took it as an act of mercy. But I also told him that I'll never be able to forgive him for turning his back on you, and that I actually feel sorry for him because he didn't get to watch you grow up. He looked a little deflated and told me that he's never been very good with words. I told him he wasn't so hot with actions either, finished my drink, wished him well, then said good-bye.

I didn't tell him you were here in New Orleans, Kate. I'm not sure if you'd want me to, but I could tell you were thinking about it at Galatoire's last night. I think you should do whatever you have to do. That decision is up to you, but I thought this was something you should know.

Now it's very late, and I'm very tired, and I have to fly home first thing in the morning. Boy, New Orleans sure is a great place for a gal like me who loves to eat and play.

Love,
Mom

Date: December 1
From: VioletMorgan
To: KateBogart
Subject: RE: Red Alert

Bogie: Amazing developments. Wow, just think, Ted's going to be your stepfather. Do you think he'll try to impose a curfew on you? And what have you done about your real father? If you do confront him, try to hit him up for all those missed allowances when I had to pay for the movies and the sodas when we were kids. That man robbed me of my childhood!

Good luck, whatever you decide to do.

See you in New York.
Vi

Date:	December 1
From:	KateBogart
To:	VioletMorgan
Subject:	Blue Bayou

Vi: Nice to know you're finding so much comedy in my predicament. I spent the day on a bayou tour with Jack, who's a lot more sensitive than you are, by the way. A weird and lovely landscape. We saw lots of alligators and nutria and herons. Even a bald eagle. It was all kind of spooky to me, and I kept looking out for water moccasins. Jack of course wants us to move to Louisiana so he can join the effort to preserve the bayous. Fat chance. I just don't see myself farming crawdads for a living.

As for Red, I still haven't decided what to do, but time is running out. Only two days left here. It's kind of scary, to be perfectly honest, and I don't know why. I guess it's just like the bayou, unfamiliar ground that's hard to trust.

Wish This Weren't So Hard,
Kate

Date:	December 1
From:	KateBogart
To:	GamblinRose
Subject:	God Bless the Child

Dear Mom: Well, after deliberating in that way of mine, I finally decided to go to The Columns to see Red again. Jack came with me, and we sat at a little table sipping our bourbon while the band launched into their first set. They played "Sophisticated Lady," "You'd Be So Nice to Come Home To," and "Body and Soul." They're a darn good band, but mostly my mind was on Red, and my own reasons for being there, which I still hadn't figured out at that point.

As he blew all his soulful devotion into that saxophone, I thought how wonderful it is to love something so much, the way that I love my work, and Jack loves nature, and you love your games. But when the band went into "God Bless the Child," I realized that after all these years, I didn't have anything to say to Red. I couldn't say that I ever really missed him, since I didn't really know him, and mostly I remember being a pretty happy kid, so I don't even have any deep-seated anger to unleash.

I'm glad that I saw him, glad that I know where he is, glad that the last piece of my own private puzzle has been put in its place. But let's face it, it's a little late for us to be celebrating Take-Your-Daughter-to-Work Day. Besides, I've done pretty well without a father all my life, thanks to you, and I sure don't need one now. As the song says, "God bless the child that's got his own."

After the set, we gave the band a good round of well-earned applause, and Red looked me straight in the eye. I wondered if he noticed some resemblance, if maybe some piece of his puzzle was being put in place too, but I didn't stick around to find out. Jack and I finished our drinks, sent the band a round, then went out to hail a cab back to the Quarter. Just think, if it weren't for the bourbon and that song, I might have done something that I regretted forever, setting myself up for a lifetime of frustration from which I had been previously spared. Thank God for booze and music!

Wish You Were Still Here,
Kate

Date: December 2
From: KateBogart
To: VioletMorgan
Subject: A Girl's Best Friend

Dear Vi: Read this sitting down. For my last night in New Orleans, I wanted to see the Christmas lights in City Park, so Jack and I took a taxi out to Mid-City. Magically lovely, sparkling with more little white lights than you've ever seen in one place before. Just like New Orleans to do something to rich excess, and get away with it. Decided to ride the old-fashioned carousel, where Jackson produced a shiny diamond ring in a lovely platinum setting, an antique one, so as not to contribute to the brutality of the African diamond trade, bless his heart. Then, he got down on one knee and asked me to marry him. Again.

He went on to tell me how he was so inspired by Maxwell's engagement and was planning to propose to me that night at The Columns, but then Red ruined the mood and Ted and Rose made their announcement first and he just didn't think the time was right. He said a lot of other gooey stuff that I won't share with you, Miss Snideypants, but I was moved to tears. I was also speechless. Literally.

Meanwhile, a boisterous Cajun family was riding along, watching the whole thing. They kept saying *"Oui, chèrie! Oui! Oui!"* while Jack knelt there looking up at me with his heart in his hand and those blue eyes glistening with tears. He was just irresistible. So I said *"Oui."* Then there was much applause and congratulations, and tears and kisses all around. Jack even hid a bottle of champagne in his backpack in the event of a *"Oui."* As if by magic, the Cajuns produced an accordion and two fiddles and launched into some festive dance music. I guess these are the sorts of things Cajuns just carry around with them everywhere in case a celebration is suddenly called for.

There's so much to figure out between us: where we're going to get married, where we're going to live, how we're going to work, etc. But I have to say, Jack was a rock through this trip and there was none of the loneliness I felt in Seattle. He handled Ted like a charm and he was completely patient and supportive when I discovered my father.

He's such a good friend and such a beautiful man. Let's face it, Vi, men like Jack just don't come along all that often.

Have not told Mama Rosa yet, as I want to spring it on her in person. Anyway, we're spending one more night in New Orleans to celebrate and to discuss our future plans. Would you mind looking after Truman a little while longer? Things are awfully sweet here. I'll be back in a couple of days. You're the best.

Love,
Kate

CHAPTER 16

In Amsterdam

Date: December 5
From: JackMacTavish
To: KateBogart
Subject: Who Do You Love?

Katie: No message from you on my machine, and no answer at your place. Let me know when you make it home. New Orleans was heavy, babe, between being unfairly attacked by Ted in the middle of the Thanksgiving dinner, then going through that whole situation with you and Red. Wow, rogue wave. I totally respect your decision, though. Wish I was so self-possessed. If it were me, I'd be stalking the guy until he agreed to attend some father-son healing seminars, and I'd no doubt be dragging the old coot up some mountain somewhere for some moon-howling therapy.

Having you accept my proposal in the park with all the lights twinkling and the music going and the Cajun people getting involved was more than I could have ever asked for. Boy did it make up for all the other stuff, and I'm so glad I waited. I guess things just have a way of working out. Sharmi is right: The universe takes care of us if we just put our trust in its perfection.

But then there was the incident last night. Katie, I'm really concerned about this. I mean, there I was rocketing past the moon and just about to touch the stars, and you call me "Maxwell"! I still can't

believe it. I thought that only happened in cheesy old sex comedies. I
don't want my life to be a cheesy old sex comedy. I love you! And I
want to know that you love me, but I'm still smarting from that one.

Love,
Your Jackson

Date: December 5
From: KateBogart
To: JackMacTavish
Subject: RE: Who Do You Love?

Jack: Just got in. I know what you mean about last night. It was like
something out of an old Doris Day/Rock Hudson movie, except they
never had sex. I don't know what came over me, Jackson, and I'm
really, truly sorry. I think it was just a right brain/left brain malfunc-
tion, that's all. Maybe some synapses were burning out, or some brain
cells regenerating. Maybe it was the bourbon or all that rich food, but
please accept my apology and don't take it too personally. I just think
my whole system was a little out of whack.

     That doesn't mean I wasn't enjoying myself last night, Jack. You
were great. You are always great. And you know that I love you. I
married you, didn't I? And I couldn't resist you even when I was trying my damndest to make our divorce work, so I'm marrying you
again. If that's not love, what is?

Wish You Were Here (So I Could Make It Up to You the Way You
Really Really Like),
Kate

Date: December 6
From: Manowar
To: KateBogart
Subject: Pressing Engagements

My Dear Ms. Bogart: How happy I was to get the news of Ted's engagement to your mother. They do seem quite right together, and I have never known Ted to be as spirited as he seems to be these days. Love has made a new and better man of him, as it has of me as well.

My own engagement is moving along gracefully. Odette is moving her things in this week for a sort of practice-drill. Mynah looks a bit put out by it all, but she'll adapt. The delightful Jane Plank has been good enough to set up some meetings for me so that I might find a suitable publisher for my new book on the international cannabis trade. I do hope it bears seed, if you will forgive the expression. I hope too that your own writing is rich and fulfilling.

Best,
Miles

Date: December 6
From: KateBogart
To: Manowar
Subject: RE: Pressing Engagements

Dear Maxwell: You can't imagine how often your name came up in New Orleans! Were your ears burning? And if you think the news of Ted and Rose is exciting, you'll be ecstatic to know that Jack and I are also getting re-hitched. That's right, we're tying the knot again, and I owe part of my good fortune to you, Maxwell. Jack was so inspired by your engagement to Odette, he surprised me with a diamond ring and a proposal in New Orleans. Made the announcement to Rose and Ted last night. Mom was very happy, and Ted even forced a tight smile. We haven't worked out the arrangements, but since we were married in New York the last time, we're thinking of San Francisco this time, for the sake of symmetry. Of course, Mom is very eager for a double ceremony, but I still haven't sprung that on Jack. I'm afraid he'll actually go for it.

How nice to hear that you have found some promising work that doesn't involve outrunning armored tanks and spending weeks in a blindfold. As for me, I'm feeling some pressure to settle down for a bit and focus on one particular area. Jack is very eager to start an eco-lodge somewhere in Central America, or Brazil, or the Nunavut territory in Arctic Canada, which he thinks is going to be hot hot hot, despite the unbearably low temps. I'm sure that those places are all rich with material; I just don't know if I'm cut out for those kinds of frontiers.

But you know how our lives are, Maxwell, we're just always hunting for an angle, and they get harder and harder to come by all the time. Next time you e-mail me, I'll probably be living in an igloo, but happily married.

Wish You Were Here,
Kate

Date:	December 7
From:	TedConcannon
To:	KateBogart
Subject:	Holland Days

Kate: I have just filed for divorce from Lorraine and I feel younger and thinner already. She didn't take the news so well, 'cause she's the one who likes to initiate these things. It goes against her take-charge nature, and I do believe she's even a little jealous that I have found someone else. Her tough luck.

Congratulations again on your engagement and please extend my sincere best wishes to Jack, too. Does this mean that you'll be settling down somewhere in Patagonia, or retiring to a grass shack on stilts in some stagnant rain forest? Will you still e-mail me dispatches, if so? Or do you plan to take the long-distance approach to matrimony again? I don't mean any of these questions to be taken as skepticism or anything, just friendly concern and nagging curiosity.

It sure seems to be your lucky week. Not only have you won a new fiancé and a new stepfather-to-be, but you're going to Amsterdam too, courtesy of the *New York Standard*. The music critic was going to ride his bike from Amsterdam to Rotterdam and do a feature piece on the underground music scene in Dutch "squats," but he needed to have an emergency appendectomy. The flight is all paid for and the deposits have been made on the Pulitzer in Amsterdam. We don't want to lose all that money, so the assignment is yours. Since you're doing Paris for Christmas, you can just take the train from Amsterdam. You fly the day after tomorrow. Get out your wooden shoes and pack your bags!

   TC

Date: December 7
From: KateBogart
To: TedConcannon
Subject: RE: Holland Days

Ted: Just because you're engaged to my mother doesn't mean you can boss me around or give me the third degree. As to future living arrangements, you'll be pleased to know that Jack and I are in the midst of some very serious negotiations, and we plan to hammer out the particulars over the holidays in Paris. Once things are decided, I'll let you know where to forward my e-mail.

   Maybe I don't want to go to Amsterdam in December. Have you ever thought of that? The days are so short this time of year and the canals haven't frozen over yet, so you can't skate, and it's too darn cold to be riding around on a bicycle. But I guess I could go to the Concertgebòuw, and the city does have great flea markets, and I haven't been to the Rijksmuseum in years, and the Pulitzer is really swell, I hear. I'm packing now. Can you tell Mom?

   Kate

Date: December 7
From: VioletMorgan
To: KateBogart
Subject: Century 21

Bogie: Before you run off to Paris and I run off on the Killers' West Coast tour, let's celebrate your engagement with lunch and shopping. With all the junk food consumed on the road, I seem to have out-grown all my clothes. I can't go around wearing Shane's T-shirts all day until I drop the weight. So Daffy's, here I come!

   Please say you'll join me. It'll be so much fun, just the two of us loose in the retail wonderland that is New York. No parents, or hus-bands, or ex-husbands, or stealth fiancées, or long-lost fathers, or stepfa-thers-to-be, or annoying groupies. Just a couple of New York natives and their charge cards. Call me.

   Vi

Date: December 7
From: KateBogart
To: VioletMorgan
Subject: Rain Check

Oh, Vi, I'd love to spend the whole week shopping with you, but I'm about to hop on a plane for Amsterdam. Ted was in a pinch, as one of his other writers needed some emergency surgery, so I'm taking the assignment. But since you're going to be home for the rest of the month, would you mind taking care of you-know-who? He misses you so much. I swear he even meowed your name yesterday.

   Wish I Were Here,
   Kate

Date: December 8
From: VioletMorgan
To: KateBogart
Subject: To-Do List

Tuesday, December 8th:

✦ Buy new fat wardrobe.
✦ Christmas shopping.
✦ Check hotel arrangements for West Coast. Downgrade to motel
   arrangements.
✦ Try to make those cute little "easy-to-make" Christmas cards fol-
   lowing dyslexic instructions as laid out in *Martha Stewart Living*.
   In drunken frustration, shred and chop into little pieces. Use as
   confetti on New Year's Eve instead.
✦ Find new, reliable best friend who is not always running off to
   distant corners of the planet at the last minute just when you are
   looking forward to girling around with her.
✦ Feed her stupid cat.

Date: December 9
From: JackMacTavish
To: KateBogart
Subject: Hooking Up

Katie: Called your apartment today. Nice talking to Vi, but I really
didn't mean to whisper all those things about what I wanted to do to
her earlobes and her eyelids and her tender little ankles in my best
Barry White tones.

    Katie, why didn't you tell me you were going to Amsterdam?
Don't I even rate a phone call, or at least a quick e-mail? Thought we
talked about this, babe. First you call me by someone else's name
while we're riding the old Starship Erotica (sp?) and then you just
skip off to Europe like the world is your own big sandbox and you

don't have to share it with anyone. And Ted Concannon calls *me* a flake!

What's going on? I'm hurting here!

Jackson

Date: December 10
From: KateBogart
To: JackMacTavish
Subject: RE: Hooking Up

Jackson: Sorry if you're feeling so hurt and neglected, but as you know, sometimes my work requires me to throw my things in a bag and race to the airport. I don't like it any more than you do, Jack. Well, okay, maybe I like it a little more, 'cause I always end up some place really nifty like Amsterdam as it gears up for Christmas.

But you really shouldn't take it personally. You of all people have to understand that I need to make hay while the sun shines, 'cause there's no guarantee I'll be working next week or next month. I had every intention of e-mailing you when I got here, because I agree that we should keep each other as close as we can, especially now that we're going to be remarried.

That is why I unpacked a picture of you and put it by my bedside as soon as I checked into the hotel this morning. In the photo, you are standing in the dunes in Provincetown, in this golden Hopperesque light. The wind is billowing your red corduroy shirt and you're leaning on a spindly driftwood staff. There are little licks of sunlight playing in your tawny curls and in the wispy beach grass bowing in adoration all around you. You're looking straight at me with those deep blue eyes and there's a sly smile just breaking at the corner of your luscious mouth.

I know it's a poor substitute for having you here beside me, but I also know that any other woman would kill to give this photo pride of place on her night table. So until you join me in Paris, it will have to do. I'm truly sorry that I missed that phone call, but if you can find it

in your heart to forgive me and you'd like to try again, I'm all earlobes. And eyelids, and tender little ankles, and . . .

Wish You Were Here,
Kate

Date: December 10
From: JackMacTavish
To: KateBogart
Subject: RE: RE: Hooking Up

Whew, Katie! How can I stay mad at you? You sure know all the right
things to say. That e-mail really got to me. I'm totally inspired, babe.
Right now. I'd really love to talk to you, even at the international rate,
but Vi gave me the wrong number to your hotel. As soon as I can find
an operator who'll help me, I'm gonna get you in your room and I'm
gonna make slow, thorough love to you using just my perfect knowledge of your body and the soothing timber (sp?) and steady rhythms
of my commanding, manly voice. Don't go anywhere, baby!

Your Insecure Server,
J

Date: December 11
From: VioletMorgan
To: KateBogart
Subject: Call Girls

Okay, Bogie, what's going on with you and Jack? First he called me
on the phone whispering sweet nothings about all the things he's going to do to my earlobes, and my wrists, and my tonsils, etc. After
some embarrassed apologies and transparent excuses, he called me
back for the number to your hotel. Then, about a second later, he called
me for the number again. Then, one more time for the Netherlands'

country code. With each call he sounded a little more breathy, a little more bothered.

Isn't it bad enough that I have to sift through your cat's litter box every day and administer his hairball treatment for the next few weeks? Please assure me that fate has not also delivered me into the unfortunate role of your personal international phone-sex operator. It's really undignified.

V

Date: December 11
From: KateBogart
To: VioletMorgan
Subject: RE: Call Girls

Sorry you had to hear that, Vi. Thank heavens it's you at my apartment and not Ted! Loving Amsterdam already, though haven't really left my hotel room all that much. I'm starting out at a pretty little place on the Prinsengracht canal right between the Leidseplein and the Jordaan. Because it's the off-season, I easily landed a room with a canal view. The days are burning short but bright, and with all the trees bare, the light just pours in. I feel like a girl in a Vermeer—only one who works at a computer.

Even though I'm thrilled to be here, I've been inside much too much making naughty with Jack on the phone. Last week I made a little booboo and called him Maxwell at exactly the wrong time, if you know what I mean. Felt terrible about it, so I had to make it up somehow. But wait till he sees his phone bill. That'll cool him off.

In the meantime, Amsterdam awaits. I've got to go to the bike rental shop to pick up my wheels for the rest of the week. Then I'm going to toodle over to the Bloemenmarket and put some flowers 'round my room, just like Joni Mitchell did in that song. What fun!

I'll bring you back a wheel of gouda or something. Thanks again.

Wish You Were Here,
Kate

Date: December 11
From: JackMacTavish
To: KateBogart
Subject: After Midnight

Whew! Katie, last night was wild! I really got you with that line about tearing your hair ribbons loose with my teeth, didn't I? I'm really proud of that one. I've got some more stuff I haven't even used yet, so let's do it again. I'll call you around midnight tonight, your time. Be by your phone, okay?

Love,
Jackson

Date: December 12
From: Manowar
To: KateBogart
Subject: The Pulitzer Prize

My Dear Ms. Bogart: Just off the telephone with Ted, who informs me that you are in Amsterdam covering for another writer. Yet another bizarre coincidence in our lives, as I, too, am in Amsterdam.

I came to interview some seed smugglers and hydroponic hemp growers who were here for the Cannabis Cup, the city's yearly marijuana convention, which just concluded. I am trying to talk to Nico DeKoker, the Dutch botanist who served on the judge's panel, but he seems to have difficulty keeping appointments.

How lucky for me that you are in Amsterdam as well! Is there lunch in our near future? Or perhaps dinner? Do please rescue me from these drug-crazed riffraff. I am staying at the Pulitzer, in room 305. And where might you be?

Eagerly,
Miles

Date: December 12
From: KateBogart
To: Manowar
Subject: RE: The Pulitzer Prize

Maxwell, a lucky coincidence indeed, as I am on my way to the Pulitzer this afternoon for the high end of my stay. Luckier still, I will be right next door to you in room 304.

There is indeed a lunch or dinner in our future. Do you like spicy? I hear that the Rijsttafel at Long Pura can't be beat. We can discuss this at the Pulitzer, however. Just knock on my wall.

Glad You Are Here,
Kate

Date: December 12
From: KateBogart
To: TedConcannon
Subject: The Lowlands

Dear Ted: Why do I get the feeling that there's nothing wrong with that music critic's appendix at all? And why do I think that he was never even planning to ride his bike from Amsterdam to Rotterdam? In December! Maybe it's because Miles Maxwell just happens to be in Amsterdam at the moment, lodging at the very handsome Pulitzer. In fact, he is on the other side of the wall right now. There's no use denying it, Ted. I asked the reception clerk, who told me that the person making the reservation specifically requested the room next to Maxwell's.

The old Kate would have been infuriated by your deceptive and meddlesome ways, but the new, improved Kate doesn't really care. She is happily engaged to be married to Jack MacTavish. In fact she is so happily engaged that she can very easily enjoy a platonic date with her friend Miles Maxwell, a man who is as engaged as he is engaging, I'll remind you.

I know you think I have no control or common sense when it comes to men and that Jack and I are incompatible, but you're wrong Ted. Wrong, wrong, wrong.

Wish You Were Here (So I Could Trip You with a Wooden Shoe), Kate

Date: December 12
From: TedConcannon
To: KateBogart
Subject: RE: The Lowlands

Kate: Is that how little you think of me? Do you really think I would stoop to such underhanded manipulation as to fake an assignment—hotel arrangements and all—just to get you and Miles together? What will it take to convince you of my innocence? An inflamed appendix in a pickle jar? If so, then that's what I must do. In the meantime, enjoy Amsterdam and say hello to Miles. Whatta coincidence!

TC

Date: December 13
From: JackMacTavish
To: KateBogart
Subject: XXX

Hey, Katie, I'm lonesome for you, babe. I can't wait until Paris. Let's burn out another long-distance satellite together. Where are you staying now? Send me the number and I'll call you at midnight again. I've got some dirty, filthy thoughts I'd like to plant in your tasty little ears.

Love,
The Midnight Caller

Date: December 13
From: KateBogart
To: JackMacTavish
Subject: RE: XXX

Dear Mr. Caller, I'd really love to, but I'm not quite comfortable getting frisky over the telephone here. You see, Maxwell is in Amsterdam too, doing more research on the state of the international cannabis trade, and it turns out he's in the very next room. What if he hears me through the walls? It's a little inhibiting. But we can still send naughty e-mails. The naughtier, the better.

> Wish You Were Here Instead,
> Kate

Date: December 13
From: JackMacTavish
To: KateBogart
Subject: RE: RE: XXX

Katie: That e-mail hit me like an ice-cold shower. What do you mean Miles is in the next room? That's a pretty funny coincidence, isn't it? I'm trying not to feel jealous here, but since it was just over a week ago when you were moaning his name in my ear, I'm not doing a very good job.

All those images that I had of you and me making like the karma suitra (sp?) have been replaced by images of you and Miles making out on the canals all lit up like Christmas, or pedaling around on a bicycle built for two with your little scarves tied in those cute European knots, or rubbing noses over cups of hot chocolate at some cozy little café while the bells of Amsterdam are clanging all around you.

I hate to sound all paternalistic and possessive by saying you've got some explaining to do, but you've got some explaining to do.

> Jackson

Date: December 13
From: KateBogart
To: JackMacTavish
Subject: The Windmills of Your Mind

Dear Jack: You've got to check that jealous reflex of yours. I had no idea at all that Maxwell would be here, though I do think that Ted may have something to do with the strange coincidence.

One way or another, you have nothing to worry about. Maxwell is engaged to be married, remember? What happened between him and me is over, so you can wipe those pictures of us frolicking around Amsterdam right out of your mind. He will be chasing some elusive marijuana grower all around the city over the next few days, and I'll be busy sampling frites, visiting the boutiques on P.C. Hoofstraat, and checking out the flea markets, all on a bike very much built for one.

Please try to trust me Jack. It's very, very important to me. You know that I find possessiveness and jealousy oppressive, and when I get back to the States, we're going to have a sitdown.

Wish You Were Here (Whether You Believe Me or Not),
Kate

Date: December 14
From: Manowar
To: KateBogart
Subject: Going Dutch

Dear Ms. Bogart: What a lovely day spent with you in Amsterdam. So much more rewarding than sitting in some dark, smoky coffee shop trying to coax a coherent sentence out of the great DeKoker while he samples one spacecake after another.

The Rijksmuseum truly is astonishing, is it not? And quite exhausting, as well. And thanks too for indulging my silly impulse to bicycle out to the Bos on that ridiculous tandem. How bracing the cold air felt (you were wise to suggest those scarves!) and how delicious that cup of chocolate tasted at t'Smalle afterward. A perfect winter's day.

In truth, I thought it would be difficult for me to say good-bye to you at the end of the evening, knowing that nothing but a thin wall separates us, but it has proved remarkably easy. I now see clearly and without question that we made the right choice in choosing our partners, and how lucky I am to count you as a friend.

What would you say to dinner and a nighttime stroll to see the lights along the canals later? Knock twice for yes, thrice for no.

Miles

Date: December 14
From: KateBogart
To: Manowar
Subject: Dutch Treats

Dear Maxwell: Thank you so much for dinner at Christophe tonight. It was out of this world. Still a little tipsy from the wine and the cognac, but just wanted to say I too am very happy with the way things have turned out between us, as true friendship is such a rare blessing.

Just like you, I thought at first that it would be difficult having a room right smack dab next to yours, but I haven't been tempted by your nearness, either. Not at all. When I look at you now, Maxwell, I feel nothing beyond the warmth and fondness I'd feel for a brother, if I had one. But I don't. So you'll have to do, and you'll do quite nicely. What a relief to be finally cured of all that confusion!

Would love to return the lovely gesture. Can I take you to lunch tomorrow at Metz & Co? I want to see the Christmas decorations, and the dining room has great views over the city's rooftops. Twice for yes, thrice for no.

Glad You Are Here,
Kate

Date: December 15
From: Manowar
To: KateBogart
Subject: RE: Dutch Treats

Ms. Bogart: You still seem to be asleep, as I cannot hear you tapping away at your computer or going about your ablutions. Not that I have been eavesdropping, of course, but one can't help noticing these things—or their absence. Don't want to disturb you, so in place of a neighborly knock, do take this e-mail in acceptance of your kind invitation to lunch at Metz. Will meet you there at 12:00.

Would it be too much trouble to ask for your help selecting a gift for Odette? I'd like to surprise her with something when she arrives this afternoon. Why I might even find a Christmas present there for Mynah. Do they have a department specializing in oversized orthopedic bedroom slippers?

Glad that you are catching up on your sleep, by the way. A bit fitful last night myself. Quite restless, actually. Must have been the alcohol. Very tempted to rouse you, but whatever would we do in the middle of Amsterdam in the middle of the night in the middle of the winter?

Once again, I have to express how happy I am that our friendship has risen to this higher ground and it is so reassuring to know that you return my feelings in kind. See you at lunch, old chap.

Your Good Friend,
Miles

Date: December 15
From: JackMacTavish
To: KateBogart
Subject: Fair Warning

Okay, Katie, I'm ready for that sitdown. Couldn't wait for Paris. I'm here. In Amsterdam. At Skipall (sp?) Airport.

Went through hell changing my ticket, but I know it was the right thing to do. Decided it was very, very important for us to talk now, in person. I just couldn't wait any longer, or risk leaving you alone with Miles under such precarious conditions. I know he's a decent guy and all that, but I also think that's part of the problem. Let's face it, Katie, you don't have a lot of resistance when it comes to men.

Besides, I haven't been in Europe since college. Let's just spend the next two weeks eating and sleeping and planning our future together and walking wherever our feet lead us and looking at gorgeous art and making even more gorgeous love. Okay, babe? On my way to the Pulitzer now so we can work this situation out.

Love,
Jackson

Date: December 16
From: KateBogart
To: VioletMorgan
Subject: Eros

Oh, Vi, craziness follows me everywhere I go. When Jack found out that Maxwell and I were in adjacent rooms, all his insecurity came to the surface. Why, he even accused me of having no willpower when it comes to men! The nerve. What's most galling is that Maxwell and I have totally gotten over each other. He is even calling me things like "chum," "matey," and "old boy." Jack, however, wasn't convinced, and rather than wait until Paris, he changed his flight and came to Amsterdam.

Thing is, I had already checked out of the Pulitzer and moved over to a smaller hotel. Since I had a larger room than Maxwell's, and Odette was coming to join him, Maxwell moved over to mine. When Jack arrived, Maxwell greeted him in his underwear and Jack drew some hasty conclusions and apparently started giving Maxwell the third degree. Maxwell bristled at the accusations, of course.

Meanwhile, Odette had just arrived minutes before Jack and was freshening up in the bathroom, where she apparently found the nightgown I left behind. The very slinky one. I guess that got her mind racing and she started grilling Maxwell, too. She didn't buy his explanation and actually threw a punch at him, but Maxwell ducked and Jack took the hit. That set Jack off on Odette, and Maxwell came to her defense.

That's when I made the mistake of returning for my forgotten night-gown. Odette lunged for me, and Jack lunged for Odette, and Miles lunged for Jack. Then Odette threw a pretty little Delft blue vase at Miles, and she tore a small still life off the wall and tossed that my way. I liked the painting, but not that much, so I ducked and it hit the hotel security man who had come to quiet the storm. By that time, furniture and ashtrays and pillows and luggage and cute little Dutch knick-knacks were flying wild and we were all lost in a blizzard of goose down. When it was over, the room looked much the way it would if the Killer Abs had spent a week or two. In short, total destruction.

The hotel management was nice enough to find us other accommo-dations in an Amsterdam jail. I've stayed at better places in my travels, I must say, but I've stayed at worse too, and the Dutch are genuinely hospitable, even the police. Graciously, Maxwell made a deal with the hotel and promised to cover all the damages, and the hotel, being a classy establishment, decided not to press charges. Still, I don't think they want us back. Ever. In fact, they were pretty firm about it.

Once everything was explained, Odette was quite apologetic. Jack was, too. And so was Maxwell. I joined in too, just to be on the safe side. It was a veritable orgy of apologies, and even the hotel manager found something to be sorry for, as did the arresting officers.

Maxwell and Odette have gone in search of other accommoda-tions and Jack has joined me at a very cute budget place in the Museumplein. I had a good mind to send him to a youth hostel, but I'm a pushover. We are staying at the Hotel de Filosoof. It ain't the Pulitzer, but it's interesting just the same. Every room is designed around a philosophical theme or thinker. We've got some serious talk-ing to do, once Jack recovers from his jet lag and can think straight. For now, he more or less garbles shame-faced apologies while I glower and steam. Ironically, we have landed in the room dedicated to "Eros." Don't laugh.

Wish You Were Here,
Kate

Date: December 17
From: Manowar
To: KateBogart
Subject: The Reformation

Dear Ms. Bogart: Once again, I'd like to extend my apologies for the row at the Pulitzer. I'm afraid you have seen first-hand just how impetuous Odette can be. I do believe it's a symptom of bearing witness to so much violence and hostility on a day-to-day basis and I am sure that with time, she will regain her sense of civility. She is quite sorry for the names she called you and we're both concerned about your wounds. You'll be pleased to know that ours are healing nicely and are really almost nothing compared to the injuries we have incurred in the war zones.

You and I had been having such a lovely time in our platonic phase, whiling away those precious rainy days in Vancouver and defying Amsterdam's wintry chill together. I am eagerly looking forward to building upon that foundation of friendship in the years to come and I do hope that I have not undone that possibility. But let us now turn our attention to the task of loving our respective fiancées and repair our defects before they become unmanageable.

You'll be pleased to know, by the way, that word of our outlaw status has not apparently traveled all that far, and Odette and I were received at The Grand without incident or protest. We have pitched camp here this evening and I will have my last meeting with DeKoker and some other hemp maniacs tomorrow at 12:00, before heading back to London with my fiery betrothed. I don't know when I will be fortunate enough to see you again, but however long it takes will be much too long for me.

Fondly,
Miles

Date: December 17
From: KateBogart
To: Manowar
Subject: RE: The Reformation

Oh, Maxwell, no need to apologize at all. I'm the one who should be sorry. I shouldn't have been so careless with my lingerie. Jack feels terrible too, by the way, just as he should.

I wish you didn't have to leave so soon. I want to give you your Christmas present in person. Just a little souvenir. I don't think that will set off any world wars, do you? Squeeze me in tomorrow before your appointment. Let's meet at t'Smalle at 11:00. In the meantime, I am following your lead, and trying to talk things over with Jack in Amsterdam before we head off for Paris.

Wish You Could Stay,
Kate

Date: December 18
From: KateBogart
To: VioletMorgan
Subject: Cold Feet, Warm Heart

Dear Vi: Said goodbye to Maxwell today, and gave him a bicycle bell from the shop where we rented our tandem. I also told him that I think he's one of the finest people I ever met and that I look forward to being friends with him for the rest of my life. He said a lot of sweet things to me too, which I am too modest to repeat. Then he shook my hand and said, "See ya later, buddy," in his best American accent, which isn't that good, which, in turn, is part of his charm. Then I watched his taxi lurch off into the chaos of the Amsterdam traffic.

He and Odette are back in London by now, planning their wedding and getting ready for their first Christmas together without gunfire and troop movement. I'm very happy for them, but it made me doubt my own situation. I was supposed to go back to my hotel to continue my peace talks with Jack, but I just couldn't do it, Vi. Instead, I threw

my things together while he was in the shower, left his diamond ring
and a good-bye note with my apologies, and high-tailed it to Centraal
Station. That's where I am right now, waiting for a train to Paris.

I know it's small of me, but I just don't think I can make it work
with Jack, and the sooner it's over the better. I've canceled the accommodations we were supposed to take together, and begged Jack to
head back to California and get on with his life, once and for all. I
hope he takes my advice.

I'll let you know where I land once I'm there.

Wish You Were Here,
Kate

Date:	December 18
From:	JackMacTavish
To:	KateBogart
Subject:	The Great Escape

Katie! I just got your note. Now who's being unreasonable? This is
just classic female passive aggression and I think it's beneath you. I
promised that I would take care of my jealousy and insecurity issues,
and consult Sharmi and everything. You know me, Kate, and you
know my word is good. And this is how you treat me? Sneaking out
on me while I'm in the shower? I know I can be a pain, but I came
halfway around the world because I love you. Don't I deserve a little
more than this? Are you trying to punish me with this childish hide 'n
seek stunt? Well ready or not, babe, here I come.

J

CHAPTER 17

✈

In Paris

Date: December 19
From: JackMcTavish
To: KateBogart
Subject: *Cherchez la Femme*

Okay, Katie, this is really silly. I went to the Hôtel Caron de Beaumar-
chais where we were supposed to check in and they told me you canceled the reservation, so you're obviously somewhere else. I called
Violet, who was clearly playing dumb. You should be happy to have
such a loyal friend. She advised me to pack my bags and head home.
I changed my ticket, but I just can't do it, Katie. I really want to talk
to you face-to-face, and I know that you want to talk to me, too. It's
just not like you to be so unforgiving.

Tell me where you are, babe, so we can patch this up once and for
all. Or meet me at the Web Bar on rue Picardie. It's in the third ar-
rondisement. (sp?) I'll wait for you there, all day and all night if I
have to. Please come, Katie. Please.

Love,
Your Jackson

Date: December 20
From: KateBogart
To: GamblinRose
Subject: A Free Man in Paris

Dear Mom: I have arrived in Paris, but things have taken a little turn. Let me catch you up: When Jack found out that Maxwell was in the room next to mine in Amsterdam, he showed up uninvited with all sorts of suspicions. It caused quite a mess, but we managed to straighten it out eventually. Still, I was really smarting from Jack's accusations and his rash behavior and I had to reconsider our prospects as a couple.

Jack is a good friend, sensitive and dedicated, but as a lover, he's just too possessive. It's oppressive, Mom, and I don't want to be married to someone who makes me feel that way. Even worse, whenever I tried to imagine our future together—where we'd live, how we'd live—I just couldn't arrive at a scenario that could please us both. I don't think I could ever really be happily married to Jack; it calls for too many compromises, and I've been denying the fact that it's never going to change.

I knew Jack would resist all of this reasoning, and Lord knows he can be pretty hard to resist himself. That's how I got into this mess in the first place. So, while he was in the shower at the hotel in Amsterdam, I left his engagement ring and a note explaining my feelings. Then I threw my things in my bag and rushed off to Paris without him. I've become awfully good at packing on the fly. Maybe too good.

Of course, Jack followed me here anyway and begged me to meet him at a café. Have to admit that I felt like a terrible coward and I couldn't just let him go without an explanation, so I gave in. I apologized for accepting his proposal in the first place and admitted that it was a romantic impulse that just overwhelmed me. Apologized for running off to Paris without him too, but explained that I just didn't want to lead him on or drag this out any longer. Even though I genuinely love him, I've done the math and I just don't think our problems are solvable.

What's most surprising is that he didn't put up much of a fight. He said he never really expected me to accept the proposal in the first place, and thought it was too good to be true. He conceded that it was probably best if we parted. He didn't want to force me into something against my will, but he didn't want to end it on a hostile note, either. Then we held hands and cried together for a long, long time.

He had already rescheduled his flight, and when it came time for him to go, I put him in a taxi, and watched it blur through my tears as it whisked him off to the airport. As you can imagine, I'm awfully sad, Mama Rosa, but even more relieved. Thankfully, I have all of Paris to comfort me.

Wish You Were Here,
Kate

Date:	December 20
From:	GamblinRose
To:	KateBogart
Subject:	RE: A Free Man in Paris

Dear Kate: What heartbreaking news. You know what's best for yourself, of course, and I stand by any decision that you make. I am very sorry you have come to feel that way about Jack, but I have to admit those odds are pretty tough. I just wish there was something I could do to make it hurt a bit less.

Have to admit, I don't like the idea of you spending Christmas alone in a foreign city, but I know that you have a knack for making friends too, and Paris isn't all that foreign to you. Just know that if you're feeling lonely, you can come right back home. Ted and I are having an open house to celebrate our first Christmas together. But no pressure. You do what you have to do to get through this.

Love and Kisses,
Mom

Date: December 21
From: KateBogart
To: GamblinRose
Subject: RE: RE: A Free Man in Paris

Thanks for the support and consolation, Mom, and for the invite, too.
Honestly, I don't think I could face an open house right now. To get
me through these dark days and this grueling job, I have decided to
go on a tour of the city's chocolate shops and pâtisseries. Started today with a chocolate tarte at Gérard Mulot in the 6th, where the cakes
are just dreamy. There's no painkiller like chocolate, Mom. It might
not be as good as love, but it's the next best thing, and much less complicated, too. It asks nothing of you other than your pleasure. Why, I
feel better already.

> Wish You Were Here,
> Kate

Date: December 21
From: KateBogart
To: VioletMorgan
Subject: French Kiss-Off

Dear Vi: Thanks for trying to cover for me. You're the best friend in
the world, but I met with Jack after all and he was much more understanding than I expected him to be. He even agreed that we'd both
have to go much too far to meet each other halfway and that it's best
for both of us if we stay divorced.

Let's face it, Vi, marriage just isn't the thing for me. I never was
one of those girls who starts planning her wedding day as soon as the
training wheels are off her bike, and wedding showers always give me
that creepy, early-Polanski feeling, as if behind the seemingly benign
ritual is a secret coven waiting to sacrifice a virgin in some satanic
blood rite. The only time I have ever felt anything resembling the
hot pangs of matrimonial longing that afflict so many women—the
marriage-for-the-sake-of-it kind—are when I see the words "rates based

on double occupancy." Tempting though they may be, package discounts just aren't the best reason to tie the knot.

So, after I explained all this to Jack, we said a tearful farewell.
Then I watched him as he walked off, as beautiful and as sexy and as
graceful as ever, straight out of my life. Although I'm relieved, the
thought of giving him up once and for all still hurts plenty. To numb
the pain, I am following my sweet tooth wherever it leads me. That's
my angle for this piece—chocolate as morphine for the heart. Gotta
go. Time for my dose.

Wish You Were Here,
Kate

Date:	December 22
From:	VioletMorgan
To:	KateBogart
Subject:	RE: French Kiss-Off

Bogie: Sorry to hear the sad news, but I'm proud that you stuck to
your guns. Jealousy is as nasty as an unloved pit bull, and I don't
blame you one bit for not wanting to live with it. I know you're hurting now, but I also know that you'll be right back on the horse in no
time. You just can't keep a loose woman down. Why, I'm sure there's
an Henri or a Jean-Claude waiting just around le corner. I wonder if
your mother and her henchwomen have any bets running. Hope so. I
could use the extra Christmas cash. Calling her now.

Also, if you eat so many sweets and find that you can no longer
squeeze your ass into that cute little Vivienne Tam you got on mark-
down, I've got first dibs.

xxx,
V

Date: December 23
From: Manowar
To: KateBogart
Subject: *C'est la Guerre*

Dear Ms. Bogart: I suppose that by now you and Jack have settled into your Paris accommodations. How lucky you are to be there together.

I'm a bit less lucky this holiday season. Upon our return to London, Odette's agent called her with an offer to cover a resurgent guerilla movement in the Peruvian mountains. It was our agreement that we would, like a true couple, make all of our decisions together, and that we would not even consider any foreign assignments that involve war zones. I do believe this is the only way to shake this addiction to danger and conflict. Unfortunately, my beloved fiancée is too far gone, and she decided the skirmish was more compelling than spending Christmas with yours truly. She set off for South America in a breathless frenzy, leaving me feeling quite abandoned, I admit. In weaker moments, I have considered following her. It is indeed tempting, but for now, I am holding my ground.

Ah well, I don't mean to cry on your shoulder or burden you with my troubles, Ms. Bogart. I merely want to wish you and Jack well, to tell you that you are both in my heart, and to wish you the brightest of holidays.

Fondly,
Miles

Date: December 24
From: KateBogart
To: Manowar
Subject: RE: *C'est la Guerre*

Dear Maxwell: I'm so sorry to hear that Odette has chosen to spend Christmas with the Peruvian rebels instead of you. Can't imagine it myself, and I'm sure she'll regret her mistake as soon as the first bullet whizzes past her head. If not, she's genuinely crazy and she doesn't deserve you at all.

Thanks so much for the well wishes, but I have to admit that this isn't the idealized Parisian holiday I had planned either. After you left Amsterdam, it became clear to me that things would never work out between me and Jack. We were blinded by our sense of romance, but we both want very different things from life, and we want them more than we want each other. I came to Paris alone, but he followed me here and I sent him back to California—with his diamond ring.

It sure has made Paris a lonelier, colder place than it might have been, but I'm also relieved to be free from an impossible situation. It's a huge weight off my conscience, even if my heart and pride are smarting.

Be sure to wish Mynah a Merry Christmas for me, and don't forget to have one yourself.

Wish You Were Here,
Kate

Date: December 24
From: JackMacTavish
To: KateBogart
Subject: *Feliz Navidad*

Katie: Considered what we talked about in Paris, and I wish I could say I disagree, but when you're right, babe, you're right. In bed, we are the king and queen of the world, but in marriage we're a disaster.

Had a helluva long time to think about what I'm going to do with my life on that flight back to SF, but still came up with nothing. When I landed, made an emergency call to Sharmi in the middle of the night. She totally banged a left and took your side. Caught me by surprise. She made me see that you're just doing what makes you happy, and giving yourself what you need, which is all you can do, really. She told me I was a dope if I didn't follow your example and not to worry about the heartache 'cause time will take care of it.

She made me focus on the whole yin-yang of the experience and showed me what was gained and what was lost, and helped me to concentrate on that. I don't understand how you learn these things running a brothell (sp?) and working in the laundry of a women's correctional facility, but Sharmi's a natural wonder. She made me see what was right in front of me all along. No small feat.

Since you're recovering in your favorite place in the world, I decided I would try to do the same in mine. That's how I ended up in Lima. After all the confusion of the last few months, I was really eager to clear my head in the mountains. Figured I'd go back to doing the expeditions again, and guess who I met at the airport? Odette!

Turns out the French photo agency she works for wants her to cover some rebel factions hiding out in the mountains. When I told her that I know the trails and speak Spanish, she asked me to be her guide to get the jump on the competitors. Okay, she drafted me, really, but how could I refuse? This woman is fierce! And really compelling too, in a scary kind of way. I'm beginning to see why Miles has been so devoted to her all these years.

Odette and I are heading up into the hills tomorrow. For the first time in a long time, I'm stoked, Katie. I love the challenge of this thing. It gives my work real meaning on a global level. I don't know when I'm going to be e-mailable again. But wanted to let you know that I'm not mad at you, that I still count you as one of the best friends I've ever had, that my love for you is purer than ever, and that I'm moving on. Hope you are too, Katie, and hope that you have a very Merry Christmas, and that you find whatever it is that you're searching for.

Love Always,
Yr Jackson

Date: December 24
From: KateBogart
To: JackMacTavish
Subject: RE: *Feliz Navidad*

Dear Jack: I'm glad to hear that you're recovering so well and that you're so "stoked" to be leading Odette on her mission. When I said I didn't think we should get married, I never imagined you'd resort to something so dangerous instead. Even though I know you're in very strong hands with Odette, please promise me you'll be extra cautious. Just because I don't want to be your wife, doesn't mean I don't sincerely care about you.

Please know that my e-mail box is always open for you, Jackson. Drop me a line just as soon as you can to let me know that you're safe. Be careful, and do everything Odette tells you to do. Within reason.

Merry Christmas, and as ever . . .

Wish You Were Here,
Kate

Date: December 24
From: KateBogart
To: GamblinRose
Subject: Noël

Dear Mom: What a crazy turn of events. Don't know if you've heard, but Odette ran off on Maxwell to photograph some rebels hiding in the Peruvian Andes. And who do you think her mountain guide is? None other than Jackson Brown MacTavish. How's that for a Christmas present? Jack decided he'd get over our broken engagement in the mountains, and in Lima he met up with Odette, who just happened to need someone who knows the terrain, speaks Spanish, and looks like a Calvin Klein underwear model. Don't know if Maxwell has heard of this latest development yet, but as of his last e-mail, he didn't seem to know. He sounded pretty heartbroken about Odette's timing too, and I don't want to add to his Christmas blues.

I'm doing much better than poor Maxwell, so no need to worry about me, Mom. So busy making new friends and seeing the sights, have hardly had a moment to feel bad about the break-up with Jack. I'm having a lovely Christmas in Paris. I've moved over to a new hotel. It's a real friendly crowd here, and later, I'm joining some Australian backpackers at a little place in the Marais that serves the traditional French Christmas dinner with oysters, foie gras, goose, and a bûche de Noël. Afterward, we're all joining the throngs for midnight mass at Nôtre Dame. Go ahead and call me a tourist, but I live for this sort of stuff.

I'll call you tomorrow. In the meantime, I hope you and Ted and the Sisters of Perpetual Bingo all have a very Merry Christmas.

Wish You Were Here,
Kate

Date: December 25
From: GamblinRose
To: KateBogart
Subject: RE: Noël

Merry Christmas, honey! That's a real kicker involving Jack and Odette, but I guess that's to be expected with you types who go racing all around the globe as it if were the neighborhood playground. Miles didn't know that Odette and Jack are in cahoots, but he does now because he just got off the phone with Ted.

On the homefront, Teddyweddy and I had a lovely Christmas Eve. After filling up on Moira's killer eggnog we went to Midnight Mass at His Holy Blood, but we couldn't get the words straight to any of the carols. Afterward, we came home and opened our gifts. I bought Ted a foot massager, which we played with until the wee hours. The fun you can have with a foot massager! But you don't want to hear about that.

Today is the open house. All the Sisters of Perpetual Bingo and their families have dropped in, and so have some people from Ted's office. Violet and Shane are even coming by later. Isn't that sweet? I wish that you could come too, but you sound like you're having a great time in Paris with your new friends. I'm glad to hear it, and hope that you enjoy the rest of the holiday, too.

Love,
Mom

Date: December 26
From: VioletMorgan
To: KateBogart
Subject: Day-Old Fruitcake

Merry Christmas, Bogie! Shane and I went to your mother's open house last night. She and the Sisters were full of gossip and Moira (Or was it Althea?) told me all about Jack and Odette meeting up in Peru. This is how you treat your best friend at Christmas? Leaving me to hear about the juiciest bits of your personal life from an aging high school Phys Ed teacher? (Or was it Social Studies?)

How was my Christmas? Why, thanks for asking. Well, after filling up on gossip, booze, sugar, and sentimentality, Shane and I cut out of the open house before your mother and her cronies started playing high-stakes Pictionary. (I know a hustle when I see one.) We opened our presents this morning, sans The Killer Abs, which is probably the best present a girl could wish for. Spent the rest of the day more or less recovering from the diabetic shock of Ina's "Holiday Medley." Has this ever been inflicted upon you? It's a gloopy lumpy concoction of her own devising that includes Cool Whip, Jell-O, marshmallows, s'mores, broken candy canes, maraschino cherries, pineapple chunks, and two pounds of white sugar. No wonder you went to Paris for Christmas!

Rose told me you were taking the break-up well and having your own lovely Christmas in Paris. I hope she's right.

Love,
Vi

Date: December 26
From: KateBogart
To: VioletMorgan
Subject: RE: Day-Old Fruitcake

Dear Vi: I did tell Mom and Ted what a great time I'm having in Paris, but I lied. I didn't want Ted to get more smug than he no doubt already is over my break-up with Jack, and I didn't want Mom worrying about me being alone on Christmas.

To tell you the truth, I had just about the worst Christmas of my life since that year I had dysentery in Guadalajara. I am staying in the Marais at The Hôtel du Septième Art, a little budget place with a movie theme. Went to the midnight mass at Nôtre Dame last night with a group of drunken Australian backpackers. Helped carry one of them home while the others went out in search of young French men to corrupt. Held her hair while she threw up, then went to bed, as the rest of the Australian girls were returning with their conquests. Listened to them having what sounded like a decadent bacchanal until I fell asleep. Spent most of Christmas day in the hotel bar being hit on by an adenoidal French film geek deconstructing *le cinema de Jim Belushi* at me. Not very glamorous, I'm the first to admit, but I was happy to have any company at all.

Don't know what it is, Vi, but I'm just not my usual bubbly self. I can't explain my own malaise, but suddenly, I find myself with all this freedom, and nothing to do with it. Of course I'm sad about the break-up with Jack, but I know it's for the best in the long run. It's not the news of him and Odette meeting up in Peru, either. He sounded quite happy in his last e-mail, and I don't want anything less for him.

I'm so sorry I didn't call you yesterday. It's unforgivable of me, but I just didn't want to blow down your Christmas tree, too. Frankly, I'm just happy that the holiday is over. Now I just have to get through New Year's. I'm glad to hear that you and Shane finally got to spend some time alone, and I hope that my little Truman had a happy day, too.

Wish You Were Here So Badly,
Kate

Date: December 27
From: Violet Morgan
To: KateBogart
Subject: *Les Enfant du Paradis*

Bogie: Congratulations, you're a grandmother! Sorry you had such a bummer holiday, but figured this might cheer you up: Remember when Truman ran away? Well it turns out he sired a litter of five little Trumans with Mrs. D'Anunzziatta's cat, Number 7. She doesn't bother naming them, but there is apparently a method to her madness.

Bumped into Mrs. D'Anunzziatta in the hallway, or should say I was accosted by her. In her own quiet way, she is suing you for paternity. Actually, she's trying to sue me, since she's convinced that I live here. Anyway, before she makes a federal case of this and convinces your landlord that I'm an illegal subletter, I just volunteered to take the glorified dustballs off her hands as soon as they're weaned. She said I damn well better, which in the language of the insane means thank you, I guess. So, when you return you'll have not one cat, but six!

Love,
Vi

Date: December 28
From: KateBogart
To: VioletMorgan
Subject: Let Them Eat Cake

Truman is a father! Oh, what wonderful news! I can't wait to see the kittens. It does cheer me up, and I'm so sorry I can't be there. Naturally, I can't keep them, but I bet Rose and Ted would take one, maybe even two, and maybe the Sisters of P.B. might be good for an adoption. Of course, there's always you and Shane. Wouldn't you just love to have a little Truman all your own, Vi? Why, you can go down to that crazy woman's apartment right now, pick your favorite one, tie a bright red bow around it, and call it a Christmas gift from Truman and me to you. I insist.

Today I went to the grand Mariage Frères tearoom. The sandwiches were delicious, but they were easily upstaged by my Dôme du Chocolat, a ball of rich, nutty chocolate the size of a Girl Scout's fist. It came with a pear poached in tea, too. It was all very continental, but as my little white-jacketed waiter swooped around me with studied grace and efficiency I could swear I heard him thinking, "A woman taking tea alone? Why, she must be a 'orrible, unlovable wretch!" Also, the list of teas was perplexing to this uncouth American rube. I just know that if Maxwell had been there, it would have all been perfect.

You know I'm not the regretful type, Vi, but I can't help thinking that Ted is right: I messed things up with Maxwell months ago, letting my fears override my heart, and that's why I'm so miserable. To be perfectly honest with you, it's the real reason I broke off my engagement to Jack. Sure, I could have found some common ground with him, and I know he could have gotten his jealousy under control, but I think he suspected that I was in love with Miles all along. And I was. Am. (There! I said it!) I couldn't marry Jack feeling this way about Maxwell! It just wouldn't be fair to him.

But now it's all a big mess. Maxwell is back to mooning over Odette, who may or may not be getting cozy with Jack in a tight little pup tent, and I'm feeling lost in a suddenly strange world I used to find so friendly. Even Paris just seems old and cold and drab.

So, how do I deal with all this loss and confusion and regret? Well, I've already busted into the box of truffles I picked up for you at Christian Constant. (I'll get you more. I promise.) And the chocolate pyramid I got for Ted at Jean-Paul Hévin's shop is now more like a small chocolate doghouse. But I don't care, it puts me in Hévin, so to speak. I've also been back to Ladurée for some scrumptious macaroons, and to Angelina, that place under the arcade near the Louvre where we had those cups of thick chocolat. Remember that? I love how they serve the whipped cream in its own little silver bowl. I had two. Checked out all four branches of Dalloyau's pâtisseries this week too. *Incroyable!* I have also discovered the pâtisseries of Jean Millet in the 7th, and Gérard Mulot in the 6th, both geniuses of the confectionary arts. They are my true and only loves.

> Wish You Were Here,
> Kate

Date:	December 29
From:	VioletMorgan
To:	KateBogart
Subject:	Resolutions

Bogie: I was just sitting here reflecting on your regrets and taking stock of the year behind us. When you think of it, so much has happened. Ted has gotten out of a loveless marriage and rediscovered his heart with your mother, who ended a decades-long dry spell of her own and found a warm-blooded alternative to gambling. For better or worse, Jack and Odette have forged a partnership that seems to suit them both, and though Maxwell could be out one fiancée, he still has his new book to write. Meanwhile, Shane and The Killers have landed a recording deal, and I have finally gotten out of a self-defeating professional rut. Why, even the lazy and heretofore worthless Truman has done his bit for his species and taken the courageous plunge into fatherhood. And there you are, Bogie, right back to square one, loveless and rudderless and all alone in the big free world. Wasn't it Sartre who said that we are all "condemned to be free"?

I worry about you, Bogie. All the time. You continually fail to see what is right in front of you: that no woman is an island, no matter how much time she spends at sea. Since I know that you would never make any resolutions to change your reckless, restless habits on your own, I have come up with a set of suggestions for you. They are as follows:

1) No chocolate
2) No pastries
3) No cakes

4) No butter at all
5) No men at all
6) No obsessive worrying
7) No self-pitying
8) No frequent flying
9) No taking unfair advantage of best friend
10) No cats

If you would stick to these ten simple resolutions, your life would surely improve, and more to the point, so would mine. But we both know that you won't. Therefore, you should do whatever you must to enjoy your life without making yourself fat or sick. That probably means calling Maxwell to tell him what a dumbass you are—but a good-hearted one just the same—and just how much you'd like to see him again. Odette has given you an opening and you should seize the opportunity before she changes her mind, again. And you'd better replace those chocolates, too!

(Tough) Love,
Violet

Date: December 30
From: KateBogart
To: VioletMorgan
Subject: RE: Resolutions

Vi! You're absolutely right. How stupid of me to be pining away in Paris when Maxwell's just across the channel. Life doesn't give you many chances to correct your mistakes, and this one is not going to be lost on me. I don't just want to eat my cake, Vi, I want to have it too, dammit!

I was supposed to check into a swell hotel in Paris tomorrow, one that was reserved for Jack and me, but I think I'd be even more miserable if I went through with it now, so I've reserved a seat on the Eurostar for London. As soon as I made the decision a great weight was lifted off me, which is good 'cause I think I gained a few pounds

here. Plan to tell Maxwell everything I meant to say the last time I
was in London and set things straight once and for all. I know that he
might turn me away, and I don't really blame him if he does, but at
least I will have made my case.

Thanks so much for the tough love, Vi. I love you so much and I
don't know what I'd do without you.

Wish You Were Here,
Kate

Date: December 31
From: KateBogart
To: Manowar
Subject: Crossing Channels

Dear Maxwell: In case you haven't gotten my phone message, wanted
to let you know that I'm coming to London to see you. I know that
you have gotten the news that Jack and Odette have hooked up in
Peru. I don't know what it means or where it puts you, but as my
mother's daughter, I think I can call the odds on this one. I hope
you're not despairing over this, Maxwell. I'm certainly not. I'm not
coming to commiserate; I'm coming to tell you how I feel.

You see, Maxwell, I never really meant to put you off when I was
with Jack in Provincetown. I was overwhelmed and just wanted a little time to figure out how I really felt about the both of you. Things
sure got tangled up on Mt. Rainier, but you jumped to a hasty conclusion about me and Jack. In Vancouver, however, the time I spent with
you seemed positively charged with electricity. I never had any London
assignment at all. I flew halfway across the globe just to tell you that I
was ready to take you up on your invite, if it was still good. That's
when I met Odette. I didn't want to jeopardize your engagement,
Maxwell, especially after the two of you had been together for so long
and after you had tried so hard to get her to settle down. What kind of
person would I be?

I thought I could make it work with Jack again, but after those few days with you in Amsterdam, I realized I'd be living a lie. The thought of spending my entire life with Jack felt like the end of something, not the beginning. Yes, Jack is very, very dear to me, but he never made me feel the way you did, Maxwell.

It dawned on me in Amsterdam that you're the only man I have ever been with who didn't try to possess me, who never made me feel trapped, and I trust that you never would. You were always willing to respect that I have a mind and life all my own. What's so much more, you didn't seem to care for me despite these things, but *because* of them. It's part of what makes you such a lovely, lovely man, Maxwell, and it's why I'm racing off to the train station now.

Just because we value our freedom doesn't mean we have to live our lives alone, Maxwell! I see it very clearly now. I just never knew it until I knew you. Life doesn't offer us many second chances, let alone a third or a fourth, and I feel that I must seize this one. There's so much more I want to tell about how much you really mean to me, and why. Maybe it's too late. Maybe time and luck have conspired against us, but all I ask is that you hear me out.

Love,
Kate

Date: December 31
From: KateBogart
To: GamblinRose
Subject: Tea and Sympathy

Oh, Mom! What a fool I am! Although I'm supposed to be at the Hôtel Regina in Paris, I jumped on the Eurostar to ask Maxwell for another chance. When I got here, however, I found Mynah alone. She made me a cup of tea, sat me down, and told me that Maxwell rushed off after a long phone call with Odette. Mynah figures he's on his way to Lima.

I had left him a phone message, but he hasn't retrieved it yet, according to Mynah, the master spy. I even sent him an e-mail explaining my feelings and intentions. Once he reads it, he'll probably feel like he dodged the deadliest bullet he ever faced. I sure do have lousy timing, but at least I've finally made my heart known to him, and in some way, I'm grateful for the unburdening.

Things just don't seem to be going my way lately. Suppose I could go back to Paris and pick up where I left off, but given the circumstances, I think that will just make me feel worse. If I can switch my ticket, I'm going to forgo my high-end hotel room and the Paris fireworks and head back home from here. Wanted to wish you and Ted a Happy New Year before I march off into battle with the airline.

Love,
Kate

Date:	December 31
From:	GamblinRose
To:	KateBogart
Subject:	RE: Tea and Sympathy

Oh, Kate, I'm so sorry you went to all that trouble and that Miles has flown the coop on you, but I'm sure things will work out for you sooner or later. It's a whole new year, honey. Teddy and I were just planning on snuggling up with a bottle of champagne for New Year's. While I'd love to have you home for the holiday, I'm not sure if it's possible. I'll let Ted explain. Here he is:

Kate: Happy New Year, pal. A tough break about Miles, but let's face it, you've been in this situation before. Buck up, soldier! Your hotel room is nonrefundable and the paper isn't going to pay for any changes to your ticket. Sorry to have to bring up such practical matters while you're feeling so bad already. The part of me that is your future stepdad would love to see you home early, but the part of me that is your editor needs you to finish the job you were sent to do. I know I seem like a hardass, but I've got to handle you like any other writer. Besides, Paris on New Year's Eve can't really be that hard to take. Can it?

Sorry again, and try to have a Happy New Year. That's what you're getting paid for!

Love,
Mom and Ted

Date: December 31
From: Kate Bogart
To: VioletMorgan
Subject: *Bonne Année!*

Dear Vi: Well, sent Maxwell an e-mail to prepare him for my visit to London. Poured my heart out, but when I got there, Mynah told me he had already left for Peru. You can imagine how terrible and foolish I felt. I just wanted to return to New York and put it all behind me, but Ted insisted that I return to Paris so that the paper wouldn't lose the deposit on the very pricey hotel room. Can you believe it? So I hopped back on the Eurostar, crying and sulking the whole way back to Paris. Always a good way to get a seat by yourself on crowded public transportation, by the way.

Schlepped to the lovely Hôtel Regina, hard by the Louvre and the Tuileries, feeling down and defeated. But once I was caught up in the bustle of the lobby with its old world, art nouveau elegance and all the clocks marking the time in cities around the globe, I actually felt a little surge of cheer. A little bit of myself returned, Vi. In all my gloomy self-pity I'd actually lost sight of how privileged I am to be living this life other people only dream about. I'd even forgotten the transporting pleasures of a classic, well-designed lobby and the value of a high-end hotel room. Don't know what came over me!

Checked in feeling much better, even eager to welcome in the New Year in Paris. As I followed the porter to the elevators, I heard this familiar, insistent little ringing sound, sort of annoying, really. When I turned around, Vi, I saw it was none other than Maxwell, holding the bicycle bell that I gave him in Amsterdam! It turns out that while I was on my way to London to ask him for another chance, he was on his way to Paris to do the same. Rose and Ted were in on the plan and knew about the mix-up all along. They didn't want to ruin the surprise for me. That's why Ted played his duty-bound card. What a sweet old bear!

Maxwell and I jumped right into a kiss (our first in months, remember) and I think we actually made the poor bellman and all the people holding the elevator a little uncomfortable. You'd think they'd be used to this sort of thing in Paris!

Upstairs in the room, Maxwell said that he felt uneasy the whole time he had been engaged to Odette and as things moved along, he realized how much they'd grown apart over the past year. He said that's what all their kissing and hugging in London was about—he was trying to get back into it. But he just couldn't. She felt it too, and that's why she went off to Peru. He thought he'd lost me to Jack forever, but when he learned that we had split up, he decided to try for one more chance. But first he wanted to settle things with Odette. As it turns out, she was one step ahead of him. She and Jack had already traded her engagement ring for access to the rebels.

Maxwell begged my forgiveness for not fighting harder for me when he should have, and boy did I forgive him. Afterward, I told him about my true intentions the first time I went to London, and that I broke off the engagement with Jack because I just didn't love him the way I loved Maxwell. I begged him to forgive me for not being forthright and true to my heart, and boy did he forgive me.

Now Maxwell is in the shower and we have ordered some champagne from room service, along with many delicious things under a silver-plated dome. We have a marvelous view overlooking the Tuileries, with the Eiffel Tower in the distance. Oh! The fireworks have started! How beautiful!

Here's Maxwell now with those bangs all wet and his devilish dimples. Hello, Violet, dear. Happy New Year! (That's Maxwell, and he's being verry naughty.) Wow.

Fireworks brilliant flahsing boombooming. (Sorry for speling and typos—frisky Maxwell and firewoks.) I'm oh, so happy, Vi. Ditto (M again). Happier than Ive ever been beofre. pure, unadullllterated, unabmivalent happiness. You ought to try it.

won't be back tomor9ow as plannd. Not sure when i ll be back really, but let me know when those kittens are weened, kay? Coudl you also pay my runt for Janruary? I'll reimburse youuu. Also, if you have to hit road beefore i return, can you let Ted know so he can take care of Trumn? Yikes! Firewkrs bigandloud. And can you till my mither that I wont be returning on 2nd, and that Ill call her frum Loondon to explain? Oh and I've sssentt back some pckages from Parish. They due this week, so you might wanto keep your eye out for those too. You ar the best firnd a gilr coudlever hopfor and i ;ove you and the firieworksandmaxwellwho won't stop so i'd better goggogo happ newyearandwishyouwereheeeeeeeeeeeeeeeeeeeeeeeeeeeeeeeeeeeeeee eeeeeee k &m